SPUD ISLE MYSTERIES

Body *in the* Paddock

KAREN CULLEN, DVM

Library and Archives Canada Cataloguing in Publication.
Cullen, Karen. Spud Isle Mysteries: Body in the Paddock

This manuscript is a work of fiction. Characters, places, and events are a result of the author's imagination. Any similarities to people living, or dead, is co-incidental.

ISBN paperback: 9781778151934
ISBN EBook: 9781778151927

Published by: IV Lines Publishing

Cover Design: Britt Wilson - *Indie Publishing Group Inc*

For Melissa, Marlene and Tibby

AVC at UPEI

Class of 1992

Gone too soon

Chapter 1

DEAD BODIES AND peanut butter made for an unusual breakfast conversation. Let me rephrase that. It would be unusual in most households, but since I'd moved in with my aunt Josephine and uncle Johnny two months ago, unusual had become the expected.

"You should write a story about your life, Franny." I noted the use of my childhood nickname but didn't correct my aunt. If it had been anyone else, I would have cringed and insisted on being called Fran.

I looked up from my daily dose of toast and peanut butter to find my petite aunt Josephine, hands on hips and staring me down. I gulped down the crunchy bread with a swoosh of tea. "Excuse me?"

She didn't answer. I watched my dear old aunt, decked out

in polyester pants and a blue-and-yellow striped T-shirt that I suspect was a product of the 1980s, as she turned around in response to the sound of her toast popping up. The charcoal victim of a toaster years beyond its prime stood in the small appliance, a whiff of smoke surrounding it. "Oh dear, I've done it again." Aunt Josephine, her naturally straight hair tightly curled thanks to the perm she had the day before, fingered the edge of the burn victim. "Ouch. When will I learn not to touch burnt toast?"

"When will you learn not to turn the knob all the way to the right?" I heard myself saying. Aunt Josephine was the kindest, sweetest, most generous person I knew. She was also incredibly smart, except when it came to operating kitchen appliances.

"What was that, Franny?"

Thankful my father's older sister had inherited the family's propensity for deafening after the age of sixty—something I had to look forward to, no doubt—I chose to address her earlier comment.

"What is that you were saying about me writing my autobiography? Where did that come from? Why would anyone want to read about a big-city girl who moves to Sherwood, Prince Edward Island, to study English literature and journalism?" Sherwood, a quaint suburb of the province's capital city of Charlottetown, and handily situated only a short walk from the university campus, was my aunt and uncle's home since they had married.

Giving up on the toaster, Aunt Josephine placed a single slice of bread on her plate and joined me at the table. "Peanut butter! Why do you eat that stuff? Would you like some jam?" She offered me the marmalade.

I winced at the jar of yellow goo that resembled the contents of a used tissue too closely for my liking. "No thank you." I swallowed hard.

Was that a smile—or more of a smirk—that appeared on her face? Had making me queasy before I left for school become entertaining? If so, then I appreciated this wonderful woman more than ever.

"I was thinking about your comment last night. You mentioned trying your hand at writing a murder mystery." Aunt Josephine rose to retrieve the cream from the fridge. "I don't know why you'd want to write about something so ghastly as murder. Dead bodies are not entertaining."

"It wouldn't be gruesome—more like what's called a cozy mystery. Similar to the TV show Uncle Johnny watches." Uncle Johnny and Aunt Josephine had been married for twenty years, and in that time, I do believe their routine had stayed the same, including what they watched on TV.

"Oh, that show about that lady writer solving crimes." Josephine's brow furrowed. "Such silliness. Only police can solve crimes."

No doubt she had a point, or so I thought at the time. "You're right, I'm sure. You can rest assured, Aunt Josephine, that I won't be writing any murder mysteries soon. We're only a few days into classes and I already have two major essays to write for my basic English course. That'll keep me busy enough."

In the past, the school year started the day after Labour Day, but this year the university had initiated a new schedule that saw classes start the week before. This meant we had a week of classes followed by a long weekend filled with traditional freshman activities. With all the events meant to welcome new students like me, I hadn't had any time to work on my assignments, but I did have a lot of fun.

My silver-haired landlady, as I liked to call Aunt Josephine when she wasn't nearby, headed to the sink to wash up her few dishes. The lady employed to help around the house would be arriving soon, and Aunt Josephine didn't dare have a mess in the kitchen when someone was coming. As well as giving up trying to stop her from turning the toaster to the maximum setting every morning, I'd stopped trying to convince her it wasn't necessary to clean before the cleaning lady arrived. Having a tidy house, and being hospitable to all who entered it, was part of Aunt Josephine's charm.

Once she'd dried her dishes and returned them to their proper place in the cupboard, my encourager tapped me on the hand and held my gaze. "I'm serious, dear. You should write about your life. I would certainly buy a copy of that book."

I enfolded her hand in mine. "Thank you. I appreciate your confidence in me."

After leaving my dishes in the sink for the housekeeper, I collected my school bag and headed to my first class of the day.

Walking along Belvedere Avenue, I found myself admiring the graceful horses in the field to my right. I laughed at the thought that anything interesting enough to put into writing would ever happen in my life. As I shifted the book-laden sack on my shoulder, my eyes were drawn to red fabric in the long grass.

Another lost sock, no doubt. How people lost shoes and socks on the roads and in fields, I could never understand, but it seemed to be a regular occurrence. Perhaps it had to do with Charlottetown being a university town for nine months of the year.

The horses were sniffing at the red intruder to their playground, and I worried that one of them might ingest it. I dropped my bag to the ground, then hopped the fence. As I drew closer, I could see that the red object was indeed a sock. My heart skipped a beat when I realized that the sock was occupied by a foot, and the foot was attached to a man.

Was my future autobiography about to become a murder mystery?

Chapter 2

I KNOW IT WAS a foolish thought, but I found myself wondering where his shoes were. The horse nudging my shoulder with his nose brought me back to the seriousness of the moment. I tugged my phone out of my pocket and dialed 911.

"There's a man lying in the paddock beside the university."

I expected a rushed reply—an urgency to get emergency vehicles to the scene as soon as possible. I was baffled by the response, but maybe I shouldn't have been. While my general English course had started last week, today, the day after Labour Day, was the first official day of the new school year, and parties had been happening non-stop all over town the past few days.

"Don't you worry about him, dear. The young men from

the dorms often pass out in the field after a night out. I'm sure his friends will retrieve him shortly."

"Um, I think he's a little bit beyond passed out. And his shoes are missing." I don't why I included that last part, but it seemed important.

Apparently, the operator also wondered why. "Is that relevant, dear?"

"I don't know. It just seems odd."

Why were we talking about missing shoes when a dead body was sprawled out before me? Looking back, I was abnormally calm about being so close to it. To him. Who was he? I was tempted to peek at his identification, if he had any, but that would require touching the dead guy. I wasn't that curious. Not yet.

"Can you feel for a pulse? Are you sure he's not breathing?"

I sucked in the morning air and choked on it. She wanted me to touch him. "Can't you just send an ambulance?"

"One is on the way, but if he's still alive, I'll need you to give him first aid."

I swallowed my fear and approached his head, relieved that he was face down. My toast and peanut butter threatened to decorate the grass when I saw the gaping hole behind his right ear. "I don't think I'm going to find a pulse."

The sweet sound of sirens became audible, then grew louder. My tensed muscles relaxed as I watched the ambulance park near the fence and the EMTs exit the vehicle. They were soon joined by two police cars. I relayed to the 911 operator what I was seeing.

"Okay, dear, we can hang up now that the paramedics and police are there."

I clicked the End button. As I watched the flurry of activity at the edge of the field, I was confused by the body language of the uniformed officer rapidly approaching me. He had a look of suspicion on his face. He couldn't possibly think I did this, could he? No, that was simply my overactive imagination at work. I was the one who'd called it in, after all.

I moved forward to inform the officer of my role here. He fingered his holster. I froze, except for my hands—they shot into the air.

"Stay where you are."

He needn't have worried. Despite the unusually warm September day, my feet were firmly frozen to the ground.

Without lowering my hands, I used my left index finger to direct the officer to the body. He squinted. Did he not understand? Why was he still approaching me? I nodded toward the body. Unaffected by my gestures, or my raging desire that he check on the man lying on the ground and forget I existed, he continued coming closer.

I was soon face to face with the roughly six-foot-tall mass of muscle squeezed into a black shirt and matching pants. While approaching, he had removed his hat, which revealed a generous helping of silky wheat-coloured hair. He lowered his chin and directed his focus to the victim. Without moving his head, he looked up at me. "Why are your hands up?"

I pulled my gaze away from the day-old facial hair masking his chin and upper lip—I could only imagine that his hidden features were as well structured as the rest of his face—and glanced at his holster, where his index finger was plucking the snap that kept his gun firmly in place. I imagined a quick-draw cowboy. How fast could this officer fire his weapon? He followed my eyes. "Oh, sorry. Habit."

"Habit?" I lowered my arms and let out the breath I hadn't realized I was holding.

"There are worse habits."

"I can't think of any. I thought you were going to shoot me if I moved."

He shrugged off my concern about imminent death and approached the object of our meeting. "I'm Officer Hughes, by the way." He donned a pair of latex gloves, then leaned down and felt for a pulse on the man's neck. "When did you find the body?"

Again I felt the need to force my breakfast to stay where it was. "Just now. I called 911 right away. I didn't linger and chat with the horses first." And so my bad habit of using humour in stressful situations surged to the forefront. I don't know what the man with the gun thought, but I couldn't think of a more inappropriate setting for trying to be funny.

He eyed me. "I see." Then he rolled the body over.

Everything had been passing so fast, or so it seemed, from the moment I first spotted the red fabric in the field until now. It's odd how circumstances change our perception of time. The rolling over of the victim transported me from experiencing events at warp speed to slow motion, like in the movies. The paramedics, leaping the fence with a stretcher, appeared momentarily suspended in the air before they floated to the ground, their knees gracefully bending to prevent the weight of their torsos from jolting their lower legs. The movement of their limbs was oddly exaggerated as they approached the prostrate body on the ground.

Sweat droplets formed on my forehead, then ran down my nose. My head was spinning, reminding me of my one and only ride on the spinning swings at Sandspit, the amusement park near Cavendish. The once curious, now unsettled horses had moved to the other side of the field. I urgently wanted to join them, to sit down and lower my head—to forget what was going on around me.

Now that Officer Hughes had rolled the victim over, I gasped and lost my fight to retain my toast. Beyond the blood and bruises was a familiar face. "That's Vic." Speaking his name out loud made it all so real. This wasn't a mannequin or a passed-out-drunk student—this was a human being who'd been left for dead in a paddock.

I crumpled to my knees and held my hands over my mouth, trying to keep what was left of my stomach contents inside while stopping the brutality of the scene before me from entering my consciousness.

One of the EMTs rushed to my aid, but there wasn't anything he could do but offer me a towel and help me to my feet.

Officer Hughes straightened up and returned his attention to me. "You know the victim?" His all-business demeanour startled me—it didn't fit with the warm eyes and charmingly square chin.

After wiping my face, I held the towel close to my chest—it gave me a strange sense of security, and besides, I thought I might need it again. "I think so. I'm not sure, but he looks like Vic. I mean Victor. He didn't like being called Vic."

"How long have you known Victor? Does he have a last name? When did you last see him?"

"I only met him about a week ago at a meet-and-greet. I joined the *Golden Spud*. He's one of the writers. Or . . . was."

Officer Hughes squinted. "Is that a bar? I'm not familiar with it."

"No. It's the university's student newspaper."

"Odd name."

I shrugged.

The handsome man in uniform continued. "Last name?" He had a pad and pen in his hand now. Where did he get those? Was time speeding up again?

"Fitzpatrick."

He wrote on his pad. "Victor Fitzpatrick?"

"What?" I shook my head. "No. Sorry, I thought you wanted my name."

He scratched out his last note. "Okay. Let's start there. Your full name?"

"Francine Fitzpatrick. Most call me Fran. Or Franny. I don't care for Franny. Think about it. Franny Fitzpatrick. What were my parents thinking?" Another nervous habit—digressing. I'd been known to voice the cliche, "But I digress." Of course, saying that would have been another attempt at humour. I don't know if I was becoming aware of how childish I was being, or if I didn't want to embarrass myself any further in front of my present company, but either way, I suppressed the urge to digress again.

He scribbled. "Now that we have that sorted out, Fran, do you know the victim's last name?"

I sucked in a large amount of meadow air and held it briefly. "I only met him the once, and like I said, it was several days ago. I'm not so good with names, but it was something about"—I paused—"pants."

"Pants? His last name is Pants?"

Hoping for a clue to his last name, I looked again at Victor's face but had to turn away. I couldn't imagine who would do such a thing to him. While his face was recognizable, he appeared to have been in a fight for his life. Besides the blood and bruising, his eyes and lips were swollen, and not only was his nose pointing in the wrong direction, but I also had serious doubts about the angle at which his feet were pointing. Sadly, he'd lost that fight, but what could he have possibly been up to? I was starting to remember my meeting with him. He was obnoxious but polite. He'd been wearing a plaid shirt, similar to the one now tucked into his cargo pants.

"That's it!"

Officer Hughes exposed his palms. "What's *it*?"

"Cargo. His last name is Cargo."

The officer made a note of my revelation before escorting me to one of his colleagues. "Officer Mather will take your statement. I may have other questions for you later, so please keep your phone handy."

Seriously? Who *doesn't* keep their phone handy these days? This was more stress-induced sarcasm than humour—good thing I hadn't said it out loud.

Middle-aged Officer Mather had a gentle, kind face. Her appearance and mannerisms reminded me of my high school English teacher, Mrs. Emily White, my biggest encourager when I decided to pursue journalism as a career. While I was giving my account of the last thirty minutes to the uniformed officer, the EMTs carried the now occupied stretcher to the ambulance.

The police were doing their best to hold back the curious, but even they couldn't stop the onlookers from engaging in the distasteful practice of snapping photos. Victor was, of course, covered with a blanket, but his poor family. I wanted to be a reporter someday, so I understood the concept of documenting a story, but I hoped that his loved ones would never see those photos. Had any of the onlookers taken photos of his body before the blanket was placed over him? I didn't realize the importance of that question at the time.

Chapter 3

I GAVE MY RATHER short statement to Officer Mather, noted the phone number she gave me in case I remembered anything else, then decided to skip classes for the day. After the shock of the morning's events, I found myself re-evaluating my future. I questioned whether or not I truly wanted to be an investigative reporter. Did I have what it takes? What kind of reporter cracks jokes at a crime scene, not to mention vomits?

Perhaps Aunt Josephine was right; maybe being knee-deep in crime and tragedy wasn't something I wanted to write about. Maybe veterinary medicine would be for me. Probably not, but I'd seen the vet college from the crime scene, and it was the first alternative career that came to mind.

I wandered west along Belvedere Avenue, then turned south on University Avenue, arguably the busiest street on

Prince Edward Island, or PEI as the province is commonly called. Perhaps the multitude of fast-food restaurants and big-name chain stores comforted me. Having grown up in the suburbs of Toronto, Canada's largest city, I found the heavy car and pedestrian traffic more familiar than the quiet wide streets of my aunt and uncle's neighbourhood.

At the end of University, I turned left onto Grafton Street. This took me past Province House, commonly called the birthplace of Confederation. I wasn't in the mood for a history lesson, so I kept moving.

What *was* I in the mood for? I pulled out my phone and glanced at the time: 11:00 a.m., almost time for lunch, but I wasn't hungry. The thought of food was repellent to my stomach, and as I raised my free hand to wipe my mouth, I realized I was still holding the EMT's towel. I tossed it into a nearby garbage can and checked my phone again. I didn't have any messages, from the police or anyone else.

Of course, why would anyone be messaging me now? I was supposed to be in class. Skipping school was unlike me—in fact, this was the first time I'd ever done so. Finding the body of a recently acquired acquaintance had no doubt caused my foggy state of mind.

As I had told Officer Hughes, I'd only met Victor that one time. I had to admit to myself that while I felt awful about what had happened to him, I didn't like him. He was very sure of himself and condescending toward everyone around him. We all have character flaws, but is a disagreeable personality reason to kill someone? I wouldn't think so, or the worldwide murder rate would be much higher than it is.

Just ahead was Prince Street. This was an older area of Charlottetown, with a mixture of magnificent century-old buildings and churches, and newer structures devoid of the character and grandeur of the others. When I reached the intersection, I turned left and headed north. Just past the Presbyterian church was a two-storey modern building that housed *The Guardian*, the Island's largest newspaper. Standing there, I realized it was very early in my journalism career—one week on the school paper, and I hadn't even written a story yet. Maybe I shouldn't give up so soon because of one moment of weakness.

"Fran, is that you?"

I spun around at the mention of my name. The face before me, bearing cat-eye glasses I thought had gone out of style in the 1960s, was vaguely familiar.

"It's me, Lena. Lena Gallant." She stretched out her hand.

I followed suit and we shook hands. "I'm sorry. I'm not sure . . ." I squinted. I don't know why. How would decreasing my field of vision help me identify this woman with short dark hair, and brown eyes behind those distinctive spectacles. She was sporting a pink University of Prince Edward Island (or UPEI) T-shirt.

Lena threw her head back and laughed. "That's okay. We only met briefly."

I gave her the I-need-more-information sideways glance.

"At the student paper meet-and-greet. Last week."

Here was someone who was gifted at picking up on facial cues and body language—something I needed to work on if I wanted to be an ace reporter. "Right. I think I remember now." Did I? "You've been with the paper a couple of years?"

"No. I'm a freshman, like you." Seems I didn't remember, but Lena's smile told me she was okay with that. "Are you heading to campus? I'm going that way. We could walk together."

I wasn't convinced I was in the mood for company at that moment, but I was going in the same general direction. While I'd met several fellow students, I hadn't made any friends yet, so shunning a potential friend, especially one I'd be seeing regularly at the *Golden Spud* office, didn't feel like the right move. "Sure. I'm heading back home, but it's on the way to the university. Some company would be nice." *I'm such a liar.*

Chapter 4

I PARTED WAYS WITH my new friend when we reached Belvedere Avenue. I was glad I had taken Lena up on her offer of company. She was an interesting character, and more importantly, she informed me that there would be an emergency meeting of the *Golden Spud* staff that evening.

Uncertain of the meeting's purpose, she speculated that it had something to do with the grisly find of a body in a field. Lena asked if I had heard about it. I simply nodded without sharing that I had been the one to find Victor's body.

Did she know it was Victor? Had the police released the victim's name to the media? I had turned the notification setting for my phone off when I checked the time earlier—no wonder I didn't know about tonight's meeting—and hadn't looked at the newsfeed during my wanderings.

A few minutes later I was back at Aunt Josephine and Uncle Johnny's three-bedroom bungalow with the dark green roof and burgundy shutters. Uncle Johnny, the ultimate handyman since retiring from the Canadian National Railway, had built a porch onto the side of the house a couple of years ago. I rummaged in my bag for my keys before remembering that my aunt and uncle never locked the door during the day. Another difference between here and where I'd grown up. In my childhood neighbourhood, we'd locked the apartment door when going to the far end of the hall to throw refuse down the garbage chute.

The small closed-in porch housed a coat closet, a deep freezer, and the washer and dryer. On top of being the ultimate handyman, Uncle Johnny was also the ultimate gentleman—he designed the porch in this way so Aunt Josephine wouldn't have to go down to the basement with groceries and laundry. I'm sure he would have done the laundry for her, but she was a traditionalist. They'd had full-time jobs before retiring, but they stuck to the traditional roles at home: the woman takes care of the inside of the house, and the man takes care of the outside. And no, she wouldn't let the housekeeper do her laundry either.

I left my shoes on the porch, wondered again what had happened to Victor's shoes, then went through the adjoining kitchen, where I dropped my school bag. I could hear the television on in the living room at the opposite side of the house. Aunt Josephine and Uncle Johnny were watching the news. That in itself wasn't surprising; if there was news on, they were watching it. What was surprising was what I heard. The anchorman was talking about a murdered student, that his body was found in the paddock owned by the vet college, and that another student had been arrested this morning. How could they have made an arrest so quickly?

I moved to the hallway between the dining room and living room so I could see the TV. The image changed from the anchorman to video of a student being led from the student union building toward a waiting police car. His jacket was pulled over his head to hide his identity. Then the anchorman reappeared. "Authorities are not releasing the suspect's name at this time, but witnesses report that he worked with the victim on the student newspaper."

I gasped. This drew Aunt Josephine's attention. "Oh, you're home. Isn't it just terrible what happened? That poor child, lying there in the field. Maybe all night by the sounds of it. Dear, dear." She shook her head slowly. "Did you see anything on your way to school?"

I stared at her. Should I tell her the truth? Knowing I'd found Victor might send her into a panic. She was a worrier by nature—a trait common to the Fitzpatricks. Or she might bombard me with questions I couldn't answer. She would want to know who it was. I wasn't sure if Victor's name had been released. They'd referred to him as "the victim," but I didn't hear the beginning of the report.

I choose to avoid my aunt's question with one of my own. "Did they say who the victim was?"

Aunt Josephine rose to her feet and sped past me into the kitchen. "No. Names are being withheld until the family is notified. Standard procedure." She watched a lot more detective shows than she'd ever admit. "You must be hungry. Dinner will be ready soon, but I have some fresh biscuits here."

I followed her into the kitchen. "Your biscuits, or Uncle Johnny's?" I grinned. They were both retired, but my uncle had retired two years before my aunt. During that time, he had taken over some of the cooking and baking. Again, the ultimate gentleman. I enjoyed teasing my aunt by proclaiming that Uncle Johnny's biscuits were the best I'd ever tasted. The truth was, they truly were the best, but thankfully Aunt Josephine thought I was joking. She'd be less than pleased by the truth.

Ignoring my question, my silver-haired landlady deposited a plate of biscuits in front of me. I was quickly learning that on PEI, when you asked for one scoop of potatoes—or one biscuit, as was the case now—your hostess always heard two. She also provided fresh homemade strawberry jam and a hot cup of tea. I had to admit that I was quite fond of the Island hospitality but also feared that my waistline was going to be a concern by Christmas break. It had only been two months since I arrived, and I was already using a looser notch on my belt.

Aunt Josephine headed back into the living room to hear the weather report. "Come and join us, Franny. Boomer is giving the report tonight." Boomer was the nickname of the Island's favourite weatherman. "He's such a riot."

"On my way." As I lifted my plate and cup to take with me, my mind returned to Lena Gallant and how odd it was that I had run into her in town earlier. She never did say what she was doing down there. Or did she? Why wasn't she in class? Could she have had something to do with the murder? Maybe she'd been following me. Had she seen me in the field? I thought back to the crowd of bystanders, but I couldn't remember seeing her with them. Of course, that didn't mean she hadn't been there. Watching.

Chapter 5

AFTER OUR REGULAR supper of potatoes, chicken, and carrots, I helped Aunt Josephine clean up the dishes before heading to the *Golden Spud* meeting. Uncle Johnny had offered to drive me, but when the time came to leave, he was already seated comfortably in his recliner, the evening news turned on.

"I don't like the idea of you walking to the campus on your own at night. Especially after what happened this morning," Aunt Josephine said.

I gazed up at her as I slung my bag over my shoulder. "No need to worry. The meeting is at six thirty. I'm sure it'll be over long before it gets dark outside, and it's only a twenty-minute walk." The irony being that I'd found a dead body early in the day when the sun was shining, and on that same twenty-minute walk. I didn't share that thought out loud. Before today I would have laughed at the idea of anything dangerous happening between the village of Sherwood and the University of Prince Edward Island.

I popped my head around the corner to say bye to my uncle on my way out. His sparse head of hair was visible over the top of his recliner. The retired railroad man could predictably be found sitting there, feet up, every evening after dinner. I walked into the living room and noticed he was half asleep. The lines and sunspots on his face were evidence of his years of working outdoors in harsh weather, yet his eyes were as gentle as a deer's.

When I cleared my throat to get his attention, his eyes popped open and he looked up at me with a smirk. When his expression turned into that silly grin, I knew what was coming. "Did you hear about the accident on the bus?" I shook my head, and he continued. "A woman had her eye on a seat, and a fella came along and sat on it." He laughed. I laughed. I loved Uncle Johnny's corny jokes, and they were especially heartwarming when he related them to current events.

"Was that the lead report tonight?" I asked him.

"Nope, nope. Not the lead story." He switched to his serious mode. "They're still talking about that young man who was found today. Such a shame. You sure you don't need a ride?"

"I'm okay to walk, thanks. I have a few things to think about on my way to the newspaper office."

He rubbed his face with sausage-sized fingers that had seen a lot of hard work over the past few decades. "Call if you'd like a ride home. Especially if it's dark out."

"I will. Thanks." Reminding myself how spoiled I was to

have two such wonderful people looking out for me, I headed off to see what the emergency meeting was about, even though I was fairly certain what the topic of discussion would be.

As I approached the paddock where Victor had been lying, I thought again about his missing shoes. I was tempted to hop the fence to see if I could find them but thought better of crossing the police tape. The crowds had long since dispersed, and a tent was set up over the spot where I had made the gruesome discovery. I realized I hadn't heard from Officer Hughes since the incident. Perhaps that was a good thing. Or maybe not.

Since I'd found the body, I could be their main suspect. That's always the claim on detective shows, but who knows if that's how it works in reality. Maybe his silence was because he was checking into my record. If so, he would have had most of the day available for other tasks, as I had no record.

I shook off the Fitzpatrick worry mode, shifted the backpack to my other shoulder, and continued to the campus. I quickened my pace when, in my peripheral vision, I spotted movement in the distance, to my right. It was probably just a horse, but I didn't want to slow down to verify it. Just in case.

The *Golden Spud* office was comprised of two rooms in the student union building, joined by a hole in the wall. It was an actual hole someone had cut into the wall to join the two rooms. When I first noticed the DIY project, I smiled at the thought that it must have been made to save precious time when an important story had to be sent to the presses at the last minute. Those days of moving paper stories from a typewriter to a printer are long gone. Now reporters simply hit Send on their laptops and the story went to the paper's editor's computer for review—no paper needed.

As I approached the converted barn (commonly called the Barn) that housed the student union and newspaper offices, as well as the university radio station and campus pub, I sensed someone watching me. Tightening my grip on my laptop bag, ready to swing it at potential danger, I spun around to see if I could spot the culprit.

I can't be certain, but I suspect that my feet left the ground for a few seconds when I came face to face with the woman I'd seen earlier in the day, the one with cat-eye glasses. Had Lena been following me?

I felt forced to take a step back and place a more socially reasonable distance between us. "What are you doing?"

"Sorry." She slapped her forehead and laughed. "I've been told I have to work on that. I didn't mean to startle you, but boy, are you hard to catch up to."

I thought back to the feeling of being followed on my way here. "How long have you been trying? To catch up to me, I mean."

"Since the field on Belvedere, the one with the horses. I use it as a shortcut between my apartment and the campus. Saves a few minutes, but I think I'll have to find a new path in the winter. I hear they get a lot of snow around here."

"You use the field as a shortcut?"

She nodded enthusiastically. "Yes."

My earlier suspicions about this new friend were growing stronger. "Didn't you see anything out of place this morning on your way to school? Like a body in the field?" Victor's body wasn't far from the footpath Lena and other students had created while cutting across the field. How could she not have seen him? Had the horses blocked her view? Maybe—they'd completely surrounded him when I first noticed his red socks.

Her hand flew to cover her mouth. "Oh, wow! I hadn't thought of that. If I'd gone to classes this morning as usual, I might have seen the dead guy. That would have freaked me out!"

I noted that Lena referred to the victim as "the dead guy," not Victor. Did that mean she wasn't involved, or that she was attempting to divert suspicion from herself? I still didn't know who knew—or didn't know—I was the one to have found him. If she was privy to that information, it would make sense that she'd want to convince me of her innocence. I was giving myself a headache.

Lena tapped me on the shoulder and returned to her initial topic of conversation. "You're hard to catch up to, though. You were already walking fast, but then near the field you really started hoofing it. I had to scoot under the police tape to catch you, then snagged my pants on the fence." She lifted her leg to display the hole near her ankle. "Don't feel bad, though—it's only an old pair of leggings."

Uncertain of what she thought I had to feel bad about—I didn't tell her to trespass, cross a police barrier, and then jump a fence—I decided to ignore the comment. "How about we head into the meeting?" I opened the door to the Barn and, wanting to keep her in my line of sight, guided her through with a wave of my hand.

The office we sought was at the far end of a long hallway on the first floor. As we approached, I could see that the door was held ajar by a taped-up doorstop, giving us a full view of the large room, which held seven desks, an old photocopier, and a printer on a worn-out stand. In the far-left corner stood a water dispenser, and on a counter adjacent to it, a coffee maker.

Since we provided our own laptops, there was no need for desktop monitors and computer towers. A metal stand once used for vintage audiovisual equipment stood tall in the far-right corner, its new purpose to hold phones and laptops that needed to be charged. The white walls were decorated with old issues of the *Golden Spud* from its inception in the mid-1900s to more recently. The room's only window was positioned above the counter, and it provided a view of the university's sports field and a parking lot.

Seven desk chairs had been assembled in the centre of the room, and three of them were already occupied. I recognized the people seated; I had met them at the meet-and-greet last week.

With Lena and me present, that left two members of the *Golden Spud* staff absent: Victor, who was now lying in the Charlottetown morgue, and Terry James, our editor.

The TV news had reported that a member of the school paper had been arrested. So was Terry in jail? He had been very friendly the few times I'd met him, but perhaps that was his way of giving new students a false sense of security, to lead us to believe he was a decent guy when in fact he was a murderer. He'd made kind remarks about stories I had shared with him when I applied to be a student reporter, even saying how excited he was to have another skilled writer on board. He didn't seem like a murderer. I had to wonder if he'd been hiding his true nature. Was I completely unable to discern human character? I was again doubting my chosen career when a voice from behind made me jump for a second time that evening.

Chapter 6

"TERRY!" HALLIE HOPKINS, the paper's photographer, pushed passed Lena and me at the front of the room before rushing into the hallway and throwing herself into Terry's arms.

Unseen by Hallie, Terry, who must have been about six foot two, rolled his eyes, then gently pried her arms from around his neck and lowered the woman, probably a foot shorter than him, to the floor. Lena smirked and tapped me on the shoulder.

I stepped aside to allow Terry entry into the room, then followed him with my eyes as he high-fived the other men before taking a seat. If Terry wasn't in jail, then who had been arrested? It seemed I wasn't wrong about him after all—he wasn't the type of person who could murder someone. I released a silent sigh but again doubted myself when he addressed the room.

"They can't hold someone without evidence. My father called a lawyer as soon as the cops hauled me out of class." He turned to Andy O'Connell, a reporter with the *Golden Spud* since starting at UPEI three years prior. "Thanks for calling my dad, Andy."

"No problem. The whole class was losing it. We didn't know what was going on. Then when class ended and word around campus was that some guy was found dead, man, we all thought the worst."

I wondered why Andy would assume the worst? Did he *know* it was a murder? Or did he just suspect it was? Did he immediately believe that Terry's arrest had something to do with murder? Or were he and Terry with Victor when Victor was killed? Maybe they were the killers. Was Terry free because of lack of evidence or because he was innocent?

I wiped away the sweat that was running down my face as I made my way to one of the empty chairs. Lena was already sitting. When did she move from beside me? Was time standing still again? I stared at my shoes. Being in the room with not just one but possibly two killers wasn't where I wanted to be at that moment, but I couldn't leave without hearing more. And if I left now, the culprit might think I was on to him. Or them.

I returned my attention to the group and found Terry staring at me. I gulped and stared back. Should I run?

He folded his arms across his chest. "I didn't do it!"

I was going to have to work on my poker face. "Um . . . of course not. Did what?" I don't know why I chose to play dumb, but it couldn't hurt. Could it?

Terry rose to his feet and approached me. "I didn't kill Victor."

Multiple comments from the others. "It was Victor?" "Oh man, that's awful." "Poor guy. He was a creep, but poor guy." I couldn't tell who was saying what because my attention was fully on this tall, slim man who stood before me.

Terry turned back to face the others. "Sorry, guys." He squinted at me. "I didn't mean to blurt that out. I meant to be a bit more tactful."

I mouthed *Sorry*, but I wasn't convinced it was my fault that he'd blurted out sensitive news. After all, he had been arrested after someone was found dead, so why wouldn't people be suspicious? Are we in the media not supposed to be suspicious—even of each other?

It was Hallie's turn to give me the evil eye. "I would never believe such a horrible thing about you, Terry."

He nodded at her. "Thanks, Hallie. Anyway, turns out that after Victor's body was discovered, the police canvassed his dorm and someone there told them that Vic and I had an argument yesterday."

Our sportswriter, Greg MacLean, leaned back in his chair, almost to the tipping point. "Ack. That's dumb. If everyone who'd argued with that guy got arrested, the whole campus would be in jail." He returned the front legs of his chair to the floor, then headed to the counter for a drink. After guzzling a can of pop, he crushed the container and tossed it across the room into the garbage bin. Greg was the stereotypical jock in appearance—tall and muscular with young George Clooney looks. I made a mental note that he was someone who'd not only admitted to disliking the victim, but who also had the strength to cause the wounds I'd seen.

Great! I suspected three of my new acquaintances of murder. Make that four—Lena was still on my list of suspicious characters. I directed my attention to Hallie, the only one who hadn't given me reason to question her character.

Other than being too obvious in expressing her feelings for someone who didn't reciprocate the affection, Hallie came off as harmless. On the other hand, perhaps it was an act to fool the rest of us.

Good for me—I now suspected everyone in the room of being cold-blooded killers.

Chapter 7

I WATCHED OUR EDITOR circle the room for a fifth time, paying close attention to the back of his head as he passed me. With all the head rubbing he was doing, I was certain he must have created a bald spot by now. I almost choked on my gum when he turned around in mid-stride to face me. The guy had a well-developed sense of being watched—or was it paranoia? I was expecting another proclamation of his innocence, but he merely held my gaze briefly before changing his trajectory.

He headed to the coffee pot and filled a mug. After taking a few sips, he grimaced, returned the mug to the counter, and resumed pacing. "We need to find out what happened to Victor last night. I know I didn't do it, but I can't afford a long-term lawyer. My dad called one of those free services this afternoon, but that won't cut it if I'm charged. If the police don't find a better suspect, I might end up being their scapegoat."

Hallie leaped to her feet. "Don't you worry, Terry. We'll find out who did this terrible thing. We are reporters, after all." She looked around the room, apparently hoping for agreement from the others, but all she got were frightened faces.

I was surprised by the lack of enthusiasm. Here they had a crime, a victim, and a suspect within their own circle of friends, but none of them were on fire to get to the truth. They all looked terrified.

"Hey, man." Andy was now on his feet. "Of course we can help—I guess. Just tell us what you want us to do. I got a few bucks I can loan you." He shrugged. "I s'pose. But man, if they ain't got anything on you, it's probably okay. Right?"

Hey, man? S'pose? Ain't? I eyed Andy as he played with the zipper on his jacket. He was starting his fourth year of university and was a senior writer on the school paper. I thought back to articles of his I had read when I first considered joining the *Golden Spud*. They were brilliant and I had been looking forward to working with him. Were there two Andy O'Connells at UPEI?

"Andy's right, Terry. It'll be okay." Hallie tried to hug Terry again. He pushed her off again, then resumed pacing.

Lena had been quiet. I assumed that it was because, like me, she was new to the paper and wanted to get a feel for the group dynamics. "I'd be happy to do some investigating." As she said this, Lena was staring at Greg. Truth be told, she was practically drooling. "I think we should work in teams. Greg and I could work together."

Greg smiled at Lena and nodded. Terry rolled his eyes. I might have done the same. Terry pulled his laptop from its bag. "I'm glad you're all so willing to help. I have an idea."

We sat in silence as our editor typed into his laptop. Then, in what would have looked like perfectly synchronized choreography from someone looking in from the hallway, we all turned our heads to the right in response to the printer turning on. I marvelled at the wonders of Wi-Fi.

Once the printer stopped, Terry retrieved a small stack of papers from it and returned to his chair. He made some notes on the back of a blank page, which he handed to me, then handed each person a printed page. "I've indicated what I'd like each of you to do for me. We will be information gathering only. No need to write an article or interview anyone at this point. Do precisely what I've indicated and nothing more."

Each of my journalist colleagues reviewed their instructions, gave a nod of understanding to Terry, then exited the office. I leaned forward as our leader approached me. I steadied my legs to keep myself from bouncing around—my first assignment was to help find a murderer!

My earlier concerns that the very person who was the murderer might be among us had diminished as the meeting went on, but when I turned over the page handed to me, the sweat returned to my forehead. Terry had written a single line.

Meet me in the parking lot by the men's dorm. We need to talk.

In my confusion my jaw dropped, and I raised my head to ask Terry why, but he was gone.

Chapter 8

T HE MEN'S DORM was on the other end of the campus on the east side of University Avenue, situated between the woman's dorm to the south and the building that held the registrar's office to the north. I pulled out my phone to check the time: 7:00 p.m. I estimated another hour before sunset started.

I asked myself why Terry wanted to meet at that location. Perhaps he lived there. It wasn't what I'd call secure or isolated, but not knowing what type of danger I might be walking into, I debated meeting him versus taking my uncle up on his offer to pick me up.

I would meet Terry, but as a precaution, I opened the recording app on my phone, then shoved it into my jacket pocket. If something bad happened to me, there would be audio evidence of the responsible party. Or would there? Everyone had smartphones with voice recorders; the killer would simply take my phone to avoid being caught.

I paused between the Barn and the registrar's office as the debate raged on in my mind. But how dangerous could it be? The parking lot mentioned in Terry's note had to be the one between the two dorms, no doubt frequented by car-owning students. I made up my mind to meet him, since there would be other people around.

My assumption was wrong. When I reached the parking lot, it was empty except for a small green hatchback. *Stupid.* I slapped my forehead; yes, this was the student parking lot, but the average student couldn't afford a car. I certainly couldn't. If it wasn't for Aunt Josephine and Uncle Johnny giving me a roof over my head and a full belly, I would have had to work for a few years before I had the funds needed to attend university.

I fingered the phone in my pocket and again questioned the wisdom of meeting up with a murder suspect. Not only were there no other cars, but also no people. That meant no witnesses to whatever evil plans he might have for me.

I wanted to back out, to run, but it was too late to pull a no-show—Terry had already seen me and was exiting his vehicle. He waved me over.

I touched the screen on the phone where I hoped the Start button for the recorder was and strolled to the car. I wanted to appear unfazed about meeting him. "Show no fear," they say. Who *they* are I didn't know; nor did I know why I was following their directions.

Why was I meeting this man who had singled me out to meet him? Why had he singled me out? Maybe it was fear of authority, and being kicked off the school paper, that had brought me here. Or maybe I actually had what it took to be an investigative reporter: bravery and determination to find the truth. I hoped it was the latter. Fear of authority wasn't a good reason to put myself into danger, but getting a good story, well, that was a good reason, right?

"I'm glad you came." Terry's gaze shot to the men's dorm before returning to me. The head rubbing returned. "I wasn't sure you'd show." He nodded toward the library. "Can we walk?"

"Sure." Relieved that he didn't want me to get into his car, I took in a huge breath and felt my shoulder muscles loosen.

We made our way along the path to the library. As we passed the brown-brick structure with a tilted roof and large windows, I noticed a sunroom off the second floor. Was it possible that someone sitting up there could have seen what had happened to Victor? Might they have seen the murderer running from the field back to the campus? Or to a car waiting on the road?

Uncertain of the purpose of our meeting, I kept my questions to myself as we headed north of the building to the deserted railway tracks on the far-west side of the campus. Our path was leading us close to where Victor's body had been lying less than twelve hours earlier.

"Is there a reason you want to go in this direction?" I asked.

Terry choked out a laugh. "Wondering if I'm returning to the scene of the crime?"

I slapped my forehead, then ran my hand over my hair so that the head slap wasn't so obvious. "No. Of course not. I'm just . . . well . . ."

"Don't worry about it. I'm just kidding. Today has been such a nightmare, I thought I'd try a little humour. Guess it didn't work."

Was Terry a kindred spirit who also used humour in stressful situations? "I think we're all uptight. It's not every day a friend gets murdered."

Terry stopped and rubbed his face. His eyes were red and his cheeks flushed. "He *was* my friend, you know. We didn't see eye to eye on most things, but he was the only other real reporter on the paper. We had no choice but to work together to get enough decent stories out each week to keep the thing going."

He continued. "Three years we'd been doing this. You can't help but become friends when you spend that much time with a guy. Like I said, we didn't like each other, but we did confide in one another about school stuff, and sometimes personal stuff. Home life and all that."

I didn't know how to respond. I knew Terry and Victor less than they'd known each other—and less than Terry knew the other students on the paper. "Why are you telling *me* this and not the others?"

"The sample articles you submitted when you applied to the paper, they were really good. Much better than the rest of the gang could write. I don't know if you noticed tonight, but none of them have a good grasp on . . . well, I don't want to be critical. They all have good hearts, but writers they are not."

We continued our walk along the trail, the sun behind us bright in the clear sky. I tugged on a tall piece of grass and tied it in a knot. "What do they do, then?"

"They do some interviews and gather information. Greg supplies us with all the sports statistics we need for the sports page, and he'll occasionally interview one of the players. He records the conversation. Then Victor or I would write an article. I guess it'll just be me now."

The more I listened to Terry, the less I suspected him of

being the one to end Victor's life. In fact, from what I was hearing, he had the least motive of anyone.

"Andy and I have been friends since high school. Being on the paper gives him extra credits in his English class, and bonus points with his parents. They can be difficult. He struggled in high school to keep his grades up and please them, but I don't think they ever showed any support. He deserves better. When he offered to lend me money earlier, he would have done it, if he had any to spare."

That explained my observation about Andy's speaking versus writing abilities.

"That's rough," I said. I understood what it was like to have family who didn't recognize your efforts. It didn't mean they didn't love you, but it could be crushing to the spirit. "What about Hallie?" I suppressed a giggle. Terry was suffering enough; this was no time to tease him. There'd be time for that later.

He inhaled so deeply, I thought his lungs might explode. He held the breath, creating a dramatic pause, shook his head, then exhaled. "Hallie. I have no idea why she wanted to join the paper."

I smirked. "I think I do."

He shrugged. "Okay. Yes, she seems to have a crush on me. I don't know why. I've never done anything to encourage her. She's nice and all, but I'm just not interested in someone who's so into PDAs."

"PDAs?"

"Public displays of affection. She's always hugging me. It gets tiring."

"I can only imagine." I wasn't a fan of hugging and PDAs, as he called them, myself. "How did she find her way onto the paper if she doesn't have writing talent?"

"That was all Victor. He spotted her leaning all over me at the pub one night last winter and offered her a chance to be a"—he made air quotes—"star reporter. She's been hanging around ever since. I didn't have the heart to tell her she wasn't skilled as a writer, but she does take decent photos, so I made her our photographer."

"Do you think she knows that Victor was using her to give you a hard time? That would make any woman angry."

Terry stopped and pointed his finger at me. "See? That there—that's why I wanted to talk to you. I need help getting to the bottom of this. You have that inquisitive way of thinking. I saw it in your eyes when you were watching me at the office earlier."

"Yeah. Sorry about that. When we first started the meeting, I was suspicious of everyone in the room, but by the time it ended, I wasn't so sure any of you had motive. Well, except for you."

Terry's brow furrowed.

I gulped and raised my hands, feigning a defensive posture. "But not now. I believe in your innocence now, though I'm still confused as to why you wanted to meet with me alone."

"Because I need your help. Like I said earlier, I can't afford a lawyer, and if the police can't find another suspect, they'll come after me. I was seen arguing with Victor the night before he died. People have been jailed for less."

I wished he was wrong about that, but having spent much of my teens watching true crime shows, I knew he wasn't. Terry wouldn't be the first innocent man thrown into jail for the sole purpose of calling a case closed.

Chapter 9

"WHAT CAN I do?" I asked.

We paused in our trek when the path came to a crossroads. We could turn left and head toward the school's football field, or right and find ourselves in the paddock. The latter wasn't a place I was anxious to return to so soon.

Movement between the field and veterinary college caught my eye. Someone in blue overalls and waders was guiding one of the horses onto a trailer. The horse had a contraption on his head that appeared to be blocking his view.

Terry must have noticed my confusion. "They're called blinders. Sometimes handlers put them on a horse to focus his attention forward so he's less likely to get spooked. That's what I've been told anyway. I'm not sure—horses aren't my thing."

Whether they were his "thing" or not, he knew more about

the magnificent beasts than I did, so I accepted his explanation and returned to thinking about our path. Straight ahead led to Sherwood and my warm, comfy bed. I was starting to feel the effects of the day's events and yawned. "Why didn't you ask the others to help out?"

Terry ran his hand over his head. "I'm so sorry. It's getting late. You're probably exhausted. Let's head back and I'll give you a drive home."

I continued straight on the path. "No worries. I live over there on Ashwood Drive. It's just a short walk. I'll be okay."

Terry trotted after me. "No way. After what happened to Victor, I'm not letting you walk home alone. I can walk back to campus once you're safely inside."

Without meaning to, I stopped walking and stood there, my eyes darting along the road in front of us. What should I do now? While I was happy for the company because I didn't want to walk home alone at that time of day, I wasn't convinced that showing Terry where I lived was a good idea.

Unlike me, he was skilled at reading people. "Seriously? I thought you trusted me. I'm not going to sneak into your house in the middle of the night and kidnap or murder you."

I attempted a silly grin. "Are you sure?"

My attempt at humour failed. "I'm sure." He continued along the path—it was now my turn to trot after him. His long legs allowed him to cover a greater distance with each stride than I could. I felt like a shih tzu trying to keep up with an Irish wolfhound.

"I didn't ask the others to help me because they don't have that suspicious mind of yours. They're good people, but I worry that they'd make things worse, not better. That's why I instructed them to do only what was printed on their sheets of paper."

"What instructions did you give them?"

"To keep their eyes and ears open, and to write down anything they hear anyone say about Victor. And to keep their cellphones on in case I need them." Pretty basic stuff. It sounded as if he wanted to give them the feeling of being involved but without letting them do anything.

The path ended at Mt Edward Road. Traffic was heavy here at this time of day, with people leaving the mall heading south and others leaving the downtown area heading north. We waited a few minutes until there was a safe gap between cars, then ran across the road. I led the way through the side streets that would take us to my aunt and uncle's house.

A sudden thought ripped through my mind and I grabbed Terry's arm, startling him. He hopped twice on one leg to keep from falling into a ditch. His brows furrowed for a second time this evening. Was he starting to doubt the wisdom of asking me to help him?

"What?" He scanned the road behind and ahead of us. "The way you were acting, I thought we were about to be hit by a car."

"Lena!"

"Lena's about to hit us? Where? There's no one around."

"No. Earlier when we were eliminating the others at the paper as suspects, we didn't discuss Lena. How well do you know her?"

"I don't know her. Not really. She applied to work on the *Golden Spud* the same day we had the meet-and-greet. She didn't have any articles to share with me—said she'd show me some later—but she does have experience doing page layout.

She had a referral letter from a teacher at her high school. The layout process can be tedious, so I was happy to have someone else who was willing to do it."

"Interesting." I rubbed my chin to emphasize my comment.

Terry shrugged. "Why suspect her? She's a freshman. She didn't even know Victor until the meet-and-greet."

"Not that we know of." I jabbed my thumb back at the field. "Did you know that every morning she passes through the paddock where they found Victor's body? But this morning she conveniently"—I made air quotes—"skipped classes." Thinking I was on to something, I felt my heart rate speed up as my excitement grew. "I ran into her in town this afternoon, and she claimed she skipped classes this morning and so wasn't in the field. I found it odd she'd be in town rather than in class."

"Why were *you* in town this afternoon?"

Rats. Too much information. I remained uncertain as to who I should share my discovery of the body with, but if I was going to work with Terry to uncover the real murderer, I'd have to trust him. If he got charged with the crime, his lawyer would need to be privy to all of the details of the case, including who discovered the body. It would be better if he heard it from me.

"Terry, I have something to tell you."

As we made our way to the bungalow with the burgundy shutters, I started to share the details of my morning, minus the breakfast discussion with Aunt Josephine. I was interrupted when, five houses from home, a car came around the corner at the other end of Ashwood Drive. A white car with unlit lights on the roof and Charlottetown Police Department in large black letters across the side.

"Oh no." I started running.

Chapter 10

PLACING MYSELF IN front of a moving car wasn't the wisest thing I'd ever done; I was putting my faith in the observation skills and fast reflexes of the person behind the wheel. Surely they'd see me, flailing arms and all, as I flagged them down. I ran past Uncle Johnny and Aunt Josephine's house and stood my ground two houses farther down the road. I let out a breath of relief as the cruiser slowed to a stop in front of me and the driver turned off the ignition.

The officer turned on the flashing lights, leaped out of his vehicle, and unholstered his gun. It was Officer Hughes. When he pointed the weapon in my direction, I ducked down until I was face to face with the grille of the car.

My eyes were drawn to the assortment of dead bugs on the shiny metal before me. Wasps, ladybugs, flies, and a large-eyed, winged creature I couldn't identify that had slimy goo leaking from its torso. My nose scrunched up as I gulped down my surging stomach contents. I had to get this nausea-in-times-of-stress thing under control.

"Hands up!" I could hear the anxiety in Officer Hughes's voice. He sounded as nervous as I felt, but there was a gun involved, so without standing, I raised my hands in the air. "Not you!" he said.

I peered behind me. I'd forgotten about Terry in my haste to keep my aunt and uncle from seeing a police car rolling down their driveway. He stood frozen, hands in the air, his body trembling. I'd felt so relaxed with Terry by the time we'd made our way to Sherwood that I'd forgotten he was a murder suspect. I couldn't dismiss the possibility that he was under police surveillance and we'd been followed here.

I released the breath I'd been holding and unbuckled my knees. I wasn't the target of the man holding the gun—my new friend was. It was safe for me to stand, so I did.

As the sun sank below the horizon, the clouds opened up and released their contents on us. The three of us, soaked to the skin, stood like statues in a museum. What now? I glanced at Terry, then back at the man in uniform, then at Terry again.

Terry rubbed his face on his shoulders—first the right cheek, then the left—and I wondered if it was just the rain he was wiping away or tears as well. The approximately six-foot-tall man appeared to be shrinking back into boyhood before my eyes. Was he imagining his future ruined? His dreams lost? Years of pleading innocent to a crime the world might come to believe he committed?

Despite the cold rain, heat rushed through my body as my fingers curled into fists. I directed my newfound rage at

Officer Hughes. "What are you doing? Why are you pointing a gun at my friend? He's not your murderer. You have the wrong guy."

The lights in the house across the street came on. I didn't know if it was the flashing lights or my shouting that had drawn their attention, but I glanced up the road. The light in Aunt Josephine's kitchen came on too. I slapped my head. So much for keeping her from seeing the police car.

Officer Hughes simply shook his head and rolled his eyes. "Calm down." He reholstered the gun, then nodded in Terry's direction. "You were running toward me Ms. Fitzpatrick, and then I spotted your friend over there, and he was running too. I had to take appropriate action."

His sparkling blue eyes, lit up by the cruiser's lights, captured my gaze. I couldn't look away.

Officer Hughes released me from my trance when he redirected his attention to Terry and his brows furrowed. "You might be right. He might be innocent. But the department thinks he's our man, and we aim to prove it."

Terry lowered his arms. "I was running to catch up with Fran. Are you here to arrest me again?"

"No. I didn't even know you were going to be in this area of town." That answered one of my questions—they didn't have Terry under surveillance. "I'm here to speak to Franny Fitzpatrick." Was that a smirk on his face?

"It's *Fran*. Not Franny." I peered back at the house. No movement. The light was still on in the kitchen, but I didn't see any sign of my aunt in the window. She might have, however, repositioned herself in front of the window in the dining area to get a better view from the darkened room. I wasn't the only one in the family with an inquisitive mind.

"My apologies . . . Fran. Mr. James, you're welcome to head home. I have no questions for you at this time." He reached into his car and turned off the lights.

I folded my arms. "Terry and I were having a discussion. You can't just dismiss him like that."

Terry put his hand on my shoulder. "It's okay, Fran." As he spoke to me, he glared at Officer Hughes. "We can continue our discussion tomorrow."

Before Terry had a chance to make his exit, I heard a familiar voice in the wind. "Franny, is that you? You and your friends need to get out of the rain. Hurry up, now. I've put the tea on."

I smiled at the two men and shrugged. "You heard the lady."

Then I gave Officer Hughes my most serious face, but not knowing if he could see me in the darkness, I also used my most serious voice. "If you don't come in with us, I'll be bombarded with questions as to who you are. If you have questions for me, I'll be happy to answer them for you after my aunt fills us with tea and squares. And whatever you do, *do not* tell her I was the one who found the body."

I felt Terry's hand leave my shoulder. "*You* found Victor?"

Nuts. I hadn't gotten around to telling him that bit of news before spotting the police car.

It might seem odd that an officer of the law and a new friend who had just found out I was keeping important information from him would accompany me into my aunt's house for tea and snacks, but I could only assume that both being Islanders, they were by nature obedient to their elders. It was the Island way; when an older person invited you in for tea, you didn't refuse, no matter what the circumstances.

I showed my companions where to hang their wet coats, then hurried into the kitchen. "Aunt Josephine, it isn't necessary to invite those two in. We were having a little chat, that's all. They need to get home."

She smiled a suggestive smile. "Oh, don't be silly. I'm impressed, my dear. Not just one young fella but two, escorting you home from your meeting. Well done!"

My head tilted. "Excuse me?" She couldn't be serious. Why would friends drive me home in a police cruiser? But maybe she hadn't noticed the car with flashing lights. "They weren't escorting me home. Terry is the editor of the paper, and the other guy—"

Officer Hughes appeared in the doorway, holding his hat in his hands. "Thank you for the invitation into your home, ma'am, but I'm afraid I'm on duty and simply can't stay."

Aunt Josephine took his arm in hers. "Oh, don't be silly. A quick cup of tea and a few bites to keep you warm won't do any harm. You'll be back to work in no time."

She led him to a seat at the table, which was already set up for what appeared to be a formal tea party. In the centre was a platter that held at least four types of squares, a variety of cookies, and sliced banana bread. Three chairs sat behind three table settings, each with a teacup, a dessert plate, a dessert fork, and a napkin. How had she done all this so fast?

Chapter 11

IT WOULDN'T BE an exaggeration to say that overnight I was as restless as a chihuahua in a roomful of Great Danes.

Aunt Josephine had left Terry, Officer Hughes, and me alone after placing the piping hot teapot on the dining table, which hadn't stopped my two new acquaintances from making a quick exit—after swiping a few sweet squares from the platter first, of course.

Terry had been the first to excuse himself, and who could blame him for wanting to make his escape from the policeman who'd arrested him, the new friend who'd failed to be honest with him, and the crazy yet sweet geriatric woman who had been eyeing him as potential marriage material for someone he hardly knew? Terry had every reason to run, and a good part of my sleepless night was spent worrying that he might never forgive me.

Officer Hughes, or David as I now chose to call the man who had been sitting in my house eating my squares—okay, technically not my house or my squares, but I digress—stayed a few minutes longer after Terry left and started to ask his questions. Not wanting to let on to my aunt more than she needed to know—that I had discovered a dead body—I refused to answer his questions in her house, and we agreed to meet the next day after my last class.

I had quietly cleaned up the tea party dishes and put away the leftover treats while Aunt Josephine and Uncle Johnny snored in front of the nightly news. Once I cleared the kitchen and dining room of any evidence of my aunt's attempt to marry me off, I headed straight to my bedroom without saying goodnight or turning on the lights. I had to scream in silence when the small toe of my foot came into rapid, unforgiving contact with the desk sitting against the far wall across from the foot of my bed. It was a small miracle that Aunt Josephine had nodded off without first questioning me about my male companions—I wasn't going to risk waking her up.

I finally dozed off about 3:00 a.m., but the effects of the tea shortened my slumber, and at 4:00 a.m. I was sneaking down the hallway to the bathroom. I was happy to see that the television was off, the living room silent, and the door at the far end of the hall closed. The guilt of leaving my wonderful hosts snoozing in their recliners was one worry I could let go of before I had to start my day. Other worries, however, prevented me from returning to a dream state.

At 6:00 a.m. there seemed to be little reason to stay in

bed, so I dressed, popped a ball cap over my bedhead, grabbed my backpack, and headed to the side door. With any luck I could get out of the house before my housemates woke—I could still hear snoring coming from their room—but when I got to the kitchen, the dishwasher was running and the table saw in Uncle Johnny's basement workshop was buzzing away. How had I not heard him get up and turn on the dishwasher? I'd worry about that later; I took my chance to make an escape while he was occupied with a project and Aunt Josephine was still sleeping. I wrote them a quick note about wanting to get to the library early, then bolted out the door.

Before I made it to the street, the phone in my pocket vibrated twice, indicating a text. I was happy and nervous to see that it was from Terry. *Can you meet me at the corner coffee shop before classes start? I'll be there by eight.* The clock on the phone said it was 6:30 a.m. Great. That gave me one and a half hours to worry if my new friend hated me.

I was relieved to find that the university library opened on weekdays at 6:00 a.m. and that I wouldn't have to stand outside in the cool morning air before my meeting with Terry. It also meant I'd have time to check out the sunroom I'd noticed last evening.

Two large wooden doors, each with a vertically placed rectangular window, graced the front entrance to the library, built in 1975, as stated on the cornerstone plaque dedicating the building to Samuel Robertson. When I first enrolled at UPEI, I researched the history of the school, and Dr. Robertson was a memorable name I came across. He was a principal at the Prince of Wales College before it united with St. Dunstan's University to become the University of Prince Edward Island. According to the library's website, Dr. Robertson had a love for libraries and was saddened that his college didn't have one of its own.

Holding one of the doors open as I entered the lobby, I spotted a middle-aged lady standing under the Book Return sign. Her salt and pepper hair was braided and secured behind her head with a large flowery clip that was obvious, as she had her head down. She was reading a paper on the counter that separated her from the larger public area. A metal name tag pinned to her shirt informed me that her name was Maggie Smith and she was the librarian.

I released my hold on the door, and my presence was announced less than peacefully by the loud clunk of wood on wood when it slammed closed. Behind her large, round glasses, the librarian's eyes briefly darted in my direction.

"I'm so sorry. I didn't mean to startle you." *Way to make a first impression, Fran.*

Ms. Smith's startled expression quickly turned to a glowing, welcoming smile that would have made Mrs. Claus jealous. "Oh, don't be silly, dear. My mind was caught up in the news. They still have no leads as to what happened to that poor soul who was found in the field yesterday."

What was it with older Islanders and their constant focus on the news? Of course, in fairness, I'd only been on the Island a couple of months and, outside of family, this was the first person over fifty I'd met. I rubbed my chin. Perhaps we were related? I'd have to ask Aunt Josephine later; she knew every relative we had on the Island, no matter how distant the familial connection.

"Did you hear about what happened yesterday? I don't

think I've seen you in here before. Are you a freshman? I'm pretty good at remembering faces. And names too. Yours is?"

"Fran. Yes, I'm a freshman." Without answering the question about Victor, I approached the counter and offered my hand in greeting.

Ms. Smith raised her hand, smudged with black, palm out toward me. "Newsprint." She folded the paper and shoved it onto a shelf behind the counter. "The rest of the news can wait for tea break. I guess you young people don't have to worry about newsprint with those pocket computers you have." She laughed. "What can I do for you, Fran? We don't usually have students here this early in the morning. Well, not until exam time."

"I spotted the sunroom yesterday when I was strolling the campus. I woke early this morning and couldn't get back to sleep, so I thought I'd use the time to check it out. Is there a study area up there?"

"There certainly is. Why don't you head on up and have a peek? I'm sure you'll have it all to yourself this early in the day."

After she gave me directions on how to find the sunroom, I made my way there through the stacks of book and journals. This library was devoid of the musty smell I'd experienced in other older, larger, and less well-kept ones. There wasn't a speck of dust to be found on the shelves I passed, and the carpet, while worn in high-traffic areas, was clean. Someone truly cared about these books, and this building.

I found myself hoping it wouldn't end up abandoned as so many libraries have been in this age of online everything. E-books, e-shopping, e-stores. Everything was going online, even my chosen profession. The world of journalism has always been highly competitive, but printed newspapers and magazines were becoming a thing of the past, with online bloggers and social media dominating readers' attention. I questioned whether there was a place for traditional journalism anymore, and if there would be a job for me after graduation.

The entrance to the sunroom was ahead of me. I suppressed the depressing thoughts about my future and focused on the task before me. Might there have been a witness here when Victor was murdered? Could they have seen what happened, and who the culprit was?

Ms. Smith said that students were rarely in the library so early this time of year, but I hadn't thought to ask her if anyone had been up here at the time of the murder—whenever that was, exactly. Perhaps I'd forgotten on purpose, not wanting to discuss the case with anyone this early in the day. *Bad plan, Fran—Ms. Smith might have seen something important.* I made a mental note to talk to her on my way out.

I checked the time on the clock that was hanging on the wall to the side of the double glass doors that led to the sunroom: 7:15 a.m. I had forty-five minutes before I was to meet Terry. That was plenty of time to check out this area, then head to the coffee shop, which was sounding more and more appealing. My stomach noisily reminded me that I hadn't eaten breakfast. I instinctively placed my hand on my belly as though that would quiet its discontent, then headed into my first site of investigation.

What appeared to be only a sunroom from the outside of the building was a large study area. At the far end of the room was a step down to a welcoming space bordered by a half wall on the inner side, and floor-to-ceiling windows on the opposite wall offered a view of the surrounding campus.

Long and narrow, the space housed multiple seating

arrangements for study, reading, or relaxing. Comfort and luxury were the point here, so this room wouldn't be conducive to studying on a warm, sunny day for me. I chuckled at the thought that my snoring would break the QUIET rule posted on the entry doors.

I edged around the sleep-trap chairs to get a better view from the windows. They faced north, not east. How did I not notice this yesterday evening? I positioned myself at the east end of the room and strained to see the paddock. Negative. Even standing on my tiptoes, I couldn't see over the veterinary college. I scanned the room to make sure no one else was around, then stood on a table. I still couldn't see the field, and even if I could, why would someone here to study push themselves up against the glass while standing on a table? Nuts. This was a dead end. So much for restoring Terry's faith in me by offering up an important lead.

"Fran! What are you doing up there?"

Chapter 12

AT THE SOUND of my name, I lost my footing. I had been leaning into the window with my feet at the edge of the table when I was yanked from my thoughts. One foot slid off the edge, propelling my body forward. To keep from face-slamming into the glass, I pulled my shoulders back. The adrenalin coursing through my system heightened the energy behind my shift in position, sending me backwards.

I could feel my feet lift into the air as my head shot toward the floor. I squeezed my eyes and held my breath, anticipating the severe head and back pain that was about to become my reality—if I didn't crack my skull and end up dead, a casualty of my foolish behaviour. Were there cameras in this area of the library? Was I about to become an internet hit for those who enjoyed laughing at others' misfortunes?

I raised my hand to shield the back of my head, but before I completed the manoeuvre, I found myself lying on a cushiony surface. I closed my eyes and thanked God for the tacky plush chairs that decorated this part of the sunroom.

"Wow. That was awesome. And scary. Sorry. Guess I startled you."

I opened my eyes to see Lena standing over me, hugging a stack of books close to her chest. She pushed her glasses up on her nose, then suppressed a laugh. "Are you okay?"

I lay still as I took a silent inventory of my body parts. My head was clear, and I was free of pain. I lowered a hand to the floor to lift my torso, helping myself into a sitting position. "I don't think I hurt anything . . . well, except for my pride." I squinted at Lena. "You weren't filming this, were you?"

She waved a hand in the air. "Oh no. Of course not. I never turn my phone on until lunchtime. Those things are addictive, you know. I once missed a whole morning of classes in high school because I got caught up watching videos online." She tsked at her own behaviour. "After that I made a rule to not turn it on until lunch." She extended her left hand to me. "Need help?"

"Thanks." I grasped her hand, intending to help by rolling and pushing myself up with my other hand, but when Lena gave me a tug, I was on my feet in an instant. I was gobsmacked at the strength of her tiny body.

"What were you doing up there on the table? Is there something going on outside?" Lena peered over her shoulder and out the window. "I don't see anything."

Her gaze shifted from the garden immediately outside the library to the veterinary college and lingered there. Her expression went from curiosity to concern as she returned her attention to me. "Were you looking to see if the horse field was visible from here? Is that why you're here?"

There was no point in lying. Why shouldn't I be curious? But instead I said, "I came in early to get a feel for the library. You know, get a library card and all." A library card? What was I thinking?

"A library card? Silly. No one uses those anymore. It's all on an app now. You can get it on your phone. Let me show you." Lena tossed her stack of books onto a chair and swung her backpack around. She started to unzip the phone pocket, then stopped and cocked her head. "Oops. It's not noon yet. Sorry. I'll have to show you later."

I had the app already. A link to it came with the registration documents the university sends to all the students. "No problem. I'm sure I'll figure it out." Now it was my turn to ask the questions. "So, Lena, what are you doing here so early?"

She hesitated, then shrugged. "Nothing." Without saying another word, the cat-eye-glasses-wearing powerhouse picked up her stack of books and fled.

The whole encounter was odd. If Lena was strong enough to lift me to my feet, she'd be strong enough to bludgeon Victor. If she was the killer, she might have been here to see if the sunroom was a source of possible witnesses to her crime.

I grabbed my bag and sprinted out of the library. When I felt the cool rush of late-summer air on my skin, I realized that in my haste I had forgotten to talk to Ms. Smith. That conversation would have to wait; I ran to the coffee shop, anxious to give Terry the latest update.

Chapter 13

I'M NOT A runner; last night's rush to stop the police car was pure adrenalin. Walking fast at a time of urgency is about the closest I've ever gotten to a sprint as an adult. Struggling against rising pain in my legs, and gasping for more air as my ability to take it in diminished with each slap of my foot on the ground, I made a pact with my too-young-to-be-this-out-of-shape body to add regular visits to the campus sports complex.

Despite my efforts to keep up the pace, my muscles could take no more and I was slowing down against my will. The coffee shop was within one hundred yards. *A little farther, Fran, you can do it.* The pep talk worked—briefly. Again, adrenalin rushed through my veins and I picked up the pace. I was feeling rather proud of myself to have made it this far, this fast, but as I attempted to leap over a concrete parking barrier, the toe of my shoe caught the metal bar at the top, bringing me to an abrupt stop. *Not twice in one day.* As my body flew forward, I raised my hand to protect my face and head before flopping unceremoniously onto the gravel-laden lot.

I'd like to say that I gracefully leaped to my feet, but in reality, I rolled over to my side, placed my battered other hand on the ground, and raised myself to a crawling position before assessing myself for injuries. My feet and legs felt intact, though there was a gaping hole in my shoe where it had snagged the metal bar protruding from the top of the concrete, and the knees of my jeans had seen better days. Not all bad—the value of my jeans was higher with the tears in the fabric.

The back of my left hand and the palm of my right hand were decorated with bloody scratches and pieces of gravel. I pried the stony intruders from my skin, wincing with each one I removed, but happy that the damage was to my hands and not my face.

My backpack lay on the ground beside me, its contents safely stored in the zippered compartments. I shifted to a sitting position and scanned the parking lot for witnesses. The only other people were a young couple who were arguing. I thought it odd to be arguing in public so early in the day, but I was delighted that their focus on each other meant it was unlikely they had witnessed my tumble. I remained seated for a few minutes to catch my breath before meeting Terry.

The coffee shop, Jacob's Café, was a privately owned business on the northeast corner of Belvedere and University avenues—a nice change from the multitude of large chain doughnut and sandwich shops that had invaded many university towns over the past two decades. Aunt Josephine had told me that the owner, Mr. Scott Jacob, had been offered a buyout by one of the larger outlets, but he refused to sell the business his father had started fifty years ago. Some people thought he was foolish to not take the money and run, but his business had never suffered. This little shop was busy year round catering to students from fall to spring, and in the summer to tourists who were delighted to taste something different from what they could get back home.

Scott Jacob was one of my aunt's numerous former students. He remembered her from grade two, and he was always happy to treat her to tea and a scone in gratitude for how well she treated him when he was a young boy.

The first time I accompanied my aunt to Jacob's Café, I assumed she pretended to remember him only because he remembered her. It's much easier for a student to remember twelve teachers through grade school and high school than for a teacher to remember hundreds of students over a forty-year period. I was wrong. As we visited multiple other stores and public locations on PEI over the past few weeks, it didn't take long to realize that not only did she remember many of her former students, but also details of their lives, such as who their siblings were, what neighbourhoods they had lived in, and "who they belonged to"—as Islanders would say when describing a person's family.

The angry couple's slamming of the car doors brought my focus back to my mission. I was to meet Terry here at 8:00 a.m. I stole a peek at my phone: 7:59 a.m. I dragged my butt off the concrete barrier that had tripped me, wiped the sand off my pants, and headed in.

Terry was seated in the far corner at a table for two. I passed an eighty-something couple seated near the entrance;

no doubt this was their daily ritual. They sat quietly, each with a breakfast sandwich and a cup of tea before them, she reading a newspaper, he completing a crossword puzzle. They raised their heads and smiled at me as I passed. I nodded a greeting in return. The remaining seven or so tables were empty; most customers would be ordering their coffee and food to go at this time of day—a quick stop on the way to school or work, as shown by the long line at the counter.

Behind the glass counter was a mouth-watering array of doughnuts, biscuits, scones, tarts, and cookies, all made fresh on the premises. I eyed the chocolate scones with strawberry filling, then sighed at the lineup. I could see that Terry already had his coffee, and I didn't want to keep him waiting while I stood in line to place an order. Convinced that my grumbling stomach could wait a little longer to be satiated, I headed for my friend but stopped when I heard my name.

"Franny Fitzpatrick, is that you?" Scott Jacob was standing behind the counter wiping his hands with a towel and beaming at me. Remembering names and faces must be an Island talent—we had only met a couple of times.

I smiled back at him. "Yes. Good memory, but please, call me Fran. Only Aunt Josephine gets away with calling me Franny. How are you?"

Scott raised his hand in surrender. "Not to worry . . . *Fran*, I completely understand. My grandmother still calls me Scotty." He laughed. "And to answer your question, I'm doing well, thank you. Are you here for breakfast?"

"In a bit. I'm meeting a friend first." I looked at the line of customers. "I don't want to keep him waiting. I'll get something after we talk."

Scott waved his hand in the air. "Don't be silly. Miss Fitzpatrick's niece won't be going hungry in my restaurant. What can I get you?"

I didn't think it polite to remind him that Aunt Josephine has been Mrs. MacDonald for two decades, not when he was offering me food. "That's really sweet of you." I faked humility and tried to will myself to blush. "I'd love a coffee and one of those chocolate scones. They look so good!"

Scott puffed out his chest. "Well, you won't be disappointed. I only just added them to the menu today. My own recipe. Worked on it for a few weeks to perfect it. Join your friend, and I'll bring the coffee and scone over to you."

"Wow. Thanks so much." In Hollywood you'd have to know a big-time celebrity to be treated like royalty. In PEI, knowing a beloved school teacher is all that's needed.

Terry downed the last of his coffee as I approached the table. His face was pale, and the bags under his eyes told me that he hadn't got much, if any, sleep last night. He removed the lid to drink the last few drops.

I took the seat opposite him and waited for him to speak first. I had some news to share, but I remained uncertain as to how he felt about the revelation last night that not only had I found Victor's body, but I had also chosen not to share that information with him.

His hand trembled slightly as he held the cup an inch above the table. He met my eyes and held my gaze, then let the cup drop. A paper cup hitting a hard surface from that distance certainly wasn't loud, but the action startled me. An eternity seemed to pass before he spoke.

"That was quite the fall."

"How did you know?" I looked over my shoulder. "Oh, of course—windows."

"Are you okay?"

"Sure. Just a few scratches. No big deal." The small talk was unsettling. "Terry, I'm sorry I didn't tell you about—"

"Here you go." Scott placed a coffee cup and a plate with a scone in front of me. He also set a coffee cup in front of Terry. "And you look like you could use a refill, young man."

Terry shook his head and put his hands up to protest. "Um, no. Thanks, but I can't . . ." His face turned redder than the strawberries in my scone as he retrieved his wallet and opened it. "I haven't got any more cash on me. Sorry."

Scott waved his hand in the air again. "Oh, don't be so silly. Any friend of a niece of Miss Fitzpatrick's gets a free refill." Scott turned his head toward me and winked. Although sometimes a man winking at a woman is creepy, in this case it was sweet. Scott was trying to help a student who was clearly in need of a serving of kindness. "And Fran, yours is on the house this morning."

"Awesome. Thanks, Scott."

Terry eyed me suspiciously after Scott walked away. "How do you know him?" He pointed his chin in the direction of our host.

"Long story."

Terry narrowed his eyes and frowned. I was being evasive at a time I needed to regain his trust.

"He's a former student of my aunt's. The one you met last night."

"That wasn't a very long story."

"No, I guess it wasn't. Listen, Terry, I really am sorry I didn't tell you about Victor. I didn't know who to trust. It was scary. I mean, I found this dead guy in a field, and the police are all over the place because there's a murderer in town. Possibly someone on campus." I took a deep breath.

Terry straightened up in his seat. "It's okay. I thought about it last night, among all the other things I thought about last night. I didn't get much sleep, but I get it."

"So we're good?"

"I think so. Let's just move on. You're willing to help me out and I appreciate it." He held up the coffee cup. "And hey, you have access to free coffee."

I laughed. "I wouldn't count on that being a regular thing."

As I ate my scone, we reviewed what we already knew about Victor and his death. It didn't take long because we didn't know very much. Then I told Terry about my encounter with Lena at the library.

"What do you think she was doing there?" he asked.

I shrugged. "I don't know. I mean, she may have been there to study, but even the librarian said it was unusual to see students that early in the day this time of year. No one is seriously studying yet, or working on projects."

Terry ran his hand through his hair, then rested it behind his neck. "And she just plucked you out of a chair, stared out the window, then ran off?"

"Pretty much. I didn't admit to her I was curious about the visibility of the paddock from the sunroom, and she didn't offer any reason for being up there. I mean, if she was there to study, why did she take off?"

His hand moved to his chin and rubbed the stubble that told me he hadn't shaved this morning. "Do you think she was following you?"

I shrugged again. "Maybe. It's creepy to think someone might be following me." Was she following me? How many times do you "bump into" someone in under twenty-four hours?

"I remembered something last night. The day before Victor died, he told me he was working on a big story. Something that would put our little school paper on the big stage."

"What was it?"

Terry lifted the coffee cup to his lips, held it in place for a few seconds without drinking, then placed it back on the table. "I don't know. I didn't get a chance to get the details from him."

"Was that what you argued about?"

Terry finished his coffee. "I guess. I wouldn't call it an argument. We were outside his dorm room and he said he had this big story. I kinda laughed at him, I guess. The guy was always claiming he was going to get a big scoop someday. When I started to leave, he yelled out that once I knew what he had, I'd have more respect for him. It was odd, but his yelling is probably what made someone think we were arguing. Now that he's dead, I can't stop wondering what the big story was."

What type of information could a small-town university reporter stumble upon that would be that groundbreaking? An invisible force squeezed my lungs—a mixture of anxiety and excitement. "You have no idea what it was?"

He shook his head. "No, but I wish I did." Terry stared into my eyes. "We need to be cautious, Fran, because whatever it was, it may be what got him killed."

Chapter 14

ENGLISH LITERATURE 101: a required class for students majoring in journalism. As the lecture drew to a close, I glanced at my notebook. I saw only three words: *The Great Gatsby*. One of the many books we'd be required to read, and no doubt discuss to exhaustion, this semester. I sighed at the memory of picking the novel apart in high school, again wondering if the author, F. Scott Fitzgerald, had purposely written all that symbolism into the book, or simply written a story that English lit scholars later picked apart and complicated. My question was never answered in high school, but perhaps I'd get to the truth this year.

I couldn't recall anything the professor had discussed in the past hour; I was too distracted thinking of my conversation with Terry. We'd agreed that our time should be spent getting to know as much as we could about Victor. Everything from his bed-making habits in the morning to his aspirations. Did he have a girlfriend? Did he fold his socks before putting them in a drawer?

We would investigate projects he might have been working on. Projects that might have put him on the path of a story dangerous enough to get him killed. Was his murder related to the story, or was it more personal, or a random act of violence? The latter was the most disturbing. If he had been accosted by a stranger with no apparent motive, then everyone in town was at risk of being the next victim, and the perpetrator would be far more difficult to identify.

I shoved the notebook into my backpack and hoisted the bag to swing it over my shoulder. I felt a jolt as the bag's movement was abruptly halted. Hearing a groan, I turned to see a fellow student rubbing the side of his head. I flashed a guilty smile. "Sorry. Are you okay?"

"Yeah. It's all good." His expression didn't match his words. He wasn't about to become a new friend. I pushed my back against the desk, allowing him room to pass, then remained in place as twenty more students filed past me to the door.

As I waited for an opening in the stream of freshmen, I peered at the note Terry had given me as we were leaving Jacob's Café. He'd made a two-column list of people to interview. At the top of the first column, he'd penned his own name, and the second column was titled with mine. Our goal was to interview the first two or three people on our respective lists before the day ended. The first person on my list was Victor's roommate, Bobby Burrell. Terry had texted a photo of Victor with his roommate to me so I could recognize Bobby if I passed him on campus. Eager to start my investigation, I had planned to track Bobby down and interview him once my class ended, but as luck would have it, the second interviewee on my list was Dr. Robert Watson, whose office was in this very building.

Most of the courses in the English and Languages department were held in Murray Hall, the Faculty of Arts building, but English Literature 101 was always scheduled in the Duffy Science Centre because of the large number of students enrolled. By the end of the first year, many students would change majors, some would drop out, and the remainder would be split into different specialties within a major, eliminating the need for larger classrooms. My plans placed me in the latter group. After first year, I'd move into a track of classes focused on journalism rather than general English.

Terry had told me he'd spent his sleepless night reviewing everything he remembered about Victor, from conversations they'd had, to Victor's application to be on the school's newspaper, to the numerous articles he had written. Victor was a biology major with a special interest in archaeology and paleontology. His plan after graduation was to secure a master's degree at a university with a strong program in those areas.

Terry couldn't remember which schools Victor was interested in, but he did find out from Victor's Facebook page that he had hoped to work this past summer on a dig with Dr. Watson. He made no mention there as to whether or not that happened. Oddly, the last post Victor made was in mid-May, four months ago.

The office legend in the foyer directed me to the second floor of the science building. I eyed the staircase and sighed as I shifted the book-laden bag on my shoulders. My inquisitive mind was filled with questions. How secure was it to leave it here? Why no elevator? It was an old building, but not so old that elevators weren't a thing when it was built. *Suck it up, Fran—you're young and it's only one flight of stairs. Stop the grumbling.* The internal debate was resolved. None of my questions were relevant to the case, so I needed to stop whining and get moving. I let the heavy bag drop into my hand and started the climb. I desperately needed to get into better shape.

The staircase was at the north end of the building, while Dr. Watson's office was at the south end. I opened the metal door that had the number two centred on the tiny wire-meshed window and walked through. The stark silence of the staircase was replaced by numerous voices, the clanking of metal on glass, and the whirring of machinery. Was I in the right location? The science department of my high school consisted of skeletons and dead things in jars, none of which made any noise.

The familiar smell emanating from the first room I passed told me that I was indeed in the correct location. It brought to mind images of frogs, chickens, and . . . What was that toxic substance they were soaking in? Oh yes, formaldehyde. I wondered how any of us had survived science classes before the days of fume hoods and safety goggles.

I confidently strolled down the hall, excited about my first official interview on a murder case. Midway down the hall was a tiny alcove to my right; it wasn't much bigger than a restroom on a small airplane, but it was large enough for me to duck into when I heard a familiar voice. I peeked around the corner and noticed a pair of broad shoulders in a black uniform in Dr. Watson's office doorway.

Officer David Hughes was facing into the office. One shoulder extended forward and his elbow moved up and down. "Thank you for your time, Professor. If you think of anything else, please call me at the station. My direct line is on the card I left on your desk."

A deep, gravelly voice emanated from the room. "I will, Officer. It's horrible what has happened to Mr. Cargo. Not something any of us here in the science department would have expected."

"Of course not, Professor. I'm sure it was a shock for everyone. Thank you again." The men appeared to shake hands again before David turned on his heel and headed in my direction. I crept back behind the wall and looked for a way to hide. There wasn't one, so I stood as still as I could in the corner of my little prison and hoped he wouldn't notice me. He was staring straight ahead as he passed me. I sighed a quiet sigh of relief until—

"Franny Fitzpatrick. It's nice to see you again." I couldn't see his face as he continued down the hall, but I could hear the smirk in his voice. He stopped at the door to the staircase. "Don't forget that we're due for a chat after you're finished classes today."

"I remember, but what are you doing *here*?" Dumb question, with a snotty tone. *Good work, Fran.*

"I'm on official business. I hope you're not about to interfere with the investigation."

I stepped into the hall. David had turned around. I gulped as my heart rate quickened. "Of course not. I'm on official business too. For the school paper."

He gave me a sideways glance. "I see." And with those two words, he turned and left. Once he began his descent down the stairs, I continued my directive to interview the man Victor had spent the summer with. As I approached the office, I heard the same commanding voice. It sounded as though Dr. Watson was on the phone. Not wanting to interrupt him, but also wanting to follow my journalistic instincts and not miss the opportunity to gather information, I waited in the hallway, just out of sight but within hearing range.

"A police detective was just here asking questions about Victor and the program. I didn't have much to tell him. I'd only seen Victor a couple of times since classes ended last term."

I scratched my head, literally. If Victor had spent the summer working with Dr. Watson, why did the professor just say they'd had minimal contact since spring? Had Victor lied to Terry about how he'd spent the past few months?

"No. No. I didn't go with them. Ended up in the hospital with food poisoning or something. Doctors had a hard time figuring it out, but there was no way I could have trekked up north, even if they knew what it was that took me down."

I imagined a giant of a man sitting at his desk, and how his falling to his knees with abdominal pain would be akin to Goliath toppling to the ground after being shot with a stone by David. His illness explained his comment about not seeing much of Victor, though. It was Dr. Watson who hadn't made the trip, not Victor.

Once the professor ended the call, I counted to ten, then approached his door. Dr. Watson's voice was that of an imposing, intimidating hulk of a man, and my knees quivered at the thought of interviewing him, so when I stood in his doorway ready to introduce myself, I was rendered speechless at the sight before me.

As I'd imagined, the professor was tall, but that's where my accuracy about how he would look ended. His long scraggly hair reminded me of Medusa's head of snakes, and his thin cratered face, with an exceptionally long nose, brought to mind Ichabod Crane from Washington Irving's "The Legend of Sleepy Hollow." His long bony arms extended past his outdated tweed jacket, while worn-out suspenders held up pants that bunched at the waist.

Did he shop at a thrift store or had he lost tons of weight recently? He did mention in his call that he'd been ill. Was that why he was sweating? While I was wearing a hoodie and still felt a bit chilly, droplets were visible on his nose as he pushed his sliding glasses back into place. I wondered if sweating was a symptom of an undiagnosed illness, or a result of shaken nerves after being interviewed by the police.

Ichabod's twin shot me a smile when he noticed my presence. Poking his stalagmite-like, scruffy chin into the air, he approached with his hand out. His fingers were long and thin, the contours of the bones easily visible. As he walked the short distance across the room, his movements were awkward, as though his muscles, if he had any, were poorly attached to his bones. He looked like a clothed version of one of the biology lab's skeletons.

"Well, hello. Are you one of my students? My apologies. I do try to get to know all my students and learn their names, but it's only the first official week, so you'll have to forgive me that I haven't learned yours yet." He tilted his fragile frame at the waist and lifted his eyebrows.

After shaking his hand, I avoided the temptation to dry my own on my pants. "My name is Fran Fitzpatrick."

He ran his sweaty hand through his oily hair. "Fran. Fran." He returned to his desk, sat, and rummaged through some papers. "I don't remember seeing that name on any of my class lists. Are you sure?"

"Am I sure about my name?"

He waved at the air. "Silly me. Of course you're sure. Perhaps there was a mistake at the office." He picked up a pen. "Your name again? Do you have questions about the required texts? Lab schedules? I do expect my students to attend all labs."

"Fran Fitzpatrick." I chose not to correct him on his assumption that I was a student in the science program. Maybe he would be more talkative if he thought he'd be seeing a lot of me over the next four years. "I'm not actually here about my classes." Not a lie. "I'm working for the *Golden Spud* and had some questions about Victor Cargo."

Chapter 15

"**P**OOR MR. CARGO." Moving at the speed of a sloth after a night of partying, Dr. Watson used the edge of his desk to support his weight as he moved to, then sat in his office chair. As he closed his eyes and breathed deeply, he indicated the other chair with his upturned hand.

I sat in the proffered seat and opened my notepad. I drew a line through the professor's name in the potential suspect list Terry had made. *No way does this guy have the strength needed to bludgeon Victor to death, but he might have some information on what Victor was up to.*

"I'm sorry to bother you, Dr. Watson. If you're not feeling well today, I could come back later in the week." His face was pale and pasty. Would I be calling 911 for a second time in the span of less than seventy-two hours?

"Oh, that's fine, Fran. Is it okay to call you Fran?"

I nodded.

"Good. Good. I prefer not to be as formal as some of my colleagues are when addressing students. I feel it makes for a more congenial learning environment. I'm not sure how much help I can be with your article for the paper. You're writing it about Victor's death, I assume?"

I nodded again.

"Good. Good. Let's see." He cupped his chin in his hand and diverted his gaze to the ceiling. Seconds passed, then minutes. He seemed to be deep in thought and I didn't want to disturb him. A few more uncomfortable minutes passed, and then the professor looked into my eyes. "Did you have a question for me?"

I was again reminded that I still had a lot to learn about journalism, as well as human behaviour. "Of course. Sorry. I thought you were thinking about something and I didn't want to disturb you."

Dr. Watson squinted. "Generally, I leave the thinking until after the question is put forth." He cast a friendly don't-worry-we-were-all-beginners-once smile at me.

If I were the blushing type, I would have turned a deep shade of crimson by now. "Um . . ." *Good start, Fran.* "Victor had posted on his Facebook page back in May that he would be working with you on a summer project. Would you be able to share with me what that project was?"

"As I told the police officer who was here earlier—you must have passed by him on your way in—I did arrange the summer project but was unable to attend. I was terribly disappointed, as I had been working on the arrangements for several months, but sometimes things don't go as planned."

He shrugged, but it wasn't a rude *whatever* shrug but more of a disappointed-at-a-great-opportunity-lost-forever shrug. Sadness was evident in his sunken eyes.

"What was the project?"

The sad eyes lit up. "Well, I'd be delighted to tell you all about it. Perhaps you also might join an expedition group in the future. You and Victor are alike in some ways; science and journalism were his two greatest interests. He was very enthusiastic about paleontology." The professor shook his head. "It's quite tragic. So much potential, lost. I was sure Victor would go a long way in his career. The energy and passion that young man put into his studies was impressive."

I scribbled the words "expedition" and "where" on my notepad. "Victor was on an expedition this summer? Can I ask where? And what the purpose of the trip was?"

"Of course, of course. I had put a team of paleontologists and students together for a dig near the site of the Tiktaalik discovery on Ellesmere Island in northern Canada."

My pen hovered over the page. "Tickle licks?"

"I believe it's pronounced *Tick-ta-like*. Or perhaps it *is* lick? I've heard it said both ways. Depends a good deal on the speaker's accent. The fossilized bones were discovered in 2004. It's believed to be a sarcopterygian."

I felt my blood pressure surge as my cover was no doubt about to be blown. I didn't know these science terms. I'd made it through high school biology on a wing and a prayer.

My fears were abandoned when the deep, gravelly voice said, "Of course. Silly me. You're just starting your freshman year. I don't imagine most, if any, high schools are teaching about Tiktaaliks and their relatives."

I chuckled, then gave a sigh of relief. "No. Not my school."

Not that I knew of, anyway. "How long was the trip? Do you mind my asking who the other participants were?"

"Not at all. It's information readily available on the department's student page. You'll have access to that after our first lecture."

Dr. Watson's kindness had returned my blood pressure to normal, but my guilt at deceiving this friendly fellow was sky-rocketing.

He rose slowly and turned to the small window situated over the well-used metal filing cabinets behind his desk. "There was one other student, Laurie Lamont. Not a student, per se—she's working on a master's degree in archaeology and paleontology. Now, there's a young woman with drive. She and Victor were quite the pair."

I looked up from my notes. Was this a case of a romance gone wrong? "Were they dating?"

The good doctor's eyes widened. "Dating? Oh my, no! They were the very definition of antagonists. Both extremely driven individuals—'individual' being the key word. They each preferred to work alone. I did think it a shame, because when Victor first came to UPEI, I thought that, though a couple of years apart in their educational endeavours, the two of them would have made a good team. Laurie was a senior when Victor was a freshman. They didn't meet, to my knowledge, until last year when I introduced them, thinking Victor would make a good teaching assistant for Laurie."

Dr. Watson plucked a tissue from a container on the filing cabinet. He wiped his brow, then grabbed a few more tissues and continued to wipe. "It didn't last long. A few weeks into the arrangement, Laurie requested permission to seek a new assistant. Victor didn't seem to mind in the least, so I suspect it was a mutual parting. Then when I was assembling the team for the Ellesmere Island trip, I put them together again, despite their ongoing conflict."

"They continued to have problems even after they stopped working together?"

"It's a small department. We have over two hundred freshman science students at the start of the year, but by year's end, some of them will have switched majors, and a few drop out of university. After the second year, they will split into groups focusing on chemistry, physics, biology, et cetera. Some eventually move to the nursing or veterinary colleges. So you see, the number of students in the senior class is much smaller than in the freshman class.

"As Victor followed the same track as Laurie, they had many encounters, Victor at times being Laurie's student. He was not happy with that arrangement." Dr. Watson, looking winded from simply standing still for a few minutes, returned to his chair.

"Why was Victor so upset by that? He wasn't going to be a student forever." The irony of my words didn't escape me. His death as a student had indeed secured him that status forever. That was how he would always be remembered, as the *student* who was murdered.

"Victor was . . ." Dr. Watson took a deep breath. "How shall I say it? Don't get me wrong—he was a brilliant young man, but . . ."

"But?"

The professor's eyes widened, and he turned up his palms. "But he knew it. He believed he was smarter than everyone else. He was able to keep his attitude in check around the faculty and show them due respect, but I fear he regarded Laurie as simply another student, a peer or an equal, not a superior—intellectually or academically."

I found myself scribbling notes too fast for them to be legible. Ideas and theories were flowing onto the paper.

Dr. Watson must have read my mind, or my facial expression. *You've got to work on your poker face, Fran.*

"Oh dear, please don't misunderstand me. Victor and Laurie didn't get along, but there's no way Laurie could be responsible for what happened."

"How can you be so certain? I mean, if things were that bad between them . . ."

"It's true, as I've pointed out, that they didn't get along. They were indeed—so it appeared—each other's greatest nemesis, but that was no reason for Laurie to take such extreme measures. She has a brilliant future ahead of her in the world of archaeology and paleontology. I don't believe she would throw that away with such a violent and senseless act."

"But if Victor stood in the way of her success, could she have . . . you know . . . snapped?" I snapped an imaginary twig—not mature or professional. I wanted to roll my eyes at my own behaviour.

"My dear, if Laurie Lamont were to kill everyone she didn't get along with, or who she deemed a threat, the population of UPEI would be lessened by half. Well, the science department would be." He attempted a chuckle, but it turned into a lung-splitting cough.

I noted Laurie's name and put a star beside it. I'd talk to Terry later about adding her to our list of interviewees. I snuck a peek at the clock on the wall. My next class was in ten minutes. There was no way I'd be able to get there on time, so I settled into my interview. "Who else was on the team?"

Dr. Watson gave me the name of two other faculty members, a couple of assistants who were hired to do the grunt work of carrying shovels and other supplies, and the professor charged with overseeing the team when Dr. Watson became too ill to join them.

"Dr. Daniels has been with us for two years now. He was previously in line to be tenured in the archaeology and paleontology department at the University of Hamilton, but chose to leave that position and join us after doing a stint here as a visiting professor."

"Isn't being tenured a big deal for professors? Why would he leave before that went through?"

Dr. Watson shook his head. "I can't say I know. It's not my place to ask. People have their reasons for making the decisions they make. There have been rumours . . ." He stopped himself, then looked at his watch. "It's getting on, and I do need to prepare for my next class. I hope that I've been of help to you."

My suspicions were piqued. This up-until-now talkative and helpful man was trying to get me out of his office. Maybe he'd said something that he now thought he shouldn't have. Did it involve Laurie Lamont? Was he rethinking his belief that she couldn't possibly be guilty of murdering Victor? Or maybe it was something about Dr. Daniels. I closed my notebook, thanked the man, and made my exit. When I got to the hallway, I sent Terry a text. We needed to meet this evening, but first I'd do a little more snooping. Afternoon classes could wait.

Chapter 16

A S I CROSSED the campus, heading toward the coed dormitory that had housed Victor Cargo, I thought about Dr. Watson's reference to the science department's student page. The professor had already given me the names of the expedition participants and the trip's main objective, but I couldn't help wondering if there might be information on the page that would be useful to our investigation.

I didn't know if a student needed to be a science major to gain access to the site, and wondered if any of the *Golden Spud* reporters were enrolled in the science program. I could sign up for a biology class, but it would be difficult since I already had a full class schedule, and I didn't have the money to sign up for a course I would never attend. That latter thought reminded me that I was currently skipping classes I had paid for. One day of missed classes wouldn't hurt, would it?

I stopped and checked the time. Linguistics 101 was coming to an end at this very moment, and in thirty minutes my last scheduled class for the day would be starting in the building to the left. I peered over my shoulder at Murray Hall, the location of my Introduction to Journalism class. I must be crazy, bailing on what was very likely the most important class I'd take this semester. It was chance to meet, and possibly make an impression on, Professor Linda Gayle. The woman I'd be counting on to write my reference for admission to the journalism track. The debate raged in my mind: go to a class that could make or break my future career, or proceed to an interview, acting as though I was already a skilled professional.

I glanced from the coed dorm to Murray Hall several times, indecision taking up residence in my mind. Weighing the future and the present, I consoled myself that Victor's roommate would still be on campus when my class was completed. I hefted my bag onto my shoulder and started toward my class. I risked one last look at the dorm and immediately regretted it. What was Lena Gallant doing there? Who was that fella she was hugging? He looked a lot like the guy in the photo Terry had shown me of Victor's roommate, Bobby Burrell.

I let the heavy backpack drop into my hand, then holding it by the handle, speed-walked toward my acquaintances, new and soon-to-be-new. When I was about fifty yards from the odd couple, Lena spotted me, waved, and then whispered into her companion's ear. Bobby Burrell gave me a nasty look, then retreated through the front doors of the dorm.

Lena quickened her pace in my direction. "Hey, Fran. What are you doing here? No classes this afternoon?"

This conversation was starting to become commonplace. "Um, no. Well, I was on my way to class when I spotted you. I thought I'd say hi." *Why are you hugging a potential suspect in Victor's murder, Lena? Do you even know he's a potential suspect?* I chose to play dumb. "Who's your friend?"

Lena peered over her shoulder, then, from behind her glasses, returned her gaze to me. "Oh, him? I met him a few nights ago in the pub."

"You know, he looks a bit familiar. Isn't that Bobby Burrell, Victor Cargo's roommate?"

"Oh wow. I never made the connection." She playfully slapped her forehead. "Stupid me. He said his roommate had died, but I didn't ask for details." She shook her head. "Never made the connection."

I found myself staring into her eyes. How could she *not* have made the connection? How many students die at one university in one week? We'd had no natural disasters or outbreaks of violence. This was UPEI on PEI—still a very safe place, despite Victor's fate.

"Do you know Bobby well? Where's he from? Did he and his roommate get along?"

"No. Not sure. Don't think so." She laughed at her own humorous response to my questions, but knowing that Bobby and Victor didn't get along was a helpful piece of information.

Lena clapped her hands, then threw her arms into the air as though she was singing at a Christian revival meeting. "Well, nuts. It's time to fly off to class. Are you heading this way?" She indicated the Duffy building.

My internal debate resumed. I could still make my class,

but now I was eager to talk to Bobby. "No. My class is over there in the arts building." I pointed toward University Avenue. "I'll see you later."

"Later." As I watched Lena make her way to the Duffy building, I walked slowly—crawled might be more accurate—toward Murray Hall. Once she was out of sight, I doubled back toward the coed dorm. No point in going to class. I was too distracted now to pay attention or meet new people, no matter how influential they might be for my future.

The coed dorm, Marion Hall, was a two-storey rectangular building that ran along Belvedere Avenue on the south border of the campus. It was built in the mid to late 1900s, judging by its basic architecture: a rectangular brick building with square, evenly spaced windows. Students could make use of a staircase and exit at each end of the building, but visitors were directed to the main entrance in the middle of the building.

I pulled open one of the large glass doors and scanned the lobby for a list of student names and unit numbers. I found it adjacent to the mailboxes to my left. The tenants were listed alphabetically, and Bobby Burrell was to be found in room 201. The next name on the list was Victor Cargo, also unit 201.

I grasped the handle of the inner door and yanked, but it didn't open. It was locked—I'd need to buzz Bobby's unit to get access. My shoulders drooped and I let out a sigh. How was I going to convince him to let me, a stranger, in? Victor's personal items were probably still in his room, so I wanted to interview Bobby there in the hopes that there might be a clue among Victor's things as to what he had gotten mixed up in.

I inhaled deeply to build my courage, then pushed 201 on the intercom.

"We meet again." I could see his reflection in the glass door—Officer David Hughes. "What are you doing here? I know you don't live here, and I'm sure you're not here to interfere with the investigation. Again."

I backed away from the door and shrugged as I turned to face him. "I don't know what you mean. I'm simply here to meet a friend."

With perfect timing, a voice answered my buzz. "Yeah. Who is it?"

"It's me, Fran. I'm in the lobby. Are you ready?"

"What are you talking about? Who is this?"

David crossed his arms and nodded at the speaker panel. "Seems your friend doesn't know who you are."

I shrugged again. "I must have entered the wrong code."

"Is that so? Because that sounds an awful lot like Victor's roommate."

"I don't know what game you guys are playing, but I'm busy. Go away!" The disembodied voice sounded irritated.

"Looks like you've upset my witness." David uncrossed his arms, shook his head, and smirked. "You go ahead and buzz your friend. I'll give Mr. Burrell time to cool down."

"I'll have to send him a text. My friend, I mean, not Mr. Burrell. I don't know this Burrell person you speak of. Why would I be here to see him? Anyway, it seems I don't have the correct room number for the person I'm here to see." I checked the time on my phone. "I need to get to class. Bye."

David moved in front of the exit doors. "Not so fast. Would that be your last class of the day? Might I remind you that we need to talk about your discovery yesterday? We can meet in one hour at Jacob's. The coffee shop on the corner."

I crossed my arms. "I know where Jacob's is."

"Great. I'll see you in an hour. Unless you'd rather I meet you at your aunt and uncle's home again." He smirked and crossed his arms again.

I started to fling my bag over my shoulder, a small part of me hoping that the smug man in black might suffer the same fate as my unfortunate classmate and get smacked in the head. Sadly, the bag landed on my shoulder unimpeded. Disappointed, I brushed past him and grabbed the door handle. "The coffee shop will be fine."

I didn't wait for a response. He had foiled my plans and joked about my family to get his way. Since I wasn't going to get to interview Victor's roommate today, I decided to run for class—well, walk briskly—and risk making a late-for-class bad first impression on my professor, in the hopes it would be better than a no-show bad first impression.

Chapter 17

F ROM MY PROFESSOR'S reaction, it was difficult to tell whether showing up late for Introduction to Journalism was a better choice than not appearing at all. The outside temperature had dipped to an unexpected twelve degrees Celsius, but it still felt warmer than the look on the prof's face when I interrupted her by opening the squeaky classroom door. I made a mental note to send Professor Gayle an email with my sincerest apology, and the maintenance department a box of WD-40.

I headed toward Jacob's Café immediately after class. After I passed the women's residence, a blast of cold air from the west nearly toppled me. If this was late summer on PEI, I wasn't looking forward to the winter weather. I dropped my backpack on the ground and retrieved the burgundy hoodie I'd purchased the previous week at the campus bookstore. It had large black letters spelling out UPEI Home of the Panthers across the front. The fabric was thick and soft, the thickness another reminder to newcomers of what was to come weather-wise, and the softness a gentle way of doing it.

I caught a glimpse of the corner window of Marion Hall after closing my backpack. The light was on in the room Victor had lived in. I played with the idea of calling on Mr. Burrell, as David referred to him, but as I circled around the west end of the building, I spotted a patrol car in Jacob's parking lot. Darn. No time to interview the roommate—it would have to wait until tomorrow.

David was sitting in the far corner, a secluded spot that would allow him to interview a witness without too many ears around to pick up juicy gossip. Before joining him, I purchased a large French vanilla and a chocolate cruller. My body and mind were screaming for a hefty dose of caffeine and sugar; they were starting to feel the effects of my sleepless night and early start to the day.

I lifted my cup in a toast to David as I took my seat. He responded by raising his eyebrows. Perhaps I wasn't the only one who'd had a sleepless night and a long day.

"Hi, David. How did your interrogation of the witness go? Is he a suspect?"

"I cannot share details of the case with you, Ms. Fitzpatrick."

I noticed his formality. I'd called him David, so why didn't he call me Fran? Was he trying to make a point? Professor Gayle had touched on the concept of putting the interviewee at ease when seeking information. It couldn't hurt to try that tactic on David.

"You can call me Fran. 'Ms. Fitzpatrick' seems so, you know . . . well, cold."

"My apologies. This is a murder investigation. It's hard to be warm and fuzzy when conducting an interview related to the death of a young man."

I needed to work on tact. "Sorry. You're right. I didn't mean to imply that you're cold. I mean, it's cold outside so you might be cold, but as far as your personality, I don't know you. So anyway, I'm sure you're a very nice person when you're not intimidating witnesses. Let's start over. I'd prefer to be called Fran. Okay, David?"

I noticed a mild lifting of the corners of his lips as he stared at his notepad, then tapped it with his pen. "You're a journalism student? That was a lot of words. You have a great career ahead of you, no doubt."

I felt insulted, but I wasn't sure if that was his intent, so I let the comment pass.

"I'm not sure what I can tell you about yesterday. I've already told Officer Mather what happened. I was walking to campus, noticed the red socks, and was worried about the horses, so I entered the field and that's when . . . well, you know."

"That's when you saw the victim, Victor Cargo?"

"Yes. I called 911 right away. I didn't see anyone else around until after you arrived. Then the population of people amassing on the corner exploded." I leaned in closer and whispered, "Do you think the murderer was in the crowd? You know, like on detective shows? Do criminals always return to see the outcome of their work?"

"This isn't television, Ms. Fitzpatrick. A young man has lost his life."

My empty stomach threatened to embarrass me as I remembered the crime scene. "You don't have to tell me that—I remember very well. I was simply trying to be helpful."

"Before my colleagues and I arrived, you saw no one else?"

"I just said that. It was me, the body, and the horses. You don't think they're involved, do you?" My inappropriate humour was surfacing. I could see from David's face that he was not amused. "Sorry. No. I didn't see anyone else."

"We found several worn footpaths through the field. Do you know if students use it as a shortcut? It's private property and there are No Trespassing signs posted, but that rarely deters people from doing what they please."

Was he threatening me with a trespassing charge? "I only hopped the fence to keep the horses from getting sick from eating the sock."

"Of course. I understand that. I'm asking if you know if any other students have been 'hopping the fence.'"

Should I tell him about Lena's daily shortcut? If I did, he'd interview her and I'd lose her trust.

I looked up at David. He was staring at me as though trying to read my mind. "Well?"

"I've never seen anyone using the field as a shortcut." It wasn't a lie—not really. If my investigation with Terry revealed that Lena was involved with Victor's death, I could fess up later.

"I see." David leaned closer. "How long have you known Terry James?"

"A couple of weeks. Or so. No. Ten days, maybe?" I shrugged. Where was this line of questioning going?

"You seem to be putting a lot of faith in someone you've

only known a few days. How can you be certain you can trust him?"

"How can I be certain I can trust you?" *Good work, Fran. Alienate the lead detective.* "I mean, I'm sure you're trustworthy. I mean, it's not like you committed the murder." I gave him the most serious look I could muster. "You didn't, did you?"

His brow furrowed, and he shook his head and ignored my stupidity. Probably wise on his part. "Terry James remains the prime suspect. I can't prevent you from associating with him, but I feel the need to caution you to be careful."

"Thank you, David, I appreciate that, but I'm not afraid of Terry. I have a natural sense of a person's character." The truth was, as I was quickly learning, I didn't possess that particular gift of insight into human behaviour, but he didn't need to know that.

The fact was, I had a large suspect list of my own, and no idea who any of these people really were, Terry included. Perhaps I should heed this man's advice and be cautious. On the other hand, caution would prevent us from getting the information we needed to clear Terry's name. He must be innocent.

"Terry and I are working together on a story about the case. So yes, I'm gathering information, but I have no intention of interfering with your investigation or putting myself in danger."

"Few people intentionally put themselves in danger, Ms. Fitzpatrick." He had a point.

David scribbled a note on his pad, folded it, shoved it in his pocket, and then met my gaze. "That's all for now, Ms. Fitzpatrick." He stood and handed me a business card with his name and number on it. "If you think of anything else, give me a call." He started to walk away, then turned and glared at me. "And don't leave town."

"Seriously? Where am I going to go?" I lifted the card to return it to him. "And I already have your number." Was I a suspect now? What was with this guy?

He cocked his head and smiled. "Isn't that what they say on TV? TV Policing 101: hand your business card to a witness and tell them to stay in town?" He wrinkled his nose. "Just trying to be thorough." Without waiting for me to respond, he pivoted and exited the coffee shop.

I sat and contemplated my untouched cruller. The chill I felt from the cold wind disappeared as I let my mind wander to the stern man in uniform, who not only had the most gorgeous blue eyes, but also a sense of humour.

Chapter 18

"PUSH IT THAT way, Johnny. No, no, careful not to nick the corner." Aunt Josephine's voice, along with the smell of roast beef and potatoes, met me as I opened the door, followed by a scraping sound.

"I suppose we should have moved this into the room before assembling it." Uncle Johnny sounded winded.

What were the two of them up to? I dropped my bag and made my way to the commotion past the kitchen. My dear ole relatives were moving a wooden box into my room. "Hello. What's up?"

Aunt Josephine snapped her head up, a sheepish look on her face. "Oh dear, Franny. I was hoping to have this set up for you before you got home."

I cocked my head. "A box?"

She waved her hand at me and laughed. "No, no. Don't be silly. Johnny has been working on this for you for Christmas, but after last night, I thought we'd give it to you right away."

Uncle Johnny shot me a knowing smirk. "It'll still need to be painted, but Josey couldn't wait."

"Don't call me Josey." She reached over the wooden container and gave him a playful slap on the shoulder, and he mimed falling.

"This is a hope chest, Franny. You'll be needing one. Or do you have one in Toronto?" She looked concerned, then proceeded to push on the box, sending Uncle Johnny scurrying farther into the room to avoid being run over.

"What's a hope chest?" I feared that I knew, but thought I'd better ask. I could be wrong.

"For your future home, dear. After all, you brought not just one, but two men home with you last night. It's time to start collecting linens and other necessities. Of course, at your age, you might have already started."

I wasn't wrong. Had I encountered a mystical wormhole on my walk home? I scanned my surroundings in fear that I'd been teleported to an Amish community, or perhaps an earlier era. One in which women dreamed of marriage and motherhood above all else. It seemed a strange gift from my child-free aunt who'd had a career and didn't marry until her mid-forties.

I shuddered at the thought that Aunt Josephine was planning my future with one of two men I barely knew, and one a murder suspect. True, she didn't know that Terry was a suspect, and I was intent on keeping it that way, but she didn't know anything else about him either.

"What do you mean by *my age?*" I wasn't sure if I should

be offended or not. Was a single woman in her early twenties still considered an old maid in my aunt's mind? She herself would have been considered an old maid at one time. "Did you have a hope chest, Aunt Josephine?"

"Did she?" Uncle Johnny beamed. "By time we married, she had an entire rental unit!"

Aunt Josephine's brow furrowed and she gave my uncle the side-eye. "You're lucky you're trapped in there, Mr. Mac-Donald." She stared at him for a few seconds, and then her lips curled up into a smile and she shook her head. "Perhaps we'll leave you in there until after dinner."

He didn't seem worried—he was doubled over laughing.

Changing the subject seemed a good idea. "Speaking of dinner, it smells amazing."

"Oh dear, I almost forgot about the roast. It'll be dry if I don't get it out of the oven right away." Aunt Josephine wiped her hands on her apron and hurried toward the kitchen. "Franny, you help Johnny while I get dinner on the table."

"Sounds like a plan." I smiled and shook my head at Uncle Johnny. What I'd learned about him in the few weeks of living here was that he was a man completely dedicated to his wife, but at the same time he loved to tease her.

Dinner was as delicious as it had smelled, but the initial dinnertime conversation was less appealing. Aunt Josephine had observed my early-morning departure and was very insistent on knowing the reason. I used the excuse that I had wanted to get to the library early. It was the truth, with only one tiny cloud of deceit—I left out the reason for my urgent trip there.

She was satisfied with my explanation, and the conversation soon turned to the important question of squares versus ice cream for dessert. Uncle Johnny and I voted for both.

As I sat in my room after supper wondering what to fill the unpainted new wooden box with—I had no intention of filling it with linens and face towels—my phone buzzed. Terry was finally responding to my earlier text and wanted to meet to discuss our findings of the day. As expected, my aunt and uncle were in the living room watching the news. More precisely, Aunt Josephine was watching the news and Uncle Johnny was napping.

"I'm heading back to the campus to meet a friend and work on a project." I was getting good at telling the truth yet omitting the true meaning of my words. Perhaps this journalism thing wasn't as far out of reach as I'd felt it was yesterday.

Aunt Josephine swivelled her recliner around until her eyes—they had a suspicious gleam—met mine. "Sure, dear." She smiled. "Will your *friend* be picking you up? Uncle Johnny can give you a ride if you wish."

I stopped myself from rolling my eyes. "No to both, thank you. There's still plenty of daylight left, and I need to walk off that delicious meal." Not to mention the two scoops of ice cream on top of the rhubarb-strawberry squares. If this kept up, I'd be a candidate for that TV show about obesity before the school year ended.

When I arrived at the *Golden Spud* office, Terry was frantically typing at his desk.

"Hey, what are you working on?"

His hands flew off the keyboard while his body jerked

around. When his chair bent back against his weight, the sudden movement nearly propelled him to the floor.

"Sorry." I ran the short distance from the door to steady him, but he'd already righted himself.

He took a deep breath. "That's okay. I've been so wrapped up in making notes from my interviews today, I didn't hear you come in. Thanks for coming."

I pulled a chair up to his desk and sat. "For sure. I brought my own notes so we can compare."

I filled Terry in on my day's activities. Earlier at Jacob's Café I'd shared with him my run-in with Lena Gallant at the library, and her strange behaviour. I added to that by relating the story of Lena's friendship with Bobby Burrell, and her evasive response to my questions. In my opinion, this put her back at the top of our suspect list.

"Do you think she and Bobby are both involved in Victor's murder? We don't have any proof that they were. Lena may be telling you the truth. One thing I've learned in this newspaper business is that when people make up wild stories, they're probably lying to cover something up, but not necessarily the something you *think* they're lying about."

I had to think about that jumble of words for a few minutes. Terry might be right about Lena's claim that she didn't make the connection between Victor and Bobby's dead roommate, but I questioned if she was hiding something else. Or was she not as clever as I'd been giving her credit for and truly had no clue that the two dead students she'd heard about in a single day were the same person?

"Sadly, I didn't get a chance to talk to Bobby before Officer Hughes appeared."

Terry stiffened at the mention of David's name.

"I did get to talk to Dr. Watson in his office after Hughes left."

"Is that policeman following you?"

I had to think about that too. Was David following me? I couldn't imagine why. Surely he had more important things to do. "No. I don't think it's so unusual that we're interviewing the same people. I told him we're doing a story on Victor's murder for the paper and promised we wouldn't interfere with his investigation. He seemed okay with that for now."

"Did you get any useful information from Dr. Watson?"

"Well, speaking of unusual . . ." I proceeded to tell him about my meeting with the science professor, including his details about Laurie Lamont and Dr. Daniels.

"Should we add Dr. Watson to our suspect list?" Terry had his pen poised over the growing list.

"No. The phone call I overheard raised my suspicions of him, but the man could hardly lift a pencil. I can't see him swinging a rock large enough to cause the damage I saw to Victor's skull."

As soon as the words left my lips, I readied myself for a wave of nausea that didn't come. Perhaps I was getting better at controlling my visceral responses. I had mixed feelings about that realization. On the one hand, a young man had been brutally murdered—that fact alone should have made me sick. On the other hand, if I wanted to be a journalist, I'd have to learn to control my reactions—in public, anyway.

"We should add Laurie and Dr. Daniels to the list."

Terry jotted Laurie's name on his notepad. "Why Dr. Daniels?"

"He led the expedition Victor was on." I shrugged. "Maybe something happened while they were on Ellesmere

Island? I can't stop wondering why he left the University of Hamilton when he was in line to be tenured."

Terry rose and paced the room. "There could be a million reasons. Relationship with a student that went south? Conflict with the administration, or other profs?"

"True. Maybe he didn't like the food in the cafeteria."

Terry wisely ignored my attempt at humour as he strolled over to the coffee maker and poured a cup. "But I agree. Whatever his reason for leaving the other school, it could be related to Victor's claim that he had a big scoop that would rattle not only UPEI, but also the scientific community."

Adrenalin surged through my body. "Really? What scoop?"

"I don't know yet."

"Then how do you know there *is* a scoop?"

"I'll get into that when we go over my findings. Let's finish up with yours first."

"I'm done. Like I said, I didn't get a chance to talk to the roommate. Then I had to meet with David."

"David?"

"Officer Hughes."

"You're on first-name basis now?" Terry turned his palms up and lifted his shoulders. His motions reminded me of my first class with Dr. Gayle—she had introduced the subject of determining an interviewee's mood by their body language. Was Terry annoyed? Surprised? I'd have to pay closer attention in the next class.

"No, not really. I called him David during our meeting in an attempt to soften him up so he'd let us investigate unhindered, but I don't think it worked. He kept calling me"—I lowered my voice and made air quotes—"Ms. Fitzpatrick."

Terry smiled. "Great! I mean, okay. Um." He lifted the

small stack of papers on his desk and tapped them on the table several times. "Let's go over my findings. I started by looking over Victor's emails."

"How could you do that without his password?" The room darkened as grey clouds moved across the sky and blocked the sunbeams that had been streaming through the window. By the looks of things, rain was a certainty, and I hoped I'd be able to get home before it started. I didn't want to disturb Uncle Johnny for a ride.

Terry's voice brought me back into the room. "Andy. His writing skills are lacking, but he's become quite skilled with computers. After what I saw today, he may be very useful to us in this investigation."

I cocked my head. "Meaning?"

"He hacked into Victor's *Golden Spud* email with very little effort." Terry glowed like a proud parent. "Depending on where our interviews take us, we may need a computer hacker."

"Computer hackers suck. They hurt people. Please don't tell me that Andy aspires to be one of them."

"Of course not. True, most hackers are horrible people who are out to steal and destroy, but Andy isn't like that. He's got a total Superman complex—he'll use his skills for good." Terry beamed at his superhero reference.

He seemed so certain about Andy's character, and I hoped he was right. While I was happy to help him clear his name, I wasn't thrilled at using illegal methods to do it, especially if that meant encouraging a future hacker.

"Anything interesting in Victor's email?"

"Interesting doesn't do it justice. It looks like he was running a sports gambling scam. I say scam because a lot of the teams mentioned don't exist. I checked with Greg to confirm that, and he hadn't heard of them either. Greg is one hundred percent focused on sports, including anything to do with a ball, so if he hasn't heard of the teams or some of the players we found mentioned, then they don't exist."

"If Victor was scamming people, that could seriously lengthen our suspect list." I pushed my chair out and eyed the coffee maker. "Any left?"

Terry nodded. "Help yourself. Milk's in the fridge."

I poured a cup but skipped the milk. I'd need my caffeine undiluted if I was going to remain awake while Terry worked his way through his tower of papers. I took a sip and my face crinkled at the strong, bitter taste that assaulted my tongue. I added milk, then returned to my seat at Terry's desk.

"A more interesting find was an email Victor received from the university's financial administrator, Dr. Christine Hogg. Her main responsibility is to help professors gain funding for their research projects and department programs."

"Wouldn't it make sense that she'd have contact with Victor, then? I mean, he was involved in research in the science department."

"True, but he wouldn't be looking for funding at this point in his studies. Dr. Hogg generally works with professors and postgraduate students, not undergrads. It was the content of the email that piqued my interest."

"Like what?"

"A request that he reconsider his views, as they might harm the university's financial health, followed by a warning that if he continued in his plans, it could negatively affect his future career."

"What plans and views?"

"She didn't say—it was just a single sentence telling him to back off or else."

I added Dr. Hogg's name to the growing suspect list.

Chapter 19

TERRY AND I spent another hour in the *Golden Spud* office going over our findings and formulating a plan for the next few days. A flash of lightning, followed shortly by a clap of thunder, alerted us to the storm that had moved in while we were too focused on our investigation to pay attention to happenings outside of our little world.

To my relief, Terry offered me a ride home. I happily accepted it—a twenty-minute walk in a thunderstorm was not appealing. Talking wasn't possible while we rushed through the heavy downpour, using plastic bags to keep our heads dry. It was all we could do to hold on to our backpacks and push our way through the gale-force winds to the parking lot. The clouds were now almost black, and visibility was poor as the wind blasted heavy rain into our faces. I gave up my attempts to hop over or run around the large puddles that were forming, for fear of falling into one of them. Wet feet were a better option than a broken tailbone.

When the car was in sight, Terry clicked twice on the fob. The sound of the doors unlocking was beautiful music to my ears. He jumped into the driver's seat as I darted into the passenger seat, but closing the door was a challenge. The wind grabbed it before I could close it and, despite my best efforts, yanked it open. I held on to the handle, worried that if I let go, the door would be ripped off its hinges. There I sat, rain pouring into the car, losing the battle for control over the door. I glanced over my shoulder to tell Terry I couldn't close it, but his seat was empty. Before I could look back at my door, it slammed shut, throwing me farther into the car. I was clubbed in the face by my own shoulder.

Terry ran around to his side of the car and was soon behind the wheel.

Rubbing my shoulder, I quietly said, "Ouch."

"Sorry." He shook the water from his hair. "I didn't have a chance to warn you before shoving the door closed. One of the hinges was about to snap. Hopefully it wasn't too damaged and will hold the door closed until we get to your place."

That door was the only thing between me and the road. "Yes, hopefully."

Terry began the slow drive to Sherwood. The volume and force of the rain on the windshield was too much for the wipers to handle, making visibility almost non-existent. I called the house to let my aunt and uncle know that I had a ride home. Terry and I continued our conversation about what to do next. We only hoped that the rainstorm would end before morning so our investigation wouldn't be halted by a school closure.

Terry relayed his plans to follow up on the information he'd received from one of Victor's few friends on campus—a student named Jennifer Thompson who had met him in their first-year biology class. Unlike many of the students Victor had met over the past three years, Jennifer had remained friends with him, mainly because, in her words, she enjoyed the challenge.

"Jennifer told me Victor was excited about a big story idea he had."

"We already know that." I used my hood to dry my face, only to realize that it was as wet as the rest of me. "Sorry about the car. The seats are soaked."

"That's okay. Fall on PEI can be interesting. Big storm one day, and a couple of days later, the sun will be blazing like it's the middle of summer. When that happens, I'll leave the windows open to dry things out." Terry shifted gears to manoeuvre around one of the Island's roundabouts, the number of which was growing. "Jennifer told me that this big scoop of Victor's was something that would make him famous in both journalism and paleontology. He said that a big discovery in evolutionary paleontology would be a major journalistic accomplishment."

"What do you think he meant by that?"

"No idea, but with Victor, it could be anything. We should find out more about that expedition he went on in the summer. Can you track down and talk to Dr. Daniels tomorrow?"

"I'll make that my priority. What about Dr. Christine

Hogg? Do you think she might have been unhappy with Victor's news?"

"It's possible. I'll interview her tomorrow. I have another appointment in the building her office is in, so I can make the excuse that I was in the area."

I was bending over to retrieve my bag from the floor so I could update my interviewee list when the car swung abruptly to the left, causing me to slam into Terry's shoulder. I could feel his arm jerk the steering wheel clockwise, and I braced myself as I was thrown against the door with the weak hinges. My arm smashed into the door, and I released a huge breath, unsure if it was from relief that I wasn't lying on the road, or from having the wind knocked out of me.

"Did-did you see that? That car came right at us." Terry's hands were trembling, and when he glanced up at the rear-view mirror, I saw fright in his face.

"They probably didn't see us. It's hard to see anything right now." The car accelerated and I did something I should have done when I first got in: I fastened my seat belt.

"They spun around and they're behind us now. Approaching fast." Terry hit the emergency brake, throwing the car into a one-eighty turn, then took the next right up a side street.

I braced myself against the back of the seat. "Are you sure it's the same car?"

"It's still behind us, so yeah, I'm sure."

I held my seat belt tightly to steady myself as Terry made a couple of sharp turns through the side streets. When we abruptly decelerated, then jerked to the left, I was grateful for the vinyl strap locking me in place. We squeaked past a parked car mere inches from my window.

"Good eye. That would have been nasty," I said.

"No kidding. The rain's blocking out the street lights, but I think we lost them. I'll stop here for a bit. This downpour can't last forever." He pulled alongside the curb in front of the car we'd almost obliterated, but within minutes headlights appeared in the side windows.

"Oh no." Terry shifted the gear into drive. The wheels squealed as we pulled back onto the road.

"Maybe it's not them. It's probably just someone heading home from work." I knew I was wrong when the car behind us copied not one, but three turns we made, keeping close to our rear bumper. They were definitely following us, but who were they? Between the weather and our pursuers, the night was becoming increasingly creepy. If it had been misty, I would have expected zombies to jump out in front of us.

"Can you see who's driving?" Terry flicked on the right signal light, then turned left. It didn't fool the driver, who remained on our bumper through the intersection, cutting off a pickup truck that fortunately was able to stop despite the water pooling on the road.

"No. The rain is making them all blurry. Probably not a zombie, though."

"What?" Terry gave me a sideways glance. "What are you talking about?"

What *was* I talking about? Perhaps I was cracking up under the pressure of dead bodies and car chases. And the only body that had jumped out at me lately was Lena's.

"How many people in the car?" Good—Terry was choosing to move on from my childish observation.

"I can't say for sure. At least one?" I shrugged to emphasize my uncertainty.

"Not helpful!" He tried the trick with the emergency

brake again, but this time the wheels left the pavement, sending the car into a spin. After three or four rotations—I lost count while screaming—our momentum was halted by our collision with a chain-link fence. Terry hit the gas, and as he did, I could hear metal on metal as the fence reluctantly released the back bumper. The banging and scraping told us that the bumper was barely hanging on, but stopping to check it wasn't an option. The other car, having spun a few times itself, was once again in pursuit.

"I have an idea." Terry slowed enough to take the turn onto the next street without hydroplaning again, then sped up.

I glanced behind me. The driver was staying farther back than they had been previously. Perhaps the loose bumper was working in our favour.

When I turned back to face front, I could see our destination up ahead—the Charlottetown Police Department. "Let's see if they follow us into here." Terry pulled into a parking spot beside a police cruiser, but we remained in the locked car until the small cherry-red four-door sedan, lit up by a street light, sped by.

Entering the police station, I spotted a familiar face behind the counter: Officer Mather, who had interviewed me after I found Victor's body in the field. She recognized me right away.

"Fran Fitzpatrick. What brings you out on an evening like this? Do you have any more information for us?" She met me with a warm, welcoming smile, then turned her attention to Terry with an expression of mistrust. She nodded slightly. "Mr. James."

Terry was still trembling, but he straightened to his full

height before speaking. "Officer." If he was trying to appear calm, his vibrating voice betrayed him. "I'd like to report an incident that—"

Before he could finish his sentence, I tugged on his sleeve and raised my chin at some photos on the wall over Officer Mather's shoulder. They appeared to be photos of a car rally, with various officers standing in front of cars and holding trophies or ribbons. The photo in the centre raised an internal alarm, and I needed Terry to stop talking. "Terry, let's just let it go. It's just a minor scratch."

"If you want to report vandalism to your car, you can fill out one of these forms." Officer Mather bent down to retrieve something from under the counter.

While she was out of sight, I jabbed my finger repeatedly in the air to get Terry to look at the back wall. It worked. I could see from his expression that he was thinking the same thing I was.

Officer Mather finished shuffling through some papers, then stood up and slammed a form and a pen onto the counter. "Fill this out." She shoved the paper toward Terry.

"You know, Franny's right."

"Fran!"

He glared sideways at me. "Sorry. *Fran* is right. It's just a scratch."

Officer Mather shrugged, then grabbed the paper and threw it below the counter. "Have it your way. Anything else?" She must have believed he was guilty; she wasn't the same gentle, kind woman who had spoken to me yesterday.

"Yes." He stared at the photos. "Is that Officer Hughes in that picture?"

"It is. Why?"

"Oh, just admiring the car. Is he in? I'd like to ask him about it."

"No. He's off duty right now, and I don't believe it would be appropriate for him to discuss his personal vehicle with a murder suspect."

Terry backed away from the counter and raised his palms toward her. "You're right. Not sure what I was thinking. It's just that that shade of paint is hard to find. I thought he might share where he had it painted."

Officer Mather shook her head and her brows furrowed. "It's red. Lots of cars are red. What's the big deal? Anything else? I've got other things to do."

The big deal was that the car in the photo of Officer David Hughes and his colleagues was the same size and colour as the car that had been chasing us. Was David trying to run us off the road? If so, why? Were we getting too close to something he didn't want us to find out?

<h1 style="text-align:center">Chapter 20</h1>

WHEN WE EXITED the police station, the rain had subsided enough to improve visibility. Across the street, parked in a private driveway and facing us, was a car resembling the one that had followed us. The front bumper sported a massive dent in the middle, suggesting that the owner may have had an unexpected meeting with a light pole or tree. I could see a figure in the driver's side, but it was too dark to make out the person's features. The lights of the house were off, suggesting that it was empty or the residents had an early bedtime.

The occupant of the car switched on the headlights, then the high beams, effectively blinding us. I heard the screeching tires before I saw the car heading for us. Terry grabbed my jacket and pulled me back toward the police station seconds before the four-door bullet flew by. We were sprayed by a splash of cold, dirty puddle water, but despite the oily grime deposited on my face, I was grateful we hadn't been hit by the car.

"All units, be on the lookout for a red sedan. Partial plate ETW." I was confused by the voice. "Are you two okay?" David, who was as soaked as we were, was standing a couple of feet behind Terry.

Terry and I glanced at each other, then at David, then behind him at a parked red car. Relief flooded through me, and it was all I could do not to hug the man in uniform. He hadn't been the one trying to run us off the road earlier, or to run us over just now.

"Did you see that?" It was my turn to have a trembling voice. "That car's been chasing us."

David escorted Terry and me back into the police station with an offer of towels to dry ourselves off with before we headed to my aunt and uncle's place. I wasn't convinced a towel would be of much help—I needed a hot shower and a change of clothes—but Terry seemed eager to go back inside and immediately accepted the offer.

Officer Mather was typing away at a computer monitor on the front desk. A smirk crossed her face when she looked up and saw the three of us. I'm sure we looked as though we'd just been rescued from a desert island during a tsunami.

"I see you two found Officer Hughes. Was he bathing in one of the puddles?" She laughed at her own joke, then directed her attention to her colleague. "How many times have I told you not to play in the puddles?"

"Ha, ha. Funny lady." David flipped up a portion of the

counter and joined Officer Mather on the other side. He gave her a playful punch on the shoulder. "I'm going to see if we have any towels for our friends here."

I found myself confused by my sudden mix of feelings. The interaction between the two officers suggested they might be more than colleagues. I wondered if they were dating, but why should I care? David was trying to pin a murder on my friend Terry, so he was the enemy.

They couldn't be more than friends and colleagues—Officer Mather appeared to be in her mid-forties, while David couldn't be older than his early thirties. However, my paternal grand-mother was ten years older than my paternal grandfather. I was completely lost in my swirling thoughts when a hand touched my shoulder.

"Are you okay?" asked Terry.

I sheepishly looked from him to Officer Mather, hoping they couldn't read my thoughts. "I'm fine. Just cold."

"This should help." David appeared from the back with a couple of towels, and more importantly, four cups of steaming liquid with the pleasant aroma of chocolate. I couldn't remember him leaving our company, but I was happy he was back with a treat.

He placed the tray of mugs on the counter and I greedily snatched one up. The smooth, hot liquid warmed me up almost instantly. "This is definitely helpful. Thank you."

Terry reached first for a towel to give his hair and face some attention, then grabbed his own mug of chocolatey delight. After taking a couple of gulps, he raised the mug to David. "Yes. Thanks. This is so good! I guess we were wrong about . . ." Terry paused and stared at the photo of David at the car rally.

Officer Mather doubled over and clapped one hand over her

mouth; her laughter filled the small reception area. "You thought *David* was the one chasing you?" She pointed at her fellow officer. "Him? A car chase? In the rain?" She struggled to compose herself and catch her breath. "I'm sorry, David, but . . ."

I pointed to David's photo. He was hoisting the largest trophy. "He won a car rally, and he's a police officer. Two things that must require excellent driving skills."

Officer Mather straightened up and waved a hand in the air. "Oh, don't get me wrong—Officer Hughes is an excellent policeman and a fine detective, but his driving skills . . . Well, most of the precinct is convinced he cheated at the rally."

David put his mug on the counter with enough force to draw our attention. "Okay, enough. Why would I try to run you two off the road?"

"To keep us from interfering with your investigation?" I didn't want to tell him that Terry and I had briefly suspected he might be the murderer. I'm not sure why I thought accusing him of being dangerously petty was a better choice.

Terry wisely interrupted. "Any word on the partial plate? Were you able to identify the driver?"

David shook his head. "No. None of the Island plates with ETW are registered to a red four-door sedan. There's a two-door hatchback and two pickup trucks. The plates are probably stolen. We'll check our system later for reports of stolen plates and stolen cars to see if that takes us anywhere, but it's doubtful. The driver who tried to run you down has probably already dumped the vehicle somewhere. If we find it, we can check it for prints."

"And DNA?" I was trying to be helpful.

David gave me one of those sideways you're-such-a-goof glances. "Sure. Just like on TV."

Chapter 21

I ARRIVED HOME EXHAUSTED and with clothing saturated with dirty water, and I might have been a little grumpy. Someone had tried to run Terry and me off the road and then run us down. Were they just trying to scare us, or quiet us forever? As I rode home with Terry, he wanted to go over what we knew so far, hoping that something might lead to a clue as to who the other driver was, but all I could think about was David's cutting remark about TV and DNA.

David, having insisted on escorting us back to my aunt and uncle's house, had followed us in his squad car. When we reached our destination, Terry pulled into the driveway. We planned to meet up the next day and said our goodbyes as I grabbed my backpack from the back seat. I exited the car to find David standing by the rear bumper.

"I'll walk you to the door to make sure you get in safely."

"That won't be necessary. I'm sure I can manage the few feet on my own." Who did he think he was making snarky remarks, then trying to act chivalrous?

I closed the passenger door, bent down to wave goodbye to Terry, then turned on my heel and stormed away. Despite my act of courage, I had to admit I was happy that neither of my companions left the driveway until after I was safely inside the house.

When I pushed open the door, the sound of the nightly news was emanating from the living room. I peeked around the kitchen corner and was relieved to see that the curtains in the living room were drawn. With any luck, Aunt Josephine hadn't seen my official city escort. I softly lowered my backpack onto the floor, then moved as stealthily as I could into the far room. The tightness in my neck muscles loosened when I saw that my aunt and uncle were both asleep in their respective recliners. Heads back, eyes closed, legs up, looking as peaceful as two wee babes.

I turned back toward the kitchen, intent on heading to my room, when I heard it: the familiar squeak of Aunt Josephine's green striped recliner being returned to a sitting position. I froze and slowly peered over my shoulder. There she was, my silver-haired landlady, standing beside her chair with a welcoming grin and her arms outstretched. She came toward me, grasped my shoulders, and said, "Good. You're home. Have you eaten? Let me get you some tea."

Before I could respond, the kindly woman, who mere seconds earlier had been sound asleep, bounced into the kitchen and put the kettle on. I was about to suggest she return to her chair and allow me to make my own tea, but before the words made it from my brain to my mouth, she had plates, cups, and cutlery on the small kitchen table we enjoyed most of our meals on. How had she done that?

"You'd better get out of those wet clothes."

I headed to my room and made a quick change. When I returned to the kitchen, cold chicken, homemade potato salad, and squares were ready for the taking. The unsettling grumbling emanating from my abdomen confused me; I'd eaten dinner earlier. *Well, Fran, your body is telling you that you need nutrients.* The food laid out before me was too appealing to decline, so I happily sat down and filled my plate, then my stomach. I'd worry about my waistline when I wasn't being chased by maniacs in red cars.

Uncle Johnny joined me at the table as I dove into my second helping of Aunt Josephine's potato salad. He selected two date squares from the plate of sweets to accompany the tea she had poured for him. Then she joined us and filled her own plate with a cookie and a lemon square.

"I'm afraid I wasn't able to get the hope chest painted today." Uncle Johnny stole a glance at Aunt Josephine and tried to keep a grin from forming on his lips. He wasn't successful.

The two of them were up to something, but I already had enough mysteries on my hands; the mystery of the hope chest would have to wait until another day. "That's not a problem. I like the natural wood colour, but I must confess, I'm not sure what I'd put in it."

They smiled at each other and Aunt Josephine patted my hand. "You'll think of something, my dear." They both laughed, confirming to me that they were indeed up to something.

"Thanks for the tea. I have a project due in a few days. I'd better get to work on it this evening."

I moved to the bedroom and sat on the edge of my bed, thinking about the day's events while eyeing the hope chest that was now tucked in the corner between the window and my desk. I couldn't imagine filling it up with linens and towels in preparation for a future domestic lifestyle, but perhaps some-day it would be a useful place to store sensitive information during an investigation for a story. Its clasp could accommodate a combination or keyed padlock. I made a note in my phone to purchase one at the school bookstore the next day, in case the need for security arose during my current investigation.

I moved over to the desk, determined to get some school work done, and attempted to ignore the new piece of furniture in my room. The chest would be empty—or so I thought— but curiosity forced me to lift the lid.

It was now filled with the throws, sheets, and towels used in the summer at my aunt and uncle's rental cottages on Lupin Lane, near Brackley Beach. I giggled at their joke; this wasn't a hope chest for me but storage for cottage bedding that couldn't be kept in the basement for fear it would smell musty. But something still didn't add up; even accounting for the bedding and towels, there appeared to be less room inside the chest than you'd think there was looking at the outside.

Being of an investigative mind, or just nosy, I removed the occupants of the cedar-scented storage unit and placed them on my bed. At the bottom was a thin, flat board with a leather strap in the middle, resting on raised corners. I tapped on the board; it sounded hollow, so using the strap, I lifted the false bottom out of the crate. The true bottom was made of a row of two-by-two-inch cedar pieces that ran from the back to the front, and in each corner was a six-inch-tall piece of the two-by-two wood. It secured the thin board, creating a secret compartment.

To my great disappointment, the compartment was empty. No wartime letters revealing juicy family secrets or a family hero I'd never heard spoken of lost at sea. No interesting old maps or black-and-white photos of times long gone. I allowed my mind to wander to all the possible treasures a person might find in a secret compartment, but I was brought back to the present when the phone rang in the kitchen.

"Franny, it's for you," Aunt Josephine called, then knocked on the door.

I quickly returned the wooden board and other contents to the chest, feeling guilty for snooping. But wasn't the joke that this was a gift to me? I closed the lid and headed to the phone. After a long chat with a high school friend from Ontario, we said our goodbyes and I headed to bed, the secret compartment forgotten until later that week.

Chapter 22

THE NEXT DAY, my last class ended without incident—I kept my backpack by my side until I was outside to avoid claiming any more victims with it. Once free of the crowds of students exiting Duffy Science Centre, I headed to the *Golden Spud* to meet with Terry and the rest of the gang. Terry had sent us all a text first thing this morning wanting to meet; it had been two days since he'd passed out the notes to each member of the team. While he hadn't given any of them actual assignments, he wanted to know if they had heard anything on campus about Victor's murder, possible suspects, and what people were saying about him.

My planned meeting with Dr. Daniels hadn't happened, because when I arrived at the professor's office for our scheduled meeting at 1:00 p.m., his secretary said he'd been called out on a departmental emergency. I couldn't imagine what type of a work-related emergency an archaeology and paleontology professor might have, but my time wasn't wasted. I ran into Laurie Lamont on my way out of the science building, and she agreed to meet with me early the next day at Jacob's Café. Now, as I travelled across campus, I wondered if Terry had been able to speak with Dr. Hogg.

The heavy downpour of the previous evening became a speck in history, superseded by today's blessing of sunshine and emerald-green grass. Winter was only about three months away, but the warmth of the air, mixed with the smell of nature mimicking a spring day, gave me a renewed sense of hope as I made my way to the student union barn.

I hadn't seen any sign of Lena Gallant since our encounter outside Marion Hall. As for the rest of the staff of the school paper, I hadn't seen them since the day I found Victor's body in the field. Had Terry shared with any of them that it had been me who'd happened upon Victor that fateful morning?

I had my answer as soon as I stepped into our office. Lena, at the back of the room pouring herself a coffee, was the first to spot me. "Fran, why didn't you tell me you found Victor? That must have been so gory." I was soon smothered in a hug I didn't want.

I pulled back. I'm not naturally someone who hugs people, including family, and certainly not someone I considered a murder suspect. Lena's explanation of her friendship with Bobby Burrell remained questionable. "No reason. I wasn't sure if the police wanted that information shared with others. I guess Terry told you?"

Lena shook her head, then straightened her glasses. "No. Terry isn't here yet. Andy told me."

As if on cue, Andy and Greg joined us from the adjoining room. Greg had to duck to avoid hitting his forehead on the drywall. The person who'd been put in charge of creating the makeshift doorway must have stood less than six feet tall.

Andy retrieved his phone from the charging station. "Yeah. Terry called me late last night and filled me in on some stuff."

Andy took a mouthful of coffee, then looked at me with suspicion in his eyes. I wondered how much Terry had shared with him. Had Terry told him I hadn't been upfront with him, that he himself had only learned I'd found the body when I blurted it out to David outside my aunt and uncle's house?

I decided to de-escalate the situation. "I'm sorry I didn't speak up when we all met the other day. I didn't know what I was allowed to say about my involvement. I wanted to tell Terry myself, and I was about to tell him when Officer Hughes showed up and—"

Andy raised his mug and took another sip, then cringed in disgust. "Ugh! This is awful. Who made this?" He poured the almost transparent liquid into the sink. "It tastes like dirty water." He grabbed the carafe and emptied it. "I'll make some fresh stuff."

As Andy measured out coffee grounds into a new filter, Lena briefly eyeballed the ceiling, a goofy grin on her face. I looked from her to the coffee maker and whispered, "You?" She nodded and I almost laughed but decided to remain professional. I still wasn't sure how mad Andy was about my hiding information from them.

Andy finished filling the water compartment, then flicked the switch on. "Sorry, Fran, what were you saying? That coffee, it was, well . . . never mind. Like I was saying, Terry filled me in last night. He said you weren't allowed to say nothin' to us the other day, but that cop on the case told him it would be okay to fill us in on a few details."

The tension I'd been feeling quickly evaporated. Andy wasn't upset with me—it was the person who'd made the coffee he was suspicious of. I rolled his comment around in my mind; Terry and the cop, who must have been David, had been chatting after Terry dropped me off last night. What had they been talking about? I'd have to ask Terry about that later.

The object of my questions walked into the office at that moment, and I wondered if we were following some script where the various characters enter on cue. This character wasn't alone—Hallie was hanging on to Terry's right arm as though they were a couple on a date. I felt a burning sensation in my chest, and a desire to push Hallie into the other room and fill in the hole with new drywall to prevent her escape. Why was she hanging on to him like that? Didn't she know he wasn't interested? Why did I care?

Terry pried Hallie's arms from his own and headed for the coffee. I was starting to understand why there were all those black scuff marks making a trail from the door to the back counter that was home to the coffee maker.

"Sorry I'm late. Hallie and I arrived in the parking lot at the same time, and she was showing me some photos she took for this week's edition. I suggested that we wait until we can all have a look and give our input, especially since many of them are sports related. Greg, maybe you could go over them with her for now?"

Greg shrugged. "Sure."

While Greg appeared indifferent to his new task, Hallie responded with a fiery glare that could have singed the hair off Terry's head had she been standing any closer to him. "I thought we were *all* going to go over the photos?"

Terry waved his hand in the air. "Sure, we will, but why don't you two get started with the photos from last night's game?"

Hallie pressed white knuckles against the package she was carrying and opened her eyes so wide, she resembled a lion ready to pounce on its prey. "Fine!" She marched over to Greg and grabbed his arm. "Come on, Greg, let's work in there."

She dragged him to the hole in the wall and yanked on his sleeve. Her aggression must have taken him by surprise because he forgot to duck; he was going to feel that later.

Chapter 23

GREG AND HALLIE used a laptop in the adjoining room to scour the photos on her camera's memory chip, while the rest of us sat in a circle, as we'd done a couple of nights ago, ready to share information and ideas. Terry and I were both hoping that someone in our group of amateur reporters had heard something to lead us to the murderer and clear his name.

"Sorry, man. I got nothin'. Nobody knows anything, or if they do, they're keeping it to themselves." Andy was the first to speak up, the disappointment of not being able to help his best friend obvious in his hunched posture and shaking head. "I'll keep asking around, though. One of the seniors in the math department is having a party this weekend. A few drinks may loosen some tongues." He shrugged.

"Thanks, Andy. I appreciate your keeping your ears open."

Terry swept his hand through his hair, then directed his attention to Lena. I was impressed by how neutral his face was—a true poker face that wouldn't reveal that he knew I'd seen Lena with Bobby Burrell. Would she assume I had already told Terry? "What about you, Lena? Any gossip over a cafeteria lunch?"

I was taken aback by Terry's wording and tensed up. Gossip? Why do guys assume women are sitting around gossiping? Surely men gossip too.

Lena, who had been sitting quietly listening to Andy only moments ago, sprang to life. She slid to the front of her chair and clasped her hands together as if ready to cast a spell on an unsuspecting victim. "Gossip? You bet! Not only are people talking, but they go on and on." She looked over at Andy. "Maybe they're quiet around you because you're Terry's friend?" She turned back to Terry. "I'd say it's fifty-fifty. Some kids say you're a good guy and would never do something so horrible. Others agree that you seem nice, but . . . you know"—she made air quotes—"anyone can snap."

Then she rose from her seat, took the seat beside Terry, patted his knee, and leaned into him until her face was only a few inches from his. In all seriousness, she said, "Did you snap, Terry? You can tell us. We won't tell anyone."

He leaped to his feet, narrowly missing smashing his forehead into Lena's. "What are you talking about? What are you implying?"

From the corner of my eye, I saw Andy, who'd been sitting to my right, rising with a forward momentum. I attempted to grab his belt to prevent Lena from experiencing the wrath of Terry's best friend, but he was too quick for me. "Are you insane?"

Lena's eyes widened and she scrambled to get behind her chair. As the distance between her and Andy lessened, she ended up against a wall. Andy positioned himself directly in front of her and raised his hand.

I was terrified, thinking he was about to strike her, but instead of a fist, he threw his index finger in front of her face. "Be very careful what you say about my man Terry. You don't know us. You're the new kid here. Don't forget it." He dropped his arm to his side and inhaled deeply. "And what do you mean, 'We won't tell'? You think Terry's a murderer and that the rest of us would just go along with it and cover it up?"

The corners of Lena's lips formed a grin and she laughed. "Chill, man. I was just kidding. It was a *joke*. Can't you take a joke? See, this is why no one's talking around you. You two stand up for each other."

They glared at her for a few seconds. The tension in the room was palpable, and I feared what might happen next, but a voice coming from the other room drew everyone's attention away from the crazy woman with the cat-eye glasses and the Cheshire cat grin.

"I think we found something," Greg stepped through the hole in the wall, rubbing his forehead and ducking this time. He handed Terry the laptop. "Look at that photo there," he said, pointing. "The guy with the backpack. He's got a stupid grin on his face. Hallie said she thinks she saw him talking to Victor last week."

"Not just talking, but arguing." Hallie positioned herself beside Terry and clung to his arm. She caressed his face. "I may have just saved you, Terry. Why would that kid be grinning when an ambulance, police, and a dead body were nearby?"

Terry pulled free of her and wiped his cheek. "Do you

know who he is? What they were arguing about?" He passed the laptop to Andy. "Any idea who this is?"

Andy shook his head. Lena reached for the laptop, but Andy merely gave her a dirty look before handing the computer to me.

I felt a rush of adrenalin. "Hallie may be on to something here." I leaped up and rushed to show Terry and Andy the photo they had been looking at seconds earlier. I handed Terry the laptop and pointed to the grinning man. "That's Bobby Burrell, Victor's roommate. His hair is different in this photo than the one you sent me yesterday, Terry, but I'm sure it's him. I spotted him earlier today, but this isn't the backpack he was carrying. This one is tie-dyed. White and dark red, or is it purple? The one he had today was green."

I looked over at Lena. Her grin had vanished, and she was still pressed so firmly against the wall, it appeared she was attempting to disappear into it.

"Lena, you know Bobby. That's him, right?" I asked her before thinking about my audience and what had transpired moments earlier.

Lena slowly nodded in confirmation.

Remembering Andy's current feelings about Lena, I stepped in front of her to block his access. I didn't know how he might react to the news that not only did Lena know Victor's roommate, but also that she hadn't volunteered that information.

When I peered over my shoulder at Andy, he was squinting at Lena, nostrils flared and hands forming fists. His chest rose and fell heavily several times. Then he huffed and walked to the back of the room.

Andy had a temper, and while he had just shown he could

control it, earlier he had nearly been physical with Lena. I hoped that he'd stopped short of violence because it wasn't in his nature to hit someone, especially a woman, but I couldn't be certain that it wasn't because there were witnesses. If Andy had known about Terry and Victor's argument the night before Victor was murdered, would he have attacked Victor in Terry's defence?

The room was eerily quiet for what seemed an eternity before Terry spoke. "Okay. There's a lot going on. I think we should all calm down and take a seat." He motioned to his best friend. "Come on, Andy, I'm sure we can talk this out and find out why Lena's friend Bobby was in the crowd that day."

The sun was setting outside, creating shadows of the tree branches on the wall, and the wind was picking up, causing the branches' movements to take on a sinister appearance. I felt a chill over my body as I stood still, trying to use my common sense to assure myself that shadows couldn't hurt us, but it was difficult because I knew that several people in that darkening room *could* hurt *me*.

Lena was about to speak. I faced her and made a "sh" motion with my lips, unseen by the others, suggesting that she might want to keep quiet until tempers simmered down. I reached over her shoulder and flicked the light switch on, then nodded toward the centre of the room. "Let's take a seat."

Lena followed me to the circle of hard plastic chairs, and before sitting, moved hers closer to mine. She was obviously as unnerved as I was by Andy's behaviour, but I didn't know why. Did she also suspect he might be Victor's killer, or was she concerned he'd find out that she was somehow involved in Victor's demise?

As I glanced around the circle at my journalist colleagues, I once again wondered if one of them was the murderer.

Lena was keeping secrets about her friendship with the roommate, and Andy had a volatile temper. I had no reason to suspect Greg, but what about Hallie? I thought back to our meeting a couple of days ago; she hadn't mentioned being in the crowd when the police and EMTs arrived at the field where Victor's body was lying. She'd taken photos, but this was the first we'd heard of it. The only reason we now knew she had photos from that day was because Greg was looking for the sports-related photos with her and came upon the one he'd just shared with us.

Terry's eyes met mine, and he scrunched up his face and shook his head in a she-doesn't-have-it-in-her way. I could only guess that he had seen me staring at Hallie, clearly wondering. We would have to talk about her later, in private. Why would a woman so keen to be his girlfriend not mention she had information that might help clear his name?

My question was soon answered by Hallie. "That's so weird. I remember seeing all the people on the corner the other day, and all the handsome men in uniform." She looked in embarrassment at Terry. "Sorry, Terry. I know I shouldn't be using the paper's camera for personal use, but this one ambulance guy . . . well . . . he was so cute. I thought I'd sneak a photo of him and try to find out his name later." She turned the laptop, which she had taken back from Terry, to face him. "See, he's there in the front of the picture. That Bobby guy was standing in the background, I guess." She giggled. "A lucky shot. Greg says it might be important."

Was Hallie a smart, conniving murderer who thought quickly on her feet, or was her most devious intent to stalk an

EMT? While the latter possibility was creepy, it wasn't relevant to our problem.

Terry rose and poured himself a coffee. "It might be important, Hallie. Can you email that picture to me, and any other photos you took that day?"

She gave Terry a huge, smug smile. "Sure."

With all the tension that had developed during the *Golden Spud* meeting, we accomplished little more after retaking our seats. Hallie emailed the photo in question to Terry. She claimed she had been on her way to classes that fateful morning when she noticed the ambulance with its light on, so she stopped to see what was going on. She barely noticed the gurney being carried across the field, and claimed she hadn't seen me at all. Her mind was focused on the cute EMT, she said; she wanted to find out his name and marital status. Oddly enough, while she was telling us this, she was still clinging to Terry's arm.

Andy remained quietly fuming through the rest of the meeting, shifting his glare between Lena and Hallie. Greg grabbed a glass of water, asked around for an aspirin, happily accepted one from Lena, swallowed it, then sat rubbing his forehead.

When the others were distracted by a noise outside, Terry caught my eye and nodded at the coffee maker. I met him there and, even though it was getting late to be drinking coffee, poured myself one. He whispered, "I'm going to offer Andy a ride home, then call you afterwards if that's okay. I didn't get a chance to see Christine Hogg today, but I'll try again tomorrow."

I raised my cup and took a sip. It was cold, strong, and bitter, but I swallowed it anyway. "Sounds good."

"Do you need a ride home?"

"No. I need to pick up a few things at the bookstore. I'll call my uncle Johnny and see if he'll pick me up. He's always offering, so I should take him up on it." I wasn't about to get into a car with Terry and Andy.

We all said our goodbyes and parted ways. I found the book I was looking for in the bookstore, then waited outside its main entrance for my uncle to arrive in his pickup truck.

From my vantage point, I could see the window to Bobby Burrell's dorm room. The light was on, and a person stood near the window. As I watched, the figure moved deeper into the apartment, then returned to the window with company. They hugged. Then the visitor sat on the sill and they appeared to be talking. Was that Lena? I was too far away to be certain, but the time I'd spent in the bookstore would have afforded her plenty of time to get to the coed dorm.

I pulled out my phone to call Lena to see if the person in the window answered at the same time she did. I scrolled to her name in my contact list and was about to touch the call button when my uncle's navy-blue pickup truck pulled up.

"There you are." Uncle Johnny pushed the passenger door open from his seat. I climbed up into the vehicle and closed the door.

I'd need to come up with a new plan to determine whether or not that was the woman with funky eyeglasses I'd seen hugging Victor's roommate, again. This time she couldn't claim she was unaware that the room had been occupied by the murder victim. What was Lena Gallant hiding?

Chapter 24

M Y ALARM SOUNDED the start of another day, but realizing it was my half day of classes, I hit the snooze button and pulled the covers over my head. I'd purposely scheduled one day a week with afternoon-only classes so that once projects were due, I'd have a morning each week to work on them. As I lay snuggled up in my homemade country-style quilt and flannel blankets—two of the luxuries I'd discovered after moving to PEI—I daydreamed about everything from peanut butter on raisin toast, to blue-eyed men in uniform, to the beauty of my new environment. Back home in Toronto, I'd never imagined living a few blocks away from country fields and stunning horses.

Horses. Soon the beauty of my thoughts turned to the gruesome memory of what I'd found in the field only three days ago. My sleepy, dreamy, relaxed mood soon shifted to worried and anxious. We had so many suspects and so little information to help us.

Terry hadn't been able to meet with Dr. Hogg yesterday, and my appointment with Dr. Daniels had been abruptly cancelled. Our meeting last night at the *Golden Spud* had been full of surprises. We learned that Bobby Burrell had been at the crime scene and Andy had a quick temper, and then there was Lena's behaviour. Was she as naive as she appeared, or was she hiding something? Was that something a relationship with Victor's roommate?

I threw the covers off and sat up; any hope of catching up on lost sleep from the past few restless nights was gone as facts and questions about the happenings of the past few days rattled around in my mind like an unbalanced washing machine.

One positive event from yesterday was my chance encounter with Laurie Lamont. I had recognized her from her picture on the university's website Dr. Watson told me about. Her photo and bio, as well as her academic achievements and interests, were detailed in the section devoted to graduate students. Laurie had been pleasant when I introduced myself and had happily agreed to a meeting this morning.

I shot to my feet and grabbed my phone to check the time—7:00 a.m.! I opened the calendar app to confirm my fears. There it was, scheduled at 8:00 a.m.: *MEET LL AT JACOB'S*. I had an hour to get showered, grab everything I'd need for the day on campus, and get to Jacob's, a twenty-minute walk.

I opened my bedroom door and listened for noise. The sound of an electric drill came from the basement, and my aunt's snoring resonated from the far end of the hall. Aunt

Josephine was normally up and dressed by 6:30 a.m. every day, but she had stayed up late last night watching a movie. I breathed a sigh of relief that my aunt seemed to be embracing retirement—staying up late and sleeping late—and that I might get out of the house without breakfast, or having to explain why I was in a hurry. I jetted to the bathroom and got ready for the day.

Once my feet hit the driveway, I had exactly twenty-two minutes to get to Jacob's Café. I had left a note for my aunt and uncle explaining that I'd headed to the campus early to do some research. It wasn't a lie—more like a misdirection of information. I *was* doing research—into Victor's murder. They would assume, of course, that it was related to my studies.

I exited the house, gingerly closed the door behind me, then glanced over at the garage that housed the bicycle I had purchased when I first arrived on the Island. Using the bike, I could get to Jacob's much faster, but opening the garage door might draw Aunt Josephine's attention. I flung my book bag over my shoulder and headed, on foot, for my meeting with Laurie.

I reached my destination on time, but I was winded. When I burst through the glass door, I was relieved to see only two people in the order line. I surveyed the tables for Laurie while I awaited my turn at the counter; she wasn't here.

I felt the textured nylon of my bag as I tapped my fingers against it. Was this going to be another waste of time? Another cancelled meeting? Maybe Laurie, like Dr. Daniels the day before, had an archaeological and paleontological emergency. I took a couple of deep breaths to calm my nerves. The smell of coffee and chocolate helped, and when I returned my thoughts to the menu board, I was met with a silly grin from Scott Jacob himself.

"Are you ready to order, Fran, or are you simply admiring the decor?" He laughed.

I stepped forward, no doubt to the relief of the people bunched up in the space behind me. Where had all these people come from? I mouthed *Sorry* at the group, then returned my attention to my host. "Sorry, Scott. I'm meeting another student here, but it looks like she hasn't arrived yet."

"I'll keep an eye out for her. In the meantime, let's get you a coffee and you can find yourself a seat. Remind me what you take in your coffee?"

"Two milks, please."

"Anything else?"

"A chocolate scone. I see they're on the menu again today."

My guilt at creating a backup of customers lessened when two employees appeared from the back and each manned an order station. Scott greeted the two ladies, who were sporting smocks with Jacob's Café embroidered on the lapel, placed a Closed sign by his register, then directed the individuals behind me to the other stations.

"Noreen and Catherine normally cover the morning rush hour, but they were trapped because of construction on Highway 1, the new Cornwall bypass, this morning. Coming in from Clyde River can be a chore some days." Scott was referring to the small community situated a few miles west of Charlottetown. "In the winter it's snowplows and salt trucks, but this time of year it might be tractors and trucks hauling produce to the market, or, like today, construction. The construction will probably last a few weeks, but thankfully it wasn't an accident."

Scott's words filled me with momentary guilt. Perhaps Laurie had been in an accident? And here I was getting frustrated that my interviewee wasn't here yet when I'd rushed to arrive on time.

I gathered up my coffee and scone, placed them on a tray, then added two little restaurant-size packets of strawberry jam. Coffee and a chocolate scone didn't constitute a healthy breakfast, but I convinced myself that adding the gooey treat in the little package would help; after all, strawberries are a fruit, and Canada's Food Guide suggests several servings of fruit a day. Or does it?

A table in the far corner that would afford me a wide view of both the parking lot and the entrance was unoccupied. I sat there picking away at my scone and making a mess with the jam—I had forgotten to procure a knife from the plastic utensil container—while awaiting Laurie's arrival.

As I popped the last tidbit of the sugary breakfast into my mouth, the door flew open. The crowd appeared to move in sync to the side to make way for the woman brandishing a flashy laptop bag and what looked like a designer purse.

Laurie Lamont, all five foot two or so of her, stood tall while she gazed around the room looking, I presumed, for me. I waved when her head turned in my direction. She nodded at me, then shook her head to fling her long black ponytail away from her face.

When I ran into Laurie the previous day in the science building, she'd been wearing a white lab coat, running shoes, and protective lab glasses. Today, this woman Dr. Watson had described as a brilliant academic had the body language and aura you might expect of a Parisian fashion model. To complement her fancy accessories, she was wearing designer jeans, high-heeled shoes, and a faux leather jacket. Or were the accessories complementing the clothes?

As Laurie approached me, I noticed she was carrying a takeout cup from the expensive coffee chain up the street, as well as a paper bag that would be filled with a baked treat from there. Laurie wasn't delayed because she'd been in an accident; rather, she'd been in a long line at one of Scott's competitors. I couldn't show her my frustration—or more accurately, anger—at her behaviour; I needed to find out what she knew about Victor's murder.

She sat in the chair opposite to me and placed her items with the competitor's logo on the table. She bent down to set her laptop bag and purse on the floor while I looked apologetically at Scott. He shrugged it off and I understood. While it was poor etiquette to consume something from one restaurant in another, Scott was busy enough, and mature and confident enough in his business, to allow the occasional faux pas to pass.

Chapter 25

I HAD MENTALLY PREPARED for my conversation with Laurie Lamont on my sprint to the café that morning. I would start off by exchanging pleasantries: "Hello, how are you?", "It's nice to meet you," and "So you're in the master's program—interesting. I'm a freshman in the arts with a focus on journalism." That was the plan, but that was not how it went.

When Laurie straightened up in her seat after ensuring her laptop bag was safely tucked under our table, I extended my hand to her. "Hi again. Thank you for joining me this morning."

Laurie raised her hand and waved it in the air. "Sure, sure. Listen, I don't have a lot of time to chit-chat with you, but I'm happy to help with your little article on Victor." She focused her eyes on mine, then narrowed them. "Especially if it'll expose what a little dirtbag and rat he really was."

I was literally at a loss for words, not a good position to be in when performing an interview. The man had bled out in a field not more than three—or was it four?—days ago, and she was out to get what little blood he had left. I couldn't imagine what it must have been like for Victor, or the rest of the expedition team, to spend the summer in close quarters with someone so cold.

My gut reaction was to stand up, tell this narcissistic woman off, and leave, but a surge of sadness for Victor helped me regain my voice. No matter how obnoxious he was, he deserved better than to be brutally beaten and left to die alone in a paddock.

Laurie removed the lid from her coffee, rolled her eyes, and left the table to retrieve the milk carton at the communal coffee station. After adding milk to her cup, she set the carton on our table and returned to her seat.

"What is it you want me to tell you? As I've said, Victor was a rat. He didn't care who he hurt or upset—it was all about him. I can't believe how some people can be so self-focused, but it happens."

I couldn't suppress my grin. "It does, doesn't it? The world is made up of all kinds of people."

"On that we can agree. I suppose you want to know what Victor was studying and researching."

I glanced at the milk carton, then back at Laurie. People generally took their coffee mugs to the counter to add milk, but she had robbed the morning patrons of adding extra milk to their beverages. I returned my attention to my selfish companion. "Tell me, Laurie, did you grow up in an affluent household?"

The question confused her. "My folks did okay. Why? What does that have to do with anything?"

"Oh, nothing. My journalism professor said in class the other day that we should start an interview by getting to know our interviewees."

"Your professor should mind her own business."

I was sure Dr. Gayle would have agreed with Laurie that the question was inappropriate, but since it was unlikely the two women would ever meet, I felt safe letting my prof take the heat.

I questioned Laurie about the purpose of the expedition, and about the other members of the team. The information she provided was what I had already learned from Dr. Watson.

"I met Dr. Watson the other day, and he told me he was originally meant to be the leader of the project, but he became ill."

"Yes. It was unfortunate because Dr. Watson is an intelligent man, and a true expert in archaeology and paleontology. Some in the academic world look down on those who choose to work at a smaller university, but Dr. Watson is at UPEI by choice. He makes a point of getting to know the senior science students, and those of us in the master's and Ph.D. programs. He goes as far as hosting several functions in his home each year. In fact, it was spring, after our last get-together, that he started to feel ill. Just a couple of weeks before our Ellesmere Island trip."

"And when he was unable to go on the trip, Dr. Daniels took over as leader of the expedition?"

Laurie rolled her eyes and shook her head. "Yes. Good ole Dr. Daniels."

"You don't like him?"

"It's not a matter of liking or not liking him—it's a matter of his qualifications."

"Dr. Watson told me that Dr. Daniels was on his way to being tenured at the University of Hamilton. That sounds like a big deal. He must have had excellent qualifications to get tenured at a large institution like that."

Laurie rolled her eyes and shook her head again. I was certain that this was meant for me this time. "The two have nothing to do with each other. If you spend enough time in an academic setting, you'll see that promotions and seniority have a lot more to do with unseen factors than actual qualifications."

"I'm sure that's true in many aspects of life." I sighed at the truth I heard come out of my own mouth. When had I become so cynical?

"Dr. Daniels and the team worked well together for the first couple of weeks, but then our mighty leader became impatient with our lack of results."

"What do you mean?"

"We were digging near the site where the Tiktaalik was discovered. Dr. Daniels wanted to find more specimens to cement the creature's place as the link between fish and land animals."

My knowledge of science, including the origins of life, was scant, but my interest in this potential proof of evolution was piqued. "The Tiktaalik is a missing link?"

There was the eye roll again. "Such an overused term. It's one piece of a very large puzzle. The Tiktaalik has features of both a fish and a land animal. Our goal was to find additional specimens, but as I said, we weren't finding anything useful and Dr. Daniels was becoming agitated. He wanted to move to a new location, but Victor and some of the others protested."

"Haven't people been looking for a missing link . . . sorry, pieces of the puzzle . . . for generations? Why would he get upset so soon?"

"I don't know. I guess the guy was trying to prove his genius. There's a lot of competition in the world of science and research. It can be cutthroat."

"Do you know why he walked away from a tenured position?"

"I don't know, and I don't care. It has nothing to do with me."

"Did your team move to a new site?"

"Yes, after Dr. Daniels contacted Dr. Watson. Even though Dr. Watson hadn't been able to join us, he was still in charge of the expedition. Dr. Daniels had us move closer to an Inuit settlement. I was a bit uneasy about intruding on their land, but he assured us we were on crown land and were okay to proceed, so we started exploring the area. I must admit, he did make a smart decision, because after another week we made what might be one of the biggest discoveries in paleontology to date."

"Another Tiktaalik?"

"Something far more exciting, and it will change the focus on Ellesmere Island for years to come. I am not free to discuss details with you. New discoveries must be put through the proper channels of scientific verification and publication."

Laurie was excited but vague—similar to the way Victor had been when talking about his big story, according to Terry. I wondered if Victor had been referring to the discovery his group made, and if he had been planning to steal the glory for himself by leaking the details before they were ready to go public.

As I was mulling over these questions, a hairy arm reached across the table and retrieved the milk carton. I looked up to see

Scott frowning at Laurie while he gauged the temperature of the carton with his palm. "Still cold. We do prefer to keep the milk on the counter over there, in the ice bucket. So it's"—he stared intensely into Laurie's eyes—"COLD!"

She shrugged.

"Speaking of staying cold"—Scott straightened up—"I couldn't help but overhear a bit of your conversation. Tell me, this Tiktaalik . . ." Scott pronounced it the same way Dr. Watson had. "You say it came from the waters around Ellesmere Island, then one day crawled onto land and turned itself into a land animal?"

Laurie huffed. "It's obviously more complicated than that. These things don't happen instantaneously. It takes millions of years."

"Yes, of course. Silly me. But tell me, when this fish crawled up onto the land, did it already have a fully developed respiratory system, the type needed to breathe outside of water?"

"The gills would have evolved into lungs over time."

"I see." Scott rubbed his chin. "Did the lungs develop in the water or on land? And what about the trachea and bronchioles?"

I was lost. Bronchioles?

Laurie puffed out her chest. "I wouldn't expect a mere barista to understand something as complicated as zoology and the evolution of life."

Scott playfully slapped his forehead. "My apologies. Just one more question though, if you don't mind."

It was obvious Laurie was getting frustrated. When she pulled out her phone to check the time, I worried that she was going to leave before I'd finished my interview with her. I was surprised when she encouraged Scott to continue.

"Most authorities on evolution claim that man came from Africa. If this first land animal started out on Ellesmere Island, how did it get all the way to Africa? I'm not as versed as you must be on all this science stuff, but I find the theories on the origins of life fascinating. I imagine scientists have found fossils of life forms between the Tiktaalik and humans to show the progression?"

Laurie's nostrils were flaring so wide, I thought the paper towel on the table would be sucked toward her face. "The Tiktaalik didn't"—she made air quotes—"*turn into humans.* There were millions of intermediary forms."

"Yes, but . . . ." Unlike Laurie, Scott seemed to be enjoying the conversation. And unlike Laurie, he remained respectful and polite, his demeanour calm and his facial expression reflecting innocent inquiry. "If this creature somehow made it to land and survived, and then over millions of years its gills turned into lungs, and its fins turned into limbs, how did it get back off the island to then further evolve elsewhere on the planet?" He cocked his head at Laurie.

I thought she had made her case, and so I attempted to answer Scott's question. "There must be millions of fossils in the records showing the transition. That's what we were taught in grade school. Those illustrations of a monkey turning into a man, and a fish turning into a frog." They both ignored me.

Scott took the empty seat beside me. "Yes, there must be millions of fossils in the records." He rested his chin on his fist and stared at Laurie.

"Some scientists believe that humans evolved in different parts of the world. That would explain how fossils have been found in various locations that aren't geographically suited to the progression." Laurie looked as if she'd just won a Nobel Prize.

"Really? Wow." Scott sat back in his chair as though he'd been blasted by a wave of indisputable information. Then he leaned forward again. "I'm no mathematician, but how unlikely must it have been for humans to evolve not only once but several times in multiple locations, and to have us all turn out exactly the same anatomically and in all the other ways that make us human. Wow!" He shook his head. "That's mind-boggling."

Laurie still looked frustrated. "I didn't say I believed it, only that some people do. The odds are astronomically against it. Anyway, don't you have something better to do than harass customers? What are you even doing over here?"

Scott rose and started heading toward the counter that housed the milk and cream but paused briefly. "If the milk had been where it belonged, I wouldn't have been over here to overhear."

I had my pen poised to take notes on a subject I was now interested in. "How many Tiktaaliks were found on Ellesmere Island?"

Laurie shuffled in her seat. "One that I know of—the partial skeleton that was discovered several years ago. As I've already told you, looking for more specimens was the original purpose of our work this summer."

Laurie typed into her phone, then glared toward the front counter where Scott had returned to help Catherine and Noreen restock the display shelves. "Is that guy one of those intelligent design enthusiasts?"

I hadn't heard that term before, but time was ticking by fast and I still had questions about the expedition. "I don't know. Why?"

She shook her head, then reset her ponytail. "He must be some kind of religious nut."

It was true that most of the conversation was above my unscientific head, but Laurie's assessment of Scott was rather harsh. "Why? Because he asked a few questions?"

She huffed again. "I wouldn't expect a freshman, especially one majoring in arts, to understand. He seemed to know you."

I chose to ignore the insult and focus on the latter comment. "He's the owner of this café. My aunt was one of his grade school teachers. When do you think your team will be ready to present your findings?"

"It takes a long time. We need to compile our findings, present them to Dr. Watson since he's the lead, then to the other department heads, and then we'll work on a paper for publication. That's how we share our findings with the rest of the scientific community. It takes a long time. It's not like an art project—we can't simply slap some paint onto a canvas, nail it to a wall, and voila, a presentation."

For someone who was so cocky about her own field of study, she was dim-witted about mine, but I took the high road and again ignored the insults. I now understood Dr. Watson's comment about half the university being at odds with Laurie Lamont. She might have a bright future in archaeology and paleontology ahead of her, but this scientific genius would remain on our suspect list.

Chapter 26

AFTER GATHERING A few more interesting facts about the expedition from Laurie, including an intriguing tidbit about Victor related to Dr. Daniels, I flew out of the café on a high of caffeine, chocolate, and what I deemed useful information. Scott had kindly refilled my coffee cup a couple of times; I suspect that his generosity had something to do with wanting to overhear more of my conversation with Laurie. More important than the free beverages was finding out that something big had happened on Ellesmere Island. All Terry and I had to do was find out what it was. How hard could that be?

Like a handy coincidence straight out of a TV murder mystery, Terry was exiting Marion Hall at the same time I was rushing past the two-storey brick building. I waved at him to gain his attention, hoping he would have time to talk.

It was still early in the day and I didn't have any classes until one o'clock, so I thought this was perfect timing until Andy come around the corner. I remained uncertain how to react to this guy who seemed to have two separate personalities. The Superman-like, loyal friend Terry referred to when talking about Andy's computer-hacking skills, versus the quick-tempered person I had witnessed the previous evening.

Terry put his arm around his pal's shoulders in what I took as a this-is-my-friend-and-he's-a-good-guy message to me. Andy pushed him away and they approached me, laughing and hitting each other like a couple of good ole boys.

Andy stopped about two feet from me and lowered his head. "I'm sorry about last night, Fran. This whole thing . . . you know, Victor's murder, Terry being accused, and people whispering when I'm around . . . well, it's really getting to me. I didn't realize how much until I kinda lost it last night."

I folded my arms. "*Kinda* lost it? I thought you were going to knock Lena's head off. We were both terrified."

"Yeah, I know. You're right. I shouldn't have done that, and I'm sorry. I hunted Lena down at the cafeteria earlier and apologized to her. She forgave me. I hope you will too."

Andy's choice of words sent an icy shiver up my spine. He "hunted her down"? Had Victor been hunted down? I didn't want to hold a grudge against Andy; I didn't know him well, and Terry had indicated that he'd had a difficult upbringing. But a hard childhood was no excuse to threaten people.

"Sure, Andy, I can forgive you." *This time, but while you're not on Terry's suspect list, you are still on mine.*

Andy extended his hand; I accepted it and we shook. "Great. I appreciate it. I really do." He turned around to look at the library, then turned back to Terry and me. "I gotta run.

I have a study group in a few minutes. Terry, I'll meet up with you later to work on that other project, okay?"

Terry slapped Andy on the shoulder. "Sure, bud. See you later."

I watched Andy dash off to the library, empty-handed. "He has a study group?"

"Yeah. Why? You don't believe him?"

"It's not that—I'm just used to students having a back-pack or laptop bag when they have a study group."

Terry frowned at me, shook his head, and started to walk away.

"Sorry, I didn't mean to imply that Andy was up to something." I didn't mean to imply it *out loud*, but I did wonder if he was up to something devious.

It wouldn't be unheard of for a person to have an evil side that even their best friend didn't know about. There are many cases in history of people who had no idea that their spouse—the person they shared their life with, shared their bed with, and had children with—was a serial killer. How hard could it be to hide an evil side from a friend?

Terry had spoken like a proud parent about Andy's ability to hack computers. This might be how Andy was able to remain at UPEI. Perhaps his passing grades weren't a result of studying hard, but rather a product of pounding a keyboard late at night, when no one was watching, to change his marks. Victor might have found out about Andy's computer-hacking skills and threatened to report him to the university administration.

Terry slowed down so I could catch up to him. "Let's not talk about Andy right now. How did your meeting with Laurie Lamont go? Did she show up?"

"She did." As I drew closer to him, I shared Laurie's information about the troubles between Dr. Daniels and Victor over the summer.

We were alone in the parking lot where I had met Terry after the *Golden Spud* meeting the night of the murder, so I wasn't concerned about being overheard. "What's more interesting than their tiff—I suspect Victor had tiffs with a lot of people—is this big discovery his friend mentioned to you, and that Laurie told me about today too. She said Dr. Daniels had caught Victor sneaking out of his tent shortly after they moved their camp to the second location, and the two had argued. Do you think that might have something to do with Victor's murder?"

Once I had caught up with Terry, he had met my pace and we made our way north toward the administration building. "It might. The email from Dr. Hogg warned Victor to back off. Maybe he had threatened to leak information about the team's discovery." Terry stopped abruptly. "I'm heading to see Dr. Hogg now. I can meet you after your classes and give you a rundown of what she says."

Was he trying to get rid of me? Up until now he'd been anxious to get my help, but now he seemed happy to send me off to class. I checked the time on my phone—11:00 a.m.—I still had plenty of time before Sociology 101.

"Why don't I accompany you? You wouldn't mind, would you? It's a beautiful day to meet and interview an administrator, and I have no commitments until this afternoon." I wasn't going to let him dump me that easily.

Terry shrugged. "Sure. That'd be great." He hadn't hesitated at all. In fact, his eyes lit up at the suggestion, as though he was happy to have me along. *Great, Fran, you're misreading people again.*

We entered the single-storey grey-brick building called R.E. Irving Hall, situated a couple of hundred yards north of the men's dorm, from the west-facing entrance. This structure, named after UPEI's retired drama professor, not the oil tycoon, housed the college administration and registrar offices, as well as classrooms for math and business courses.

I perused the lobby's name board for Dr. Hogg's office number. "Here it is, Terry. Room 104." I was met with silence and glanced over my shoulder. "Terry?"

I looked around the building's atrium. The door to my left was clearly labelled Registrar's Office in large, bold letters on the frosted glass. A few feet into the lobby on my right was a small metal sign with Basement on it, accompanied by a downward staircase icon. I leaned over the railing to see if Terry had gone down there, but all I saw were two doors at the basement level. Each door had a tiny stick figure, one sporting a dress and the other not. Now I knew where the bathrooms were, but where did Terry disappear to?

I advanced to the far side of the lobby, giving me a view of the hallways that extended to the right and left. I turned left first, no doubt because that's the way we're taught to look first when we're learning to cross the street safely as children. Look to your left, then to your right.

My mind wandered to countries where people drive on the left side of the road, and a less-than-useful fact came to mind. Crossing the street in England could pose a danger to those of us used to cars moving forward on the driver's right. We look to the left first because the car in the near lane is coming from the left. *Clear your head of useless information, Fran. Find Terry and proceed to your interview.*

I turned to the right and screamed. Terry, who towered over me by a least half a foot, was standing so close to me that all I could see was his green jacket. I hadn't heard him approach. Where had he come from?

He put an index finger to his pursed lips. "Sh. I was calling to you, but you were staring down this hall in a trance. Are you okay?"

I stepped back so I could see his face without flexing my neck backwards. "Sure, I'm fine. You startled me is all. You can be very quiet, you know."

"I suppose I can be." He frowned at me. "Unless I'm calling out to you. Did you see something suspicious? Hear something?"

"Um, no. I was just thinking."

"About?"

I studied the ceiling and rubbed my chin. "Nothing important." That couldn't have been more truthful.

"Come on, then. Dr. Hogg's office is down this way. I thought you were right behind me when we came in."

"Actually, *you* were behind me then. I stopped to find her office number since I haven't been in here before. How did you know where to go?"

"Because I was here yesterday. Remember? I told you I tried to meet with her."

Terry did say he hadn't had a chance to meet with Dr. Hogg yesterday, but he'd made no mention of coming to her office. I decided to let it go; this wasn't the time to be petty. I remained silent and followed him down the hall.

Chapter 27

THE DOOR TO room 104 was open, and in the far end sat a well-weathered metal desk topped with stacks of paper, two mugs full of pens, and three stacked trays with more paper. I could also see the top of a woman's head resting on folded arms.

Terry tapped lightly on the door. "Excuse me, Dr. Hogg. I'm sorry to disturb you, but I wonder if you might have a minute to talk. I'm from the *Golden Spud*."

I wondered if she'd ever heard of a computer. Besides the cluttered desk and the chair she occupied, the only furniture in the room was a row of filing cabinets under the small east-facing window.

The grey-haired lady, who appeared to be in her mid-fifties, raised her head and straightened her red-rimmed glasses.

Behind the glasses, she squinted in a state of confusion, and her cheeks flushed in what I interpreted as embarrassment. Those physical signs of emotion soon gave way to an undeniable glare of annoyance.

The journalism class I'd attended was paying off. I mentally patted myself on the back for picking up on the array of facial clues Dr. Hogg exhibited, which expressed her transition from a vulnerable, sleep-deprived individual to a haughty one. *Good work, Fran.*

"I'm sorry, what? Who did you say you were?" Dr. Christine Hogg rose from her seat and positioned herself beside the cluttered desk. She was wearing a dark grey business suit that would have made Barbara Walters jealous. *How much would a suit like that cost?* Dr. Hogg tugged at the hem of her bunched-up jacket, then wiped at her pant legs as though they were full of crumbs. Seemingly assured that she appeared to be a seasoned professional, she stood tall and crossed her arms.

Terry stepped into the office and offered his hand in greeting. "I'm Terry James, and this is Fran Fitzpatrick. We're working on an article about Victor Cargo for the university's paper, the *Golden Spud.*"

Dr. Hogg's arms remained crossed. "I'm familiar with the name of the school's paper. I *am* the financial administrator for the university, after all. It's my job to know these things. The *Golden Spud*'s yearly budget is under my tutelage."

Terry raised his palms in surrender. "Of course. My apologies. We were hoping you might have time to help us out with our article. Perhaps answer a few questions?"

Dr. Hogg waved at her desk. "Do I look like I have lots of time on my hands? I have mountains of paperwork to do."

While I wouldn't call her piles of papers "mountains," she

wasn't far off. I was devilishly tempted to ask her if she'd have more time to help students if she spent less time sleeping on her desk, but I chose to remain professional and polite.

"Again, Dr. Hogg, my apologies. I'm sure you are indeed a very busy person, but if you could see your way to sparing us just a few moments of your time, I'd genuinely appreciate it." She had been staring him down, and with a gently cocked head, Terry gave the older woman a smile I hadn't seen him use before. Talk about devilish—he was attempting to be devilishly charming to get what he wanted. I doubted it would work.

Dr. Hogg blinked rapidly and broke eye contact when she lowered her head. Using both hands, she straightened her hair, then backed up toward her chair, banging her hip on the corner of the desk. "Ouch. Um. Sure. I'm sure I can spare a few minutes." She re-established eye contact with Terry, then motioned at the two guest chairs. "Please have a seat." Our hostess glanced at me. "You can sit too."

I struggled to suppress my shock that Terry's charm had worked, and my amusement at how well it had worked. I sat. Terry sat.

Dr. Hogg tugged on her jacket again, then eased herself into her desk chair, smiling at Terry. "How can I be of help with your article? I am, of course, aware of the sad circumstances of Mr. Cargo's passing, but I'm not sure how I could possibly assist you. I don't believe I'd had the chance to make Mr. Cargo's acquaintance prior to his passing."

Dr. Hogg sounded as if she might have been a fan of Jane Austen movies. Was that a hint of a British accent that suddenly appeared? I wouldn't have described it as a good accent, more of a B-movie attempt. Dr. Hogg struck me as an interesting character. One of multiple contrasts. She was dressed pristinely, but her desk was a mess. Her attempt to speak in a sophisticated manner contrasted with her weathered-looking hands. If someone had told me she was from New York City, I'd wonder if she was a socialite from Manhattan or a tough woman from the Bronx.

As I pondered her perplexing presentation, Terry stuck to the purpose of our visit. "One of my colleagues and I happened upon an email you sent to Victor in which you suggested he might want to change his course of action for fear he would cause a financial strain on the university. We're wondering if you could share with us what course of action you were referring to."

Dr. Hogg's eyes darted to the window, then back to Terry before she breathed in a lungful of air. "You have access to Mr. Cargo's emails? Are they not private? How did you obtain access?"

My heart took an extra beat or two. How was Terry going to answer without revealing that he and Andy had hacked into Victor's email? I glanced at him; he was wearing his perfect poker face.

"You sent the email in question to Victor's *Golden Spud* account. I'm the editor of the paper, and as such, I oversee not only story assignments, but also email accounts."

I was impressed. Without lying, he'd implied no wrongdoing on his part. Would she fall for it?

Dr. Hogg's eyes widened. "I see." She inhaled again. "I don't recall the email of which you are speaking, so I'm afraid I can't help you. I'm sure it was something minor."

Terry had her on the hook. "The email suggested that if

Victor didn't heed your advice, his career would suffer for it. That doesn't sound minor."

Dr. Hogg popped up from her chair, fiercely annoyed. "I don't know what you're trying to say, young man, but as I've already stated, I do not recall the email. I send hundreds of emails every day, and I cannot be expected to remember the contents of each and every one of them."

Hundreds of emails a day seemed an exaggerated claim, even for the most addicted computer geek, but coming from someone who didn't even have a computer in her office, it was a huge stretch. I had to ask, "Do you have a computer, Dr. Hogg?"

She glared at me as though I had three heads, all lacking brain tissue. "Of course I have a computer." She opened her top desk drawer and pulled out a well-worn tablet of advanced age, then held it in the air with her right hand. "See? Any more questions? I have work to do." She threw the tablet back into its metal coffin, then slammed the drawer.

Terry stood and motioned for me to do the same. "No questions, Dr. Hogg. I do appreciate your time, and we're sorry to have disturbed you."

Without moving or speaking, she maintained her stone-faced frown. Terry placed his hand on my shoulder and we exited the office.

We were halfway down the hallway when I felt giggles ready to be expelled from my chest to my vocal cords. Terry noticed and put his index finger to his lips. We rushed out of the building, then collapsed in a fit of laughter. We hadn't learned anything about what Victor had been up to, or what Dr. Hogg's email had referred too, but something about the encounter struck us as hilarious. We slowly regained our composure, and the ability to speak without breaking down into another fit of giggles.

I threw my hands in the air. "That was a bust. She didn't tell us anything, and I doubt she'll be willing to talk to us again."

Terry picked up the pace toward the parking lot. "Don't be so sure, my junior associate. Dr. Christine Hogg is hiding something. I can't imagine she's the murderer, but she definitely knows more than she's telling us."

"What good is that if she won't speak to us again?"

"I haven't worked that out yet, but I will. In the meantime, I have some work to do for this week's *Golden Spud* issue, and I could use some lunch." Terry strolled a few feet north, then stopped. "What about you?"

"I could eat, but I didn't bring anything from home."

"If you have time to join me at the paper's office for a bit, you could grab a sandwich at the pub. They have one of those coin-operated machines that dispense sandwiches instead of drinks."

My stomach turned. Was it from hunger, or from the thought of eating something mass produced that then sat in a vending machine for who knows how long?

Terry must have noticed my reaction. Had my face turned green? "The sandwiches are fresh. They make them in the pub's kitchen early in the morning, then load the machine daily. The older ones are tossed. We did a story on it last year when some students had the same reaction you're having. It's amazing what university students will spend their time protesting. Dozens of kids were holding up homemade signs declaring the dangers of salmonella. It was a hoot."

I was starving, so I chose to trust Terry's investigative skills in this matter and joined him on the trip to the converted barn. We avoided talking about the case on the way, preferring to focus on more lighthearted subjects, such as a possible budding romance between Greg and Hallie.

Terry's high spirits at the thought that Hallie might have a new romantic interest were quickly dashed when we spotted Officer David Hughes standing alongside his cruiser in front of the pub that housed our lunch.

Terry slouched. "Now what?"

Chapter 28

AS WE APPROACHED David, I noticed that Terry had clenched his fists and that his stride had become more determined. He looked like a man ready for a fight, but I couldn't understand why. The last time I'd seen him and David together, they were conspiring to keep me a damsel in distress. I liked to think that these two men were fighting over me, but despite my aunt Josephine's fantasies, it was doubtful. Neither had displayed any romantic interest in me—not that I'd noticed, anyway.

Andy had mentioned last night at the *Golden Spud* meeting that Terry and "that cop," as Andy had put it, had been talking after I left them alone on my aunt and uncle's driveway. With all the excitement of Andy's erratic behaviour, then today's interviews, I'd completely forgotten to ask Terry what they were talking about. From Andy's comments it sounded innocent enough, but Terry's current stance suggested they'd had an altercation of some sort.

Whatever it was they had butted heads over and were now going to discuss, I hoped they would deal with it swiftly. My stomach was demanding nourishment, and I couldn't miss another class.

On second thought, did I even need to be here for their conversation? I thought not. As we reached David, Terry stopped by the cruiser, but I waved and carried on to the entrance. "Nice to see you again, *Officer*. I'm heading in for lunch." I opened the door and, hoping I had cash on me, headed inside in search of the vending machine that held the suspect sandwiches.

I expected to hear the door close behind me, but what I heard instead was David's voice. "Hold on, Franny, I have a few questions for both of you."

I stopped, rolled my eyes at the mention of the name he knew I hated, then whirled around, hands on my hips. "Yes?" Was he antagonizing me on purpose? Did he get some kind of weird pleasure out of annoying me?

I stood my ground as I watched these two men, neither of whom I'd known for long, yet who had been demanding so much of my time the past few days, make their way down the hall.

The wall to their right was lined with bulletin boards littered with thickly stacked colourful advertisements, both old and new, pinned up haphazardly, making the subject of each item indiscernible. The chaotic nature of it made me desire to scream. Why were there so many ads? Why were there so many choices? Why were there so many suspects in our investigation? And why were Terry and David constantly on my mind?

David was in the lead, his brilliant blue eyes accentuated by his smart, dark uniform. Sure, he was handsome, but he was also obnoxious and infuriating. I couldn't quite pinpoint why I found him so annoying, but that didn't matter—he simply was.

Terry brought up the rear, his hands in his pockets, his head tilted back, and his lips fluttering as he blew air toward the ceiling. The man who moments ago had been laughing and focusing on work looked defeated.

Terry didn't have David's movie star looks, but he was still a handsome guy, and much easier to get along with. From what I'd seen, he was loyal to his friends, honest, and an amazing driver.

Officer Mather implied—no, she asserted—that David wasn't much of a driver. I glared at him. *Take that, David. Terry could outdrive you just like that!* I tried to snap my fingers, a skill I'd never possessed and still didn't.

David stopped in front of me and squinted, then smirked. "Something on your mind?"

I turned around and continued down the hall toward the pub. "No. I'm just hungry. I'm going to grab a sandwich. Is that okay with you, David?"

"Not a problem. I could go for a sandwich myself, and we can have a chat in there. I don't imagine the pub's very busy this time of the day."

We made our way past the university bookstore, student union office, and the *Golden Spud* offices before reaching the pub at the end of the long hallway. David and I headed for the vending machines, but Terry went into the men's room.

I fished into my bag for cash. Nothing. I threw up my hands in defeat and headed for one of the tables.

David reached into his pocket and pulled out a handful of gold-coloured coins. "My treat. I cleaned the loonies out of my piggybank this morning. Not really a piggybank, of course—just an empty marmalade jar used for holding change until laundry day."

Marmalade? Ick. My impression of him wasn't improving, but I'd happily let him buy lunch.

"What would you like?" He perused the options. "It looks like they have egg salad, tuna salad, or chicken salad. Pick your poison."

"I'm not sure that's the best choice of words, but keeping food poisoning in mind, I'll take the egg salad, thanks."

David purchased three sandwiches and three cups of coffee from the hot beverage vending machine, then joined me at the table.

Hoping Terry would be a few more minutes, I decided to interrogate the policeman. "Why is Terry so mad at you? Did you say something to upset him?"

David popped open the plastic container that held his tuna salad. "I don't know why he's cranky, and no, I didn't say anything to upset him the other night."

That wasn't the helpful response I'd been hoping for. "If you didn't say anything after I left the two of you, then why is he mad at you?"

David shrugged. "I don't know if you've noticed, but your friend Mr. James has been mad at me since he was arrested and taken to the station. Does that surprise you? He was handcuffed, driven to the station in a police cruiser, put in a cell for a few hours, and accused of murdering a friend. It shouldn't surprise you that he's upset at the officer in charge of the investigation."

"That doesn't bother you?" I took a bite of the egg salad, winced, and quickly washed it down with coffee. The coffee was no better in quality than the sandwich was. In fact, they didn't taste much different from one another. I questioned Terry's claim that the food was prepared on site, but if this was accurate, I wouldn't be eating at the pub anytime soon.

"Nope. It comes with the territory. It's not my job to make people like me. It's my job to get to the truth. I suspect it's not unlike being a journalist. Do you want to write articles so that people will like you? Or do you want to write articles that tell the unbiased truth—that offer both sides of a story without prejudice?"

He made a good point. Traditionally, journalists were part of a respected profession and known for their unbiased storytelling and their fearless search for the truth no matter the repercussions. They weren't supposed to pander to those who held one viewpoint, even if it was the most popular one. I thought about some of the news stories I'd seen online and on TV recently, and wondered if the members of my chosen profession still followed that simple guideline of unbiased reporting.

"I want to write the unbiased truth."

"Even if what you're reporting is in direct conflict with your beliefs?"

"Yes. Of course."

"It's not so easy. When I'm making an arrest, I can't let my personal feelings direct my actions. I must follow the law, and the evidence. Whether or not I think Terry James is guilty doesn't impact how I do my job. Far too many examples throughout history demonstrate the reasons for that. When police officers allow their feelings about a case or a suspect to direct the investigation, innocent people can go to prison and guilty people go free. Neither is an acceptable outcome."

I knew what he was saying was true. I'd recently watched a true crime documentary about the multitudes of innocent people who had been convicted of crimes over the past century because the investigation focused on one suspect, which excluded finding the real culprit. And each time an innocent person was sent to jail, a guilty person got away with a crime.

I thought back to the horse wearing blinders at the vet college; the headgear forced the animal to focus in one direction. Is this what some journalists were doing, or some police officers? Focusing on one suspect or one possible scenario, while blocking out anything that might upset a preferred outcome, making it predetermined?

"Are you sure you're not focusing too much on Terry and giving Victor's real murderer a chance to get away?"

"I'm very sure I'm not doing that. That's one reason I'm here to talk to the two of you."

My eyebrows rose to the middle of my forehead. "Oh."

Laurie Lamont's reaction to Scott's comments earlier today came to mind. She had been so defensive when someone was politely asking her to explain her beliefs. Was she also wearing blinders? Was she so focused on what she thought she believed, what she wanted to believe, that she was uncomfortable at the thought of another valid argument? Another theory to explain our origins?

Chair legs scraping across the floor brought my mind back to my companions. Terry had rejoined us, and David rose to greet him, hand outstretched.

"Mr. James, please join us. I don't know if you've eaten,

but I went ahead and purchased one of the establishment's finest egg salad sandwiches and a coffee. I thought you might prefer chicken salad, but Ms. Fitzpatrick felt that was too risky an option." David smiled. I appreciated his attempt to lighten the mood, but the expression of misery on Terry's face told me it wasn't working.

"Thanks." Terry sat.

David sat. "As I was explaining to Ms. Fitzpatrick . . ."

"Oh please, can we stop with the *Ms.* this and *Mr.* that? It feels so formal and unnerving. If you're here to chat, call us Fran and Terry. If you want to formally interrogate us, call us Ms. and Mr., but shouldn't we do that in a darkened room with a two-way mirror?"

David flashed a smile my way. "My apologies . . . Fran. You're right—we can drop the formalities." He looked at Terry. "As I was explaining to Fran before you joined us, I'm not out to prove you're guilty. My goal is to find the person who murdered Victor Cargo, and to do it before they flee. One advantage is that we're on an island and it's not tourist season, so for the past few days, we've been able to track anyone leaving PEI via the Confederation Bridge or the airport."

"That sounds like an invasion of privacy. How can you do that? Especially on the bridge?" Terry sounded like a social justice warrior.

"Calm down. We aren't frisking people. Perhaps 'tracking' is too strong a word. We have message boards at the airport reminding people that they'll need identification to board a plane, and alongside those message boards is a subtle message that we're looking for information related to a current murder investigation. Our hopes are that the guilty party trying to flee by air will be reminded that we have a record of their presence on the Island."

Terry cracked open his sandwich, put half of one half into his mouth, chewed twice, and swallowed. "I can't imagine that someone willing to kill another human being would care about a couple of signs at the airport."

I couldn't believe he hadn't choked on the wad of food he'd forced down his throat. I'd barely made a dent in my own lunch and was happy to keep it that way. Eating could wait until I got home to a tasty, healthy, and less-likely-to-kill-me meal.

David scanned the room. Was he worried we'd be overheard? "You're probably right, but we have to give the public and the media the impression we're doing something." Was he kidding? Being sarcastic? I had no idea.

I decided to push him for more details. "What about the bridge? Travellers don't have to show identification to cross it."

"No, but all vehicles have licence plates." He threw me a smug smile.

"Buses full of passengers?"

"Passenger lists." Another smug smile. The man was beyond irritating.

Terry flew to his feet, knocking over his chair. He ran one hand through his hair, then threw both hands into the air. "Why are we here? I'm sure you didn't want to talk to us about tracking people leaving the Island. Are you worried I'm going to leave? You needn't be. I can't afford to leave, financially or scholastically. I have classes. I have responsibilities. And most of all, I need to prove to you and your buddies in uniform that I'm innocent. So what is it?"

I peeked at the time on my phone. "Yeah, David. What is

it? I need to get going." I chose to ignore Terry's outburst. I couldn't blame him for being frustrated.

Terry righted his chair and returned to the table. "Sorry, man."

David lifted a shoulder in a shrug. "Don't worry about it. You're right—I should get to the point." He scanned the room again, then leaned in and talked in a hushed voice. "Before I met you at the entrance, we received a call at the station. I'd been on campus interviewing some of Victor's classmates when the call came in. Seems we had a complaint that our prime suspect was harassing UPEI's financial administrator . . . What's her name?" He flipped through his notepad. "Dr. Christine Hogg."

Terry and I spoke at the same time. "That was fast."

I let Terry continue. "I'm surprised she called you and drew attention to herself. That woman is hiding something."

I shot a look at David, expecting him to tell Terry that Dr. Hogg was a respected member of the community and not a suspect. I was surprised by his response.

"I agree, Terry. Dr. Hogg is definitely hiding something. I got that impression after meeting with her yesterday, but her unusual response to your visit has cemented my concerns. Do you have any idea what she might be keeping from us?"

David used the word "us," not "me." Was he referring to his fellow officers or to Terry and me? If it was the latter, maybe he was starting to see us as a valuable part of the investigation.

Terry shook his head, then met my gaze. Didn't he know yet that I was terrible at deciphering facial clues? I suspected he didn't want me to tell David about the email from Dr. Hogg he'd found in Victor's account, but why?

David, being a professional investigator, noticed the look

and read Terry's meaning. "I can't reveal our list of suspects." That was good—they had a list, so they hadn't mentally convicted Terry yet. "But after you were pursued by the person in the red car a couple of nights ago, I have reason to believe that you might both be in danger. The faster we can get to the truth of things, the safer you'll be."

It sounded as if David was prompting Terry and me to reveal what he *knew* we knew but weren't telling him. Terry kept quiet. I didn't.

"Does that mean you believe Terry's innocent? Good. It's about time."

"I didn't say that. I said that I felt you two might be in danger, and that we have a list of suspects."

I was lost, but Terry appeared relaxed, so I took that as a good sign.

"I'd appreciate knowing why you were at Dr. Hogg's office, and what you said to her to make her so uneasy."

Terry and I glanced at each other again. I noticed the clock on the wall behind him. It was almost twelve fifteen and I still had to locate my one o'clock class. Sociology 101 was taught on the east side of the campus in Dalton Hall, another building on the university grounds I hadn't yet visited. The acreage of the campus seemed to grow exponentially every time I had to find a new class in a new location, and was inversely proportional to how much time I had to locate it.

"I need to get going. I've skipped one too many classes already this week. Thankfully, I didn't have any classes this morning, so I could meet with Laurie Lamont." As soon as the words were out of my mouth, I wished that a hole would open below my chair and swallow me. I sheepishly peered at Terry. He frowned at me, then lifted his palms to the air. I interpreted that to mean that I might as well tell David what Laurie and I had spoken about.

When I glanced at David, he had already retrieved his notepad and pen. "Go on."

"If Laurie Lamont isn't on your suspect list, she probably should be."

I felt a lightness in my chest as my pulse sped up. I was about to share my investigative findings with a detective, and he was taking me seriously. In less than a week, I'd officially started my university career, become a junior reporter for the school paper, and was now part of a team investigating a real-life murder. Real-life murder? There was something wrong with that phrase, but I'd have to work it out later.

I shared the conflict at Ellesmere Island, including the news that Victor had been found sneaking out of Dr. Daniels's tent.

David made a note of my comment about Dr. Daniels, then pushed the end of his pen into his chin. "Hmm. I spoke with him this morning. He claimed that nothing out of the ordinary happened during the summer expedition."

My adrenalin was pumping. I had more information about what Victor had been up to this summer than the great Officer Hughes! I slammed my fist on the table in triumph. "Ha!"

Both men flinched, then frowned at me. Perhaps I was getting overly excited. I toned it down. "Sorry. According to Laurie, there was a lot of friction between various members of the team, but especially between Dr. Daniels and Victor."

David made some more notes, then sipped his coffee. "And this has led you to believe that Laurie Lamont should be a suspect?"

I wasn't sure if he was being sarcastic or genuine, so I chose to believe the latter. "Not directly, but why would Laurie be so willing to talk to me, a reporter . . . and trust me? She has zero respect for me—more because I'm an arts major, not because I'm a reporter, but I'm sure the two things together—"

"Fran?" Terry was tapping his watch. "I thought you were in a rush?"

"Right! Sorry. Laurie had no reason to talk to me but seemed eager to tell me all about Dr. Daniels. She didn't care for him, and I wonder if she was trying to cause trouble for him for some reason."

"What reason?" David sipped his coffee again.

"I don't know—that's why I said 'some reason.'"

"Okay, then." David flipped his notebook closed and tucked it into his pocket. "I think that's all for now. I appreciate you two taking the time to talk with me. I caution you again to be careful. Leave the police work up to the police."

Terry rose and offered his hand to David. "Not a problem. We'll stick to journalistic investigation and leave the criminal investigation in your capable hands."

David rose, shook Terry's hand, and pushed in his chair. He locked eyes with Terry. "You need to be careful for your safety if the real murderer gets bothered by your snooping. And you're still a suspect, so you don't want to bring further suspicion on yourself if it looks like you're tampering with evidence."

Terry nodded. "I'll be careful. Thanks."

David disappeared down the hallway as quickly as he had appeared at the entrance earlier.

I slapped Terry on the shoulder. "That's great."

He gave me the side-eye. "What's great?"

"He told you to be careful because the real murderer might be after you?"

"Being stalked by a murderer is great?"

"Well, no, but having the lead investigator telling you that there's a"—I made air quotes—"*real murderer* means that even if he can't say it directly, he doesn't believe it's you."

Terry paused and rubbed his chin. "You're right." He smiled and let out the biggest sigh of relief I'd ever seen escape a human. "And did you notice what he didn't say anything more about?"

"No. What?"

"The email Christine Hogg sent to Victor warning him to back off."

"Makes sense, I guess. Wouldn't the police need a warrant to access Victor's emails? And I'm sure Dr. Hogg isn't going to show it to them."

I headed toward the pub's exit, expecting Terry to follow me to the newspaper office, but he turned toward the staircase in the northeast corner of the building.

"Where are you going? I thought you had work to do on the newspaper."

"I do, but I want to talk to Greg first. He's got a show on the radio this time of day. Haven't you heard it?"

"Greg's on the radio?"

"Of course. He has a show every afternoon over the lunch hour. He comments on any recent sports events. You know— scores and VIPs and all that."

"That explains why I haven't heard it. I don't know if you've noticed, but I'm not very athletic."

"Come up and I'll give you a quick tour. It won't take long. Maybe you'll have a show of your own someday."

I followed Terry to the upper level of the Barn. At the top, a large open room housed a few tables and chairs scattered along the walls, as well as small shelves at waist level. "What is this?"

"Dance floor. Party place. Hangout. It's pretty lively every Friday and Saturday night." Terry pointed to the far corner. We're headed over there. The radio station isn't very big these days since there's no need for storage of vinyl records. It's all digital now."

As I followed Terry, movement outside the window on the west wall caught my eye. I drew closer to the dirty glass and wiped it with my sleeve to get a better look. My heart stopped, and I gasped before crouching down out of sight.

Terry rushed over but stopped abruptly when I shot my hand up, indicating he should freeze. I signalled for him to crouch down, then make his way to the window. When he was close enough to hear my whisper, I pointed at the dirty glass. "The car that chased us the other night—it's out there in the parking lot."

"Are you sure it's the same car?"

"There's damage to the front end, it's the same colour, and there's an *E* in the plate, so yes, I'm sure."

"Is there anyone in it?"

"Yup. In the driver's seat."

"Could you see who it was?"

I shook my head. "Whoever it is, they were holding up binoculars. Who sits in a car and watches a building with binoculars?"

"Someone who wants to see who's meeting with the police? And now they know we were."

We sat quietly, pondering our next step. David had told us to be careful—that message was now loud and clear.

Chapter 29

"I HAVE TO GET going, Terry. I can't miss another class." I could hear the unsteady urgency in my voice; I needed to leave, but that meant going outside, possibly into the path of a murderer.

Before standing, Terry and I crawled away from the window to the corner that housed the campus radio station. Beyond the window in the door, I could see Greg, one hand on the microphone, talking to his audience. His other arm was animated with gestures, as though he was telling a story about a basketball player making a shot, and then he laughed. I could only guess that it was a funny story. I made a mental note to listen to Greg's show in the future, if we got out of the Barn alive.

"I have an idea." Terry waved at Greg. I joined in with frantic arm waving of my own.

Our radio host friend spotted us after a few seconds; he nodded and raised his index finger to ask us to give him a moment. After he pressed a button on the control panel, the red On Air light above the door dimmed to off, and Greg motioned for us to enter. He rose from his seat and removed his headphones. "Hey, you two look like—"

Terry brushed past Greg to the window opposite the DJ booth, then pressed his back to the wall and peeked outside over his shoulder. He looked back at Greg and me. "They're still out there."

I felt the urge to run to the ladies' room but didn't want to leave the company of these two men. I'd just have to breathe through the nausea and hope that the egg salad sandwich would stay put. Who was in that car? Were they following us?

Greg approached the window to look out, but Terry stretched out his arm, blocking the way. Greg took a step back.

"What's going on? You two look like you've seen a ghost, and it's not even October yet." He laughed at his joke, but when he noticed that Terry and I weren't joining in, his jovial wit disappeared and he became concerned for his friends. "Okay, guys, now you're freaking me out. What's going on?"

Terry peeked out the window again. "Walk past the window naturally, Greg, like you're on your way somewhere. Tell me if you see a red car. Don't stop and look out—we don't want the driver to know that we know they're out there."

Greg cocked his head. "O-kay."

If I didn't know what was going on, I'd agree with Greg that Terry sounded like a paranoid crazy person. At that moment, I wished we were only caught up in some strange, twisted fantasy of Terry's, but we weren't. This was reality, and there was a stalker out there—someone who'd already tried to kill us, and who'd possibly killed Victor only a few days ago.

Greg retrieved a small stack of papers from the desk, then flipped through them as he passed the window. He diverted his eyes for only a second, then returned his attention to the papers. "There's a red car in the parking lot." When he was at the far side of the window, he turned around and stared at Terry. "*Now* will you tell me what's going on? Do you need me to take care of that guy for you?"

"You could tell it was a guy? Do you know who he is?" Terry raked his hand through his hair.

"No. Don't know who it is. Can't say I've ever seen him before, but he was wearing a baseball cap and sunglasses. The car doesn't look familiar either."

I was impressed by the details Greg had picked up in a quick pass-by of the window. "How did you see all of that so quickly?"

He shrugged. "When I'm reporting on a game, I need to spot details, like player numbers on jerseys, while at the same time looking at the big picture. You know, like where each player is on the field or rink, and what they're all doing. Where's the puck? Who's open for a pass? What are the other team members doing? Where's the referee? Spotting one dude in a stationary car is no big deal." Greg shrugged again, then returned to his desk. "Easy stuff. Give me a minute—I'll put another commercial on." He tapped on a few keys, then gave Terry a questioning glance.

Terry filled Greg in on the car chase and the conversation we'd had with David over lunch.

Greg rubbed the nape of his neck and leaned back in

the chair. "That's wild, man. A real-life high-speed chase. Now what?"

"I think you can help us with this, Greg. Can you make some kind of announcement, like a random prize for a car parked in the Barn parking lot? Tell your listeners you're going to look out the window, and that any car parked out there wins tickets to some event." Terry sounded desperate.

"What event?" Greg pushed some more buttons. "I'm happy to play along, but I need to say something soon. I can't keep playing commercials. And what if the guy isn't listening?"

Terry raked his hand through his hair again. If we didn't get out of the Barn soon, he was going to be bald. "Doesn't matter—just make something up. It's the only car out there, so no one else is going to claim a prize."

"Sure thing." Greg pulled the microphone close to his mouth, then flicked a couple of switches. The On-Air light came on. "Hey, gang, impromptu lotto. In a few seconds, I'm going to look out the window, and if you're the first car I see parked in the lot west of the Barn, you win. I'll make note of your licence plate, and you can claim your prize by calling and telling me what it is. You're probably wondering what that prize is . . ." Greg paused. I could only imagine the gears in his head spinning as he tried to come up with a prize on the spot—one that would fool a potential murderer but not get him into trouble with the school administration if they got wind of it.

Terry peeked out the window again, then gave Greg the thumbs-up. "He's driving away. He must have fallen for it. Thanks, Greg."

Greg let out a sign of relief, then returned to the microphone. "The prize is to be announced." He banged his feet on the floor. "Here we go. Oh man, no one's parked out there. Hmm. That's too bad. Enough silliness. Let's return to a review of last night's game."

As Greg discussed whatever game that might have been, Terry and I waved goodbye and made our exit. I checked the time on my phone. I had fifteen minutes to get to class. I shoved the phone into my pocket and flung my backpack over my shoulder.

Terry placed his hand on my other shoulder. "Not so fast. I'll walk you to Dalton Hall, then call Officer Hughes to let him know that the car was out there."

It was my turn to sigh with relief. "You'll get no argument from me."

Chapter 30

WHAT DID THAT make? I bent my fingers as I processed the past four days. No, three. Squeezing my way past my fellow students to exit Dalton Hall, I realized that I had only made it to three classes this week. I could only hope that passing grades weren't dependent on attendance.

I had to do better; I couldn't justify sitting in a classroom when a friend was potentially facing years sitting in a jail cell. I still didn't know Terry that well, but of what I'd seen this past week, I couldn't imagine him in prison. The other prisoners would push him around like a cat playing with a catnip-filled toy. I shivered at the thought of an innocent man being sent away, possibly for life. If he did get out after a few years, how much of the current Terry would remain?

The mid-afternoon sun reflected off the windows of the

surrounding buildings, taking my mind to Terry's wet car seats. He was spot on when he predicted that the wet, cool temperatures would be replaced by warmth and sunshine, giving him a chance to dry out the inside of his car. Where I grew up in Toronto, leaving your windows down would have been a risky move—there was a good chance you'd find an empty spot when you returned for your vehicle. Luckily, this was PEI, so surely leaving your car windows down must be safe.

I smiled mindlessly as I passed by vaguely familiar faces. No doubt they were classmates I'd spoken to, but I'd been so distracted by murder, car chases, and an annoying officer with mesmerizing blue eyes that I couldn't remember who I knew and who I didn't. I'm sure they all had names, but what those names were, I'd have to work on learning next week. This week I had a murderer to track down.

I walked along the concrete path that ran between the veterinary college and the library before stopping to remove my hoodie. I bent over to tuck it into my backpack, and when I stood back up, I froze. The red car that had chased us was in the parking lot just beyond the edge of the vet college. More surprising than that was the identity of the occupants. My lower jaw dropped as I watched Bobby Burrell and Lena Gallant exit the vehicle and scurry toward Marion Hall.

I dropped my bag to the ground and grabbed my phone from the front pocket. I had to call David to report this. Not only were Lena and Bobby together again, but they were also in the car that had tried to run Terry and me down. I was sure it was the same car; it was cherry red with what I was sure was the same licence plate. But maybe it wasn't the same car— more than one red car could have ETW on its plate—I'd have to get closer before making that call.

I waited until Bobby and Lena were at least a hundred yards away, then crept toward their car. Conveniently, a van parked opposite afforded me a handy hiding place. I waited until my prime suspects had walked another hundred yards or so, then made my move.

This red car had a black vinyl car bra covering the front grille and bumper. I'd heard of these protective coverings, but I thought they'd gone out of style a decade ago. The car we spotted near the Barn didn't have a bra on it, but Bobby would have had plenty of time while I was in class to put this one in place. And since Lena's glasses and clothing choices could be called retro, it wasn't hard to believe she'd be in possession of such an old-fashioned vehicle accessory.

I scanned my surroundings to ensure I wasn't being watched. Students were all around me, but none of them were paying attention to the crazy lady sneaking between the parked cars. I was grateful for their apathy. Bobby and Lena were now far enough away that, should they turn around, they wouldn't be able identify me or even tell what I was doing. I leaned nonchalantly against the driver's side of the suspect vehicle's hood, then pulled on the vinyl cover. I was right! The huge dent in the middle of the bumper confirmed it was the same vehicle.

I returned to the other side of the van and retrieved my phone from my bag. I was dialing David's number when a text from Terry appeared on my screen: *Someone put a bloody backpack on the back seat of my car.*

Chapter 31

I STOOD IN SHOCKED silence, my gaze fixed on Marion Hall in the distance, the destination of the two people in possession of the vehicle that had attempted to run Terry and me off the road. After failing at that, they'd tried to run us over in front of a police station. I didn't know what was more disturbing—someone who was out to harm you claiming to be a friend, or she and her accomplice being brazen enough to act while we were talking to a uniformed officer.

I know that Terry had left his windows open to allow his car seats to dry out, but instead of stealing his car, someone had put incriminating evidence in it. This was much worse. A car could be replaced, but someone was trying to frame him for murder. Bobby and Lena had taken the time to spy on Terry and me at the Barn and found an old car bra to cover the damage to their car. Had they also taken the time to plant evidence that could ensure Terry's conviction? I thought back to the photo Hallie had taken at the crime scene: Bobby Burrell holding what appeared to be a tie-dyed backpack. Was it tie-dyed? Or bloodstained?

I replied to Terry's text. *Compare the bag to the one Bobby is holding in Hallie's photo. If it looks like the same bag, I think you should take it to the police station and turn it in. Don't touch it if you haven't already.*

Terry replied, *Good idea. I'll keep you posted.*

I had another idea, but whether it was a good one or not was questionable. I headed for Marion Hall to confront the two people I was convinced were trying to set up my friend. Their behaviour had me fuming; that they might also be murderers wasn't foremost in my mind. I swiftly crossed the parking lot, then stopped to put my hoodie back on should I need to hide my identity.

My backpack! It was still sitting by the van. I turned to retrieve it, happy that my fellow students were still engrossed in their own business. Feeling rushed, I flung it hard over my shoulder, winced at the pain of the laptop hitting my spine, then resumed my march to defend Terry.

I didn't get very far before I heard shouting. It sounded as though Dr. Hogg was trying to whisper loudly, but she was failing miserably. When I turned back toward the main campus, several of the previously apathetic students were staring at the university administrator, who was flailing her arms like a madwoman. If her behaviour were to lead to her dismissal, she would be guaranteed a job at the airport guiding airplanes to their assigned gates.

The object of Dr. Hogg's rage was blocked from my view

by the library. When my internal pleading for that object to show itself didn't work, I ducked behind the van so I could observe the spectacle unseen. My new location afforded me a clearer view, but despite her volume, I couldn't make sense of what she was saying.

A small alcove in the library wall that housed a statue of who I assumed was Samuel Robertson was only a few yards away, and to the side of the statue was just enough space for a person of my size to squeeze into. I did the only logical thing; as soon as Dr. Hogg shifted her gaze away from where I hid, I ran as fast as I could and became buddy-buddy with the copper version of the library's namesake.

The statue was on my left, and to my right, as luck would have it, was a window into the building. More importantly, a window on the opposite side of the interior now gave me a clear view of the object of Dr. Hogg's wrath. I had my suspicions as to who it was, but I pulled out my phone and opened the faculty page on the university's website to confirm it.

It was him—Dr. Daniels. The man who had led the expedition to Ellesmere Island. The man who, according to Laurie Lamont, had had a huge argument with Victor Cargo after finding Victor sneaking out of his tent.

David had said that Dr. Hogg was crazy mad after Terry and I visited her office, and he'd asked us why she was so upset. She'd been fine until we mentioned the threatening email she sent to Victor. Was this meltdown related to that? Or was she simply a woman prone to episodes of rage?

I had to get closer to them while remaining hidden. My options were limited. A second statue—this one of a young man and woman sporting graduation caps—wouldn't provide sufficient cover. The parking lot was emptying, diminishing the number of vehicles I could shield myself with. And what would I do if the owner of a car drove away while I was hunched down beside it? That would be too risky, and embarrassing.

I settled on the row of bushes almost exactly midway between me and the two professors. I had to get there without being seen, so I'd need a distraction.

I wasn't convinced there was a God, but when the church bells in town starting ringing, I came closer to being a believer. Dr. Hogg scrunched up her face and threw her hands in the air. I suspected that even she couldn't hear her own screams over the heavenly sounds. She whirled around and marched toward the parking lot.

This was my chance. I ran for the bushes, only to find myself sliding across the wet grass and crashing into my destination. Apparently, the sprinklers had been running. I examined my scratched-up arms and grass-stained jeans—minimal damage in exchange for a prime spying location.

I assumed a kneeling position just as Dr. Daniels was tapping Dr. Hogg on the shoulder. I ducked back down when he turned his head in my direction.

"Keep it down, Christine. You have half the campus watching us."

"I don't care. I'm tired of this. When I helped you get the job here, you promised there wouldn't be any repeats of what happened in Hamilton. And now I have students hounding me."

I dared to sneak a peek. With his black fedora and black trench coat, Dr. Daniels looked the part of a Chicago mobster from Al Capone's era. He stood without wavering, hands in his pockets, as Dr. Hogg poked her index finger into his chest, her face very close to his. "You need to fix this."

He grabbed her finger and pushed it away. "We've nothing to worry about. No one's going to listen to a bunch of glassy-eyed students who can barely tie their own shoes."

Was he talking about me and Terry? Victor? I fought the urge to stand up and inform him that I was quite capable of tying my own shoes. More importantly, I was quite capable of finding out what he was hiding. Well, I hoped I was, because if it had anything to do with Victor's death, Terry's freedom depended on it.

The heated conversation ended abruptly and the two players stormed away in opposite directions. As I watched Dr. Hogg head south, my eyes were drawn to Marion Hall and I was reminded of the mission I'd been on before she caused all the excitement.

I reached the public entrance to the coed dorm, winded but still determined to confront the objects of my wrath. The commotion outside the library gave me more to think about, but it didn't take away my anger at Lena and Bobby for trying to run Terry and me down. Dr. Hogg wasn't the only woman on this campus powered by rage today.

The outer door to the lobby was my first target. With more strength than I thought I had, I flung it open, then hoped the glass wouldn't shatter. The hinge did its job and kept the door from hitting the outer wall. Perfect, but I'd forgotten that the inner door would be locked. *Now what?* Buzz the apartment and ask them to open the door so I could go up there to yell at them? I took a deep a breath. *You're being foolish, Fran. Leave it up to the police. Call David and tell him what you know.*

I opened my list of contacts and found David's name, but

before I hit the dial button, a student came through the locked door. I aborted the call, grabbed the door by its frame before it could close, and headed into the lobby. I knew Bobby's room number from my previous failed attempt to talk to him.

I sighed at the weight of my bag and the thought of climbing stairs after my race from the library. Why didn't any of these buildings have elevators? Across from me was a door labelled Janitor's Closet. I turned the handle and let out a little squeal of triumph—it wasn't locked. I tucked my book-heavy bag behind some cleaning supplies, intent on retrieving it after confronting Lena and Bobby.

The stench of the second-floor hallway—a nauseating cocktail of stale beer mixed with sweat and mould—was in stark contrast to the air of the other buildings on campus. Stains on the carpet were a testament to the hundreds of parties enjoyed by the occupants over the decades. It had probably been clean and odour-free two weeks ago, before the late-summer arrival of students and the frosh week events.

I was momentarily distracted by the many contrasts I had encountered on the UPEI campus this week. While the two professors I'd just observed could be described as unprofessional and cranky, the rest of the school employees, profs included, had been warm, friendly, and very professional.

Dr. Watson stood out as a man who truly cared about his students, his area of study, and his colleagues. Maggie Smith, the librarian, had made me feel important and cared about during our first meeting, and was someone I looked forward to interacting with regularly. Even the food had its good and bad aspects—the scary lunch I'd gagged on at the pub was nothing like the superb food I'd eaten last week at the university's cafeteria.

My observations of contrasts might make an interesting editorial someday, but I needed to refocus on my task. I quietly hurried to room 201 at the end of the hall, then knocked on the rusty-orange door to Victor's last home. I could hear movement on the other side, but as the minutes passed, I became impatient and knocked again—louder this time.

"Give me a minute, will ya?" a high-pitched, squeaky voice shouted through the door. The person sounded unhappy to be disturbed. "What do you want?"

"Hi. I'm here to talk to Bobby Burrell. I'm from the *Golden Spud*." *Think, Fran, what excuse can you use for being here?* If Lena was there, she'd know who I was. But I'd already come this far, so I pressed on.

When the door was flung open, I was surprised by the man before me. My previous sightings of Bobby were from a distance, and over the intercom his squeaky voice had suggested physical weakness. He was taller than he'd appeared earlier, his stature that of a man who'd have no problem beating Victor to death. I gulped as my heart started to pound against my chest wall. What was I doing here?

Bobby's brow furrowed. "What is it you want?"

I needed Bobby to trust me. "I'd like to offer my condolences for the loss of your roommate. Maybe talk to you about him?"

"Condolences? For what? We shared a room. No biggie."

Wow. This guy was cold. Even if he and Victor weren't friends, I expected that he'd be somewhat sad. It seemed the decent, human thing to do. His attitude increased my suspicions of him.

"Of course—I understand. I'm sorry to disturb you, but I'm writing an article on the murder and wondered if you might have any insight into what happened." I stretched out my hand.

Without shaking, Bobby stepped aside and indicated with a nod that I should enter. A scan of the room told me Lena was no longer here.

"I don't know what you want from me." Bobby threw the book he'd been holding on to one of the beds. "I already talked to the police. Victor and I shared this unit—that's it. We didn't hang out or chat. No buddy-buddy roommate stuff."

Why the hostility if they were merely roommates who'd crossed paths only occasionally?

"Was Victor easy to live with?"

He grunted. "Anything but. Guy was a narcissist."

The dorm room included a bathroom and a small kitchenette, both clearly visible from the hall door. The main area was a combination bedroom and workspace. Twin beds were pushed up against opposing walls and separated by twin desks, in turn separated by a dresser with two rows of drawers. Above each desk was a window with curtains from an era long gone.

Whoever designed this room had a thing for symmetry; however, as reflected in their differing levels of tidiness, the occupants' personalities were hardly the mirror image of each another. One side of the room had a neatly made bed accompanied by a tidy desk. On the other side the bedding was bunched in the middle and the top of the mattress exposed, while the desk was cluttered with books and scattered loose-leaf papers.

Bobby sat down at the tidy desk, then waved his hand at the messy one. "And a slob." He rolled his eyes.

I decided to try the understanding, good cop approach. I concentrated on the messy half of the room for a few seconds, rubbed my chin while gently shaking my head, then offered a sympathetic face to Bobby. "Must be tough living in someone else's mess like this. I feel for you."

He eyed me suspiciously. He wasn't falling for it. "What is it you want? Wanna rifle through his stuff? Go ahead."

Bobby wasn't wrong about Victor being a slob, so I was uncertain as to whether I wanted to rifle through his stuff—you never knew what undesirable things you might find among the belongings of an untidy college student. However, I did have an open invitation to investigate anything I wanted to on Victor's side of the room. Keeping an eye on my prime suspect, I started with the victim's desk. As I opened the top drawer, I looked over at Bobby. He was watching me with disinterest.

"Are you sure this is okay?"

He shrugged. "Cops already looked through all his stuff. They didn't find anything."

I didn't find anything either. There was no computer, no notes from his summertime expedition, no notes in his textbooks. The desk was a bust, and the bed was no help either.

Hoping to find a locked box of valuables under the bed, I got down on my knees and investigated, but all I found was a family of dust bunnies. Of course, the police would have looked under here and removed anything of value.

Next, I focused on the dresser drawer, but unless Victor's preferred brand of underwear was a clue, I struck out again. In the closet to the side of the door were several pairs of pants. I checked the pockets. Nothing. I don't know what I was expecting to find, but I was disappointed at not finding anything.

I wondered about the kitchen and bathroom. Victor may have hidden notes in one of those areas—or hidden a flash drive in the freezer perhaps.

I turned to my host to ask if he'd be open to my checking out the kitchen, but he beat me to it. "Yes, you're welcome to check in there too. Neither of us kept much food. Snacks mostly." He waved toward the small fridge. "Knock yourself out. I gotta go."

I thought—I hoped—he was leaving me alone in the dorm room, but he only disappeared into the bathroom. *Oh, that kind of "go."* While Bobby was behind a closed door, I snooped on his side of the room, but I was again disappointed in the lack of evidence.

I returned my attention to Victor's desk. A recent memory was tickling my brain: the hope chest Uncle Johnny had dragged into my room. I turned away from the desk and looked at Victor's bed. I'd been sitting on my bed the other night staring at the cedar chest.

I lifted Victor's mattress and quickly regretted it. Nothing there could be considered evidence, unless the multitude of dirty socks and what might have been a baloney sandwich long ago held clues. But might something useful be hidden inside the socks? That question would remain unanswered; having discovered the source of the room's foul odour, I decided to leave the socks where they lay and returned the mattress to rest on the box spring.

The bed wasn't the key, but I thought again of the hope chest. It had a bottom compartment—a secret compartment. Did Victor have a secret compartment somewhere in this room?

The most logical place would be the desk, so I bent down and peered under it. From this angle, the drawer appeared to be about a foot long, but when I'd searched the inside, it was only half that length. I tugged open the drawer again, this time with a hard pull. The metal track let loose and I was thrown off balance. My feet failed me and I found myself sitting on the floor, the sectioned drawer in hand.

Despite the pain in my backside, excitement rushed

through me—there was indeed a secret compartment at the back, hidden by a homemade border. Inside it was a small notebook, which I retrieved and shoved into my back pocket.

I was elated at what was under the notebook: a hidden flash drive. I could only hope that this tiny item held the key to the mystery of the big discovery Victor had been bragging about before his death. I shoved it into my pocket.

When the bathroom door handle rattled, I leaped to my feet as Bobby came out of the bathroom.

"What are you doing?" His eyebrows were so close to one another, he looked as if a caterpillar had invaded his forehead.

I wiped the floor dust off my backside. "Sorry. I guess I yanked too hard when I was checking out the desk." I shrugged in apology, then grimaced for effect. I held up the broken drawer. "Looks like I broke it. So sorry."

Bobby lifted his hands. "Whatever. Just toss it on the bed. Someone's going to need to come and clean out Victor's stuff. The cops said they're done here."

Turning away to hide my actions, I tore away the makeshift border intended to hide the hidden compartment, then tossed the whole mess onto Victor's crumpled blanket. With my head tilted toward the bed, I said, "You might want to get the cleaners to check under the mattress."

Bobby frowned at me again. Perhaps he hadn't noticed the smell. I guess if you live with something long enough, you get used to it.

I began to doubt Bobby's involvement in Victor's murder. While he obviously didn't like his roommate, he was apathetic about Victor's death. He acted neither guilty nor worried that someone was snooping around. Still, they say that psychopaths kill without remorse or guilt. Was Bobby innocent, or a psychopath? I was staring at him, uncertain how to read him, when a key unlocked the door.

The noise made me realize something I should have thought of before entering the dormitory: that I didn't know how dangerous these people could be. I felt a tightening in my chest; not only was I was standing here in a small room with a potential psychopathic murderer, but someone was entering. If Bobby Burrell decided to end my life the way Victor's was ended, I'd have little chance of fighting him off. And now I'd be outnumbered.

I had pressed my back up against the wall and was readying myself to slam the door against the newcomer when I heard a familiar voice.

"They're not too bad, Bobby. I think if we give them a good washing, they'll be fine."

She stepped into the room and closed the door. We were now face to face.

"Fran, what are you doing here?"

I forced a smile. "Lena!"

There she stood before me in her cat-eye glasses, a quirky, questioning expression on her face, a pair of blood-soaked sneakers hanging from her hand.

Chapter 32

PANIC SET IN. Drops of sweat streamed down my face as I fought to regain control of my breathing. Short, rapid breaths were all I could manage, and I was becoming light-headed. *Don't pass out, Fran—you may never wake up.* I longed for a glass of water to moisten my mouth and throat, but more than that, I yearned for a clear path to the only door that would allow my escape.

This couldn't be happening. I'd been suspicious of Lena from the moment I met her in town a few days ago, but was she capable of murder? Had she been following me that day, or was it a coincidence that we'd met? What were her motives when we met in the library's sunroom? She'd admitted she was following me the night of the *Golden Spud* meeting, the evening after I found Victor's beaten, lifeless body in the paddock.

Poor Victor—he'd been squashed like one of those bugs on David's bumper. I was irritated with David when he showed up in Sherwood that night, but now I found myself longing for him to bust through the door. I should have followed my instincts and shared my concerns about Lena with him.

You're a fool, Fran, playing detective when you're not even a reporter yet. You've only made it to one journalism class and you're acting like a seasoned investigator, and now you've gotten yourself into a dangerous position with no escape plan. No one even knows you're here.

Lena stepped closer. I tried to back up, but the wall remained solid and refused to budge. She lowered the arm holding the evidence and hid the shoes behind her back before leaning in, bringing her face within inches of mine. "You don't look so good, Fran. Are you okay? The veins in your neck are sticking out and you look kind of pale." She straightened up and addressed her co-conspirator. "Bobby, get Fran a glass of water."

Bobby Burrell immediately headed to the kitchen, and within seconds offered me a cold glass of water. I didn't know what they were planning to do to me, but obviously Lena was the boss of the operation.

After handing me the glass with his right hand, Bobby sat at his desk and lowered his head into his hand. "Oh man. What are we going to do now?"

Lena maintained her position in front of me, blocking any chance I had to grab the doorknob and make a run for it. "Why did you let her in, Bobby? You knew Fran and Terry were snooping around. You need to be more careful."

Bobby's face reddened. "More careful? I told you to get rid of those shoes. It was stupid to take them."

"Oh, don't be silly, Cuz. I told you we can clean them up

and they'll be good as new." Lena produced the sneakers and dangled them in front of my face. Was this a threat? "See, Fran. Designer. Bobby's been wanting a pair of these since he first saw them, but man, they're expensive. No way he could afford to buy a pair."

Did she just call him Cuz, as in cousin? "You two are related?"

"Of course. Why else would I be here in Bobby's stinky room, or be hugging him." She winked at me. "I know you saw us hugging the other day."

My panic was subsiding, allowing for a resurgence of my anger. "What kind of game are you playing? Is this fun for you? Victor's dead, and Terry's being accused of a crime he didn't commit."

Lena leaned in again. "Who do you think did it, Fran?" Her lips turned up to form a stereotypical evil villain grin.

I gulped. Wasn't it obvious who'd done it? Why was she asking? Was this a trick? Or just a sick mind game they were playing before they deposited my beaten body in a field?

I thought of my aunt and uncle and how traumatized they'd be once I was found. But what if Bobby and Lena hid my body and I *wasn't* found? Not knowing what had happened to me, my aunt would be a nervous wreck. I should have been upfront with Aunt Josephine and Uncle Johnny and told them I was the one who'd found the deceased student.

I should have told David about the car with front-end damage, and I should have told Terry I was planning to confront this pair of psychopaths. Why didn't I? *Because you're a fool, Fran.*

Would playing dumb help? "I have no idea who did it, Lena. Terry and I have a long list of suspects, and we're no further ahead now than we were three days ago." I crossed my fingers and clenched my toes. *Please believe me.*

"Come on, Fran, do you seriously think I believe that you don't suspect me now that you've seen me holding Victor's shoes?"

Darn. Well, I could still play dumb. "Those are Victor's shoes? I didn't realize that. He wasn't wearing shoes when I found him, so I have no idea what he usually wears. Well, other than Fruit of the Loom socks. And underwear."

Lena frowned at me. "What are you talking about? His underwear wasn't visible on his body. Bobby didn't take his pants." She turned around and stared at her cousin. "You didn't take his pants too, did you?" She wrinkled her nose. "Ick!"

Bobby grimaced and shook his head. "No. Of course not. I'm not a sick psycho." He pointed at me. "She was looking through his stuff before you got back. I didn't think it would be a big deal. You weren't supposed to still have"—he pointed at the shoes still dangling from Lena's hand—"those!"

"I couldn't throw them away, Cuz. Oh well, what's done is done. We'll need a new plan." Lena tossed the shoes into an open gym bag that was sitting on the floor at the foot of Bobby's bed. She nodded at Victor's desk chair. "Have a seat, Fran."

I sat and placed the glass of water on the desk. "Listen, Lena. No one knows I'm here." *Stupid. I just told her no one would suspect them of my disappearance. Stupid!*

"Well, until Terry gets my text." A little white lie is okay when you're trying to save your butt from a couple of psycho murderers. "But he's busy all afternoon, and if you let me go now, I can get to him and delete the text on his phone before he reads it." Would she believe it?

Lena scrunched up her face and tapped her foot. "Nah. If

you leave now, you're going to tell Terry that you think Bobby and I killed Victor."

I waved my hand in the air. "Of course you didn't kill him. Why would I think that?" The collar of my shirt was choking me. I stretched it out, but the pressure on my throat remained.

"Why would you think that?" She raised her palms and rolled her eyes. "Because of the shoes." She laughed. "Anyway, Bobby's cranky and not overly bright—"

Bobby stood. "Hey!"

"Oh, sit back down. Do you think taking the shoes off a dead body is a smart thing to do?"

Bobby didn't respond, but his pouty face told me he didn't have a good comeback for what I had to agree was Lena's sound logic. He sat.

"So you're saying that Bobby stole Victor's shoes but didn't kill him?" Wanting to throttle Bobby, I leaped from my chair, but even when he was sitting, his physique was intimidating. "You just happened to come across the body of your roommate lying battered in a field, and instead of calling for help, you grabbed his shoes and just left him there? What kind of monster does that? If you're capable of that level of coldness, I have no reason to believe you're not the one who bashed his head in."

I held my eyes on Bobby's as silence filled the room. I'd probably said too much and now they had no choice but to get rid of me. I had nothing to lose now, so I continued my rant. "The police said that Victor died after midnight, and I found him early in the day, not long after dawn. If you didn't kill him, what were you doing out there in the paddock at night?"

Bobby shifted his gaze from me to Lena, as though he was asking for permission to speak. Lena gave a slight nod. "I was taking the shortcut to campus from Lena's apartment."

Darn. That made sense. Lena had told me she often used the field as a shortcut, and the well-worn footpaths were evidence that it was a common practice among the UPEI student body.

"Why didn't you call for help?"

Bobby shrugged. "He was dead. He was a creep with a lot of enemies. It was bound to happen eventually. It was dumb to take the shoes, but once the other guy fled, I saw my chance and couldn't resist."

The other guy? Was this a ruse to throw me off, or had Bobby Burrell seen the actual murderer? "You saw someone else? Who?"

"I don't know. It was dark."

"What did he look like? Tall? Short? Are you sure it was a man and not a woman? What were they wearing?"

Bobby shrugged again. "It was dark."

The desire to throttle him returned. "It wasn't too dark to tell it was Victor, though, and it wasn't too dark to grab his shoes and run." I shoved my index finger at Bobby's face. "Think. Either *you're* the killer or you *saw* the killer."

And if you're the killer, I'm standing way too close with my hand in your face. I backed up to Victor's side of the room. The need to be cautious didn't escape me, but I couldn't back down and show weakness. I had to buy time and hope help would appear . . . somehow.

"If you saw them, you'd better come up with something more helpful than 'It was dark.'" I nodded curtly for effect.

"I don't need to come up with anything. You're not a cop, and it's your word against ours that we have the shoes. All we gotta do is soak them in some bleach and all the blood and fingerprint evidence will be gone. Then, even if the police find them in my possession, they won't be able to prove they're Victor's."

Bobby had a point. But if he soaked the sneakers in bleach,

they'd be useless as a wardrobe item, and he'd regret having done it. He was right that the bleach would ruin any evidence of who had killed Victor—whether it was Bobby or someone else. I couldn't let them erase evidence that might exonerate Terry, but what could I do? I was still trapped in this tiny room with the two of them.

I sat down and scanned my surroundings from my position at Victor's desk. There were only two ways out: the door to the hallway, and the door to the bathroom, which was shared with the adjacent dorm room.

In the time I'd been in Bobby's room, I hadn't heard any noise from the neighbours, making me wonder if the next room was vacant. If so, the door between the bathroom and that room would be locked. Or if there were female students next door (this was a coed dorm), they probably kept the door locked. No, I couldn't risk getting stuck in the bathroom. On the other hand, I could call for help from there—if there was cell service.

My best bet was to go for the door to the hallway, take a sharp turn to the left, and race down the stairs. Once I was outside, I could call for help. But what if they caught up to me before I made the call? Could I send a text to Terry without their noticing?

Bobby had gotten up and was now sitting on his bed, and Lena was still blocking my exit. The peculiar woman, and possible murder accomplice, was bobbing as she shifted from one foot to another. She was clearly uncertain of what to do with me.

"So, Lena, what do you say? Let me leave and I'll make sure Terry doesn't get that message. You know what? Let me see if he's read it already." I punched some buttons on my phone, hoping to text Terry under the pretense of deleting a message, but before I could finish, Bobby grabbed the mobile device from my hands, turned it off, and tossed it with his left hand into the same bag that held the bloody shoes.

"Taking stuff off a dead body is stupid. Letting you text someone would be stupider."

I cringed at his grammar but kept my opinion of just how stupid he was to myself.

Lena clapped her hands. "I've got it." She waved Bobby toward the kitchen. "Let's talk in here so that Fran doesn't hear us."

"You want me to tie her up first?"

"No. She won't leave." Lena thrust her face directly in front of mine once again. "You won't, will you?"

"Of course not, Lena. That would be inconsiderate of me." Was she for real? Did she seriously think I was going to simply sit here while they plotted my demise in the other room?

I patted my pocket; the notebook and flash drive were safely tucked away. I watched Lena and Bobby as they headed into the kitchenette. It was a small room, easily visible from the bedroom, meaning that not only could I see them, but they could also see me.

I eyed the gym bag that held my phone and Victor's shoes. Lena had been holding them without wearing gloves, so at least one person's fingerprints besides the victim's was on them. I couldn't leave without that bag.

Lena and Bobby stood close to each other as they whispered, devising their evil plot to get rid of me. My chance came when Lena bent down to open a lower cabinet and Bobby reached into the same space to grab something. A knife? A gun? Duct tape and rope? I wasn't going to stick around to find out. They had both taken their eyes off me, and I had to go.

I darted from the chair and ran and, in one motion, grabbed the gym bag with one hand and opened the door with the other.

I heard Lena yelling at Bobby. "You goof, you were supposed to be watching her!"

I didn't pause to listen for his response. I threw open the door to the staircase and ran faster than I'd ever run in my life. When I reached the door to the first floor, my captors weren't far behind. I flew through it and headed for the janitor's closet that held my backpack. I could hide out in there and send messages to Terry and David.

When I reached the closet, I pulled on the knob, but it wouldn't open. I pulled harder. Still nothing. Adrenalin surged through my jittery body, and my heart felt as though it wanted to make an escape of its own.

Then I turned the knob and pushed. The door opened, and I hurried in and locked it.

In the dark room, scented with disinfectant, I sank to the floor and removed my phone from the gym bag. Shivers rippled through my spine when my skin contacted the shoes with Victor's blood all over them. Poor Victor. Murdered for a pair of sneakers. When I thought of his wasted life, and how evil our world is, to the extent that materialism and greed too often outweigh the sanctity of life, I fought back tears.

I typed a text to Terry, but when I hit Send, the "Message Not Sent" icon appeared. I tried again and received the same message. My heart sank. I tried David but was also unsuccessful. The closet must have been a Wi-Fi dead zone.

My mind was spinning—what was I going to do? I was trapped in a tiny dark closet with no way to communicate with the outside world, and a couple of murderers on the other side of the door.

Chapter 33

TINY LEGS CRAWLING on my arm jolted me awake to the reality that I was still in the janitor's closet of Marion Hall. How could I have fallen asleep? And how long had I been out? I checked my phone: still no signal, and the battery was low. I had to get out of here and inform Terry and David that Lena and Bobby were the murderers.

I tried to stretch my cramped legs, but the narrow closet prevented this. I wiped my arms to rid them of creepy-crawlies, hoping that there weren't any of them in my hair or under my clothes. The thought of a spider invasion of my trapped body created tremors deep within me and threatened to send me into another panic. *Get it together, Fran. You need to get out of here.*

I inhaled deeply to calm my nerves, then regretted it when

my nostrils were hit with the stale, disinfectant-laden air. Not knowing if Lena and Bobby were still in the hallway, I stifled a cough and glanced at the phone again to see how long I'd been in here. The digital display read 4:00 p.m. My nap had been a short one, and not only had I missed my last class of the day, but I was also going to miss dinner with my family.

I had no way of knowing whether or not Terry had made it to the police station. More importantly, I hoped he was wondering where I was. Would he think to look for me here? He had no reason to think I'd be hiding in a closet in the coed dorm.

While I was chastising myself for not letting anyone know where I'd be, the quiet of the hallway transformed into a mixture of loud voices, music, and slamming doors. It was the end of the school day, and students were returning to their rooms from their classes, labs, and elsewhere.

This was my chance. Even if Lena and Bobby were still out there, would they dare grab me in the presence of so many witnesses? They'd already proven to have less-than-clever criminal minds, so I couldn't rule out the possibility that they'd try it despite the crowd. For less than a minute, the debate raged on: stay and wait for help from someone who didn't know where I was, or hope to blend into the mass of students and quietly slip away. The latter was the only viable option if I wanted to get out of here.

I tucked my legs in and used the flashlight on my dying phone to look for something to grab on to so I could pull myself to my feet. A grungy toilet plunger, sitting too close to my leg for my liking, was the best I could do.

Rising slowly, I stretched my cramped limbs before unlocking the door. My mind fought for a story to tell should any of the passing students inquire as to why I'd been in the janitor's closet. I had nothing. After the turmoil of the week, I could think of worse things than having people think poorly of me because I'd been sleeping in a closet.

With my head held high, I unlocked the door and slowly opened it. I peered out to see small groups of students at either end of the hallway, all engrossed in conversation and laughing at each other's stories. Most importantly, not one of them was looking in my direction. I scurried to escape my tiny prison and felt a rush of relief at the realization that Lena and Bobby weren't among the crowd.

As I reached the outdoors, my body convulsed into a coughing fit, my lungs anxious to rid their tiny airways of toxins I'd inhaled over the past hour. The noises coming from deep within my chest startled people around me, including one older lady who was kind enough to offer some advice.

"You should give up smoking, young lady. My goodness, if you've already got a smoker's cough, what will the next few years have in store for you, if you live that long?" She tsk-tsked and was on her way before I could declare myself a non-smoker.

A short distance away, two students, both holding cig-arettes and blowing smoke out their noses, were pointing at her and laughing. When they saw I was watching them, they raised their palms and shrugged in she's-a-nut solidar-ity. When they walked in my direction, I smiled, waved, and tapped my imaginary wristwatch. I headed away from them, but not before they smiled back and waved. Phew. I wasn't intending to offend anyone, but I had to contact David and Terry before Lena and Bobby made a getaway.

I looked over at the parking lot near the vet college; it

was almost empty now, with only a couple of cars remaining. I flung my head back in frustration when I realized that neither of the vehicles belonged to my prime suspects. Lena and Bobby had already fled, and we'd have little hope of finding them now.

One of the remaining vehicles was the van that had so effectively concealed me earlier, while the other was a dark blue four-door sedan with a gold emblem on the side that looked like a couple of mittens hanging from a string. I assumed it belonged to one of the teachers at the campus daycare—until Dr. Daniels exited from the driver's side. He threw his keys into the air, attempted to catch them with his right hand, missed, then looked around sheepishly before bending down to pick them up. He tucked the keys into his pocket, then reached into the back seat and retrieved a briefcase. He stood in place for a few minutes, staring at the field where the horses calmly grazed in the cooling air.

During his argument with Dr. Hogg, I hadn't noticed the discrepancy between the man's appearance and his faculty photo. I could only conclude that the photo, which showed a soft, pleasant face with a straight nose, was an old one, perhaps taken when he was still a student. The face of this man, who was apparently trying to set the paddock on fire with his eyes, was weathered and had a large scar across the right cheek. His nose was bent so severely that the defect was visible even from a distance. He looked more like a man who had been through many physical battles than someone who'd have a pair of mittens emblazoned on his car. Was he married to one of the daycare teachers? That must be it, and he was driving her car.

Whatever his marital status, I wanted to talk to him

to determine what the encounter with Dr. Hogg had been about. There might be a story there for the *Golden Spud*. More importantly, I wanted to know what had happened between him and Victor Cargo during their summer expedition.

It was unlikely he'd reveal anything to a student, or that he'd even talk to me, but I had to try. I slung the backpack over my shoulder, zipped up the gym bag, raised my head high in feigned confidence, and walked briskly to the blue car with the gold mittens.

Dr. Daniels eyed me suspiciously as I approached him, and when I stopped in front of him, he scowled. "What is it you want? I don't talk to my students outside of class. Make an appointment." He turned to leave.

"Sorry to bother you, Dr. Daniels. I'm not a student. Well, I'm not one of *your* students. I'm with the *Golden Spud* and I was hoping to ask you a few questions about one of your students, Victor Cargo."

The professor spun around, his hand clenched into a fist and his nostrils flared. I backed up, not knowing if he going to hit me.

"You student journalists are all the same. Picking at things you have no business picking at. The kid is dead. Leave it alone." He unclenched his hand and smoothed the front of his jacket.

"I'm sorry to have upset you." *Upset* was an understatement. Why the anger at someone asking if they could ask him some questions? Was he still boiling over from the heated discussion with his colleague? "Maybe another time?"

"Don't count on it." Dr. Daniels opened the back door of his car, pulled out his hat, plopped it onto his head, and left.

I watched the angry man storm away, his demeanour

matching the dark clouds that were appearing in the western sky. He was carrying his briefcase in his right hand; his left hand was wrapped in gauze and that stretchy brown material athletes use. When an older gentleman approached him, he quickly stuffed his left hand into his pants pocket. They nodded a greeting at each other, and after they passed, Dr. Daniels turned back with a worried expression to look at the man. He raised his bandaged hand and massaged it before tucking it back into his pocket.

What an odd man. As obnoxious as Laurie Lamont and Victor Cargo were, my heart went out to both for having to spend an entire summer under that man's direction. I would have loved to pursue the happenings on Ellesmere Island further, but I still had to talk to Terry. I sent him a message asking to meet at Jacob's Café; if I didn't eat soon, I was going to pass out.

I called my aunt and uncle's number to let them know I wouldn't be home for dinner. There was no answer, so I left a message. I wondered where they were, but I wondered more where Lena and Bobby were. Were they on their way to the Confederation Bridge to escape from the Island? Or were they hiding out somewhere on PEI? Lena had an apartment north of the campus, but I had no idea where it was.

So many questions remained, but at least I knew who'd murdered Victor. Now I just had to prove it.

Chapter 34

"EXCUSE MY HONESTY, Fran, but you look worn out. Most students don't have that look until mid-term exams." Scott Jacob placed my order of a large coffee with two milks, and a ham and cheese sandwich, on the table before sitting opposite me. "Is everything okay?"

Before responding, I dove into the tasty food and washed it down with the hot beverage. I accepted the napkin he offered and wiped my mouth. "Just hungry."

"No kidding." He nodded toward the front counter. "Should I get the kitchen to make you another?"

I laughed. I was hungry when I arrived, but I hadn't noticed exactly how famished I was until the smell of fresh food hit me. "No, but I'd love a chocolate Danish if you have any."

"Coming up. And another coffee, I suspect."

I plugged my phone into the electrical outlet under the table and nodded at the idea of more coffee; the meeting with Terry might be a long one.

"Decaf?"

"Oh no! I will very *definitely* need the caffeine. Thanks, Scott." As I watched my personal barista head to the counter, I felt a bit guilty about taking advantage of the kindness he was showing me simply because of his fondness for Aunt Josephine.

Or was there more to it? My suspicious nature was kicking in again. This morning, Scott had inserted himself into the conversation with Laurie Lamont, and I was still uncertain as to his motives. Was he interested in her romantically? Or did he simply enjoy a good debate?

He seemed very knowledgeable about the subject—but at the same time, not so much. Laurie was a Ph.D. student in archaeology and paleontology, so if she and Scott disagreed about something in that area of study, it would make sense to assume she was right, wouldn't it? An image of a horse wearing blinders popped into my mind. Was I being narrow-minded?

"Here you go." Once again Scott was placing delicious food and tasty coffee before me. "You're deep in thought. Can I ask what's on your mind?"

"Nothing important." I wasn't going to share with this man, who I didn't know very well, that I was debating whether I could trust him or his opinions.

Scott looked at the entrance. "Ah, I think I see a friend of yours. I'll leave the two of you to your meeting."

"Thanks, Scott." He headed into the back of the café after offering a greeting to Terry.

Terry placed an order at the counter, then joined me. He

looked worse than I'd ever seen him; age lines were developing on his forehead, and he had black circles under his eyes. I wondered if he'd gotten any useful sleep since all this started.

"Did you take the backpack to the station? How did it go?"

Terry looked around as if concerned about being overheard. "I did. Both Hughes and Mather were there, so I gave it to them. I told them it had been placed in my car, but I'm not so sure they believed me."

"Did you show them the picture of Bobby holding the bag?"

"I did. They looked at it, then at each other, then back at me. From the uncertainty in their eyes, I'm pretty sure they doubted me, and Hughes said that a bag with bloodstains didn't prove, or disprove, anything. He said they'd have to run some tests to see whose blood it is."

"Are they going to do that?" I licked the chocolate from my fingers and picked up one of the napkins Scott had left me.

Terry shrugged. "Beats me. They didn't seem that interested. I've been driving around wondering if I should drop out and use the rest of my college fund to hire a lawyer."

I didn't like the sound of that. Was he giving up? "I have some news that may change things. That car that chased us the other night and stalked us today—it's Bobby's car!"

"Bobby Burrell, Victor's roommate? How do you know?"

"Because I saw him getting out of it when I was leaving class earlier. Once they were far enough away, I checked it out. The plate number and the front-end damage are a match."

Terry's frown turned into a smile, and he started to rock as though his surge of energy was too much for his body to handle. "That's great news! Why are we sitting here? We need to get to the police station and tell them to pick him up."

When he placed his hand on the table to push himself up, I put my hand on his. A rush of warmth and nerves flooded through me, and I quickly withdrew my hand. "Not so fast."

"Why? We have to hurry. The cops have to arrest him before he takes off."

I hesitated; he was so excited, and now I was going to return him to his pit of despair. "They've already taken off. I'm not sure exactly when, but they left the campus while I was hiding in the closet."

Terry looked confused. He fired questions at me in quick succession. "Why were you hiding in a closet? What closet? And did you say 'They'?" I did my best to explain my encounter with Lena and Bobby.

"Lena?" Terry said her name louder than he'd wanted to, then leaned in and whispered, "Lena helped kill Victor? That's hard to believe."

"Hard to believe or not, I was lucky to get out of there alive. If it hadn't been for the creepy closet, I . . . well, I don't want to think of what might have happened. I'm sure I wouldn't be sitting here enjoying this Danish."

"You need to be careful. You shouldn't be tracking down and questioning suspects on your own."

"No kidding. I've learned my lesson." I crossed my heart. "I promise it *will not* happen again. I did, however, find something else that may be of help." I pulled the flash drive and notebook out of my pocket and handed them to Terry.

"What's this?"

I explained the hidden compartment in Victor's desk drawer, then picked up a second napkin to wipe chocolate from my lips. A note on the underside of it said *Piltdown Man*. I looked over at the counter and made eye contact with

Scott. I gestured as if to say, "What is this for?" and he gestured back what I interpreted as "Think about it." I folded the napkin and placed it into my pocket—I had enough mysteries to think about right now without adding another one to the list.

Terry flipped through the notebook. "This looks like it might be Victor's betting journal. The names in here are probably students he was taking bets from, and the numbers are either the amounts of the bets or fake scores. We already knew he was scamming people, but now we have names of some of the people he ripped off."

"Names we don't need because we already know who killed him." I picked at my dessert and finished my coffee. "I guess it's possible they may have had accomplices."

"There might be more information on the USB. I don't have my laptop with me, so we'll have to pop over to the *Golden Spud*."

"I have mine." I didn't want to go to the *Golden Spud*. It was getting late in the day, and I wanted to get home.

I placed my computer on the table and turned it on. Once the boot-up was complete, I plugged in Victor's flash drive. The Quick Access window opened automatically when the USB was detected. I double-clicked on the D drive folder that Victor had named *My Big Break*.

"I guess he really did have something big he was working on." I turned the computer so that Terry could see the screen. Unfortunately, the only thing happening was that the blue wheel was spinning, indicating that the computer was working on something. We waited several minutes before a message popped up, then let out a collective sigh of disappointment after reading *Encrypted Files. Password Needed.*

"Do you know the password?" I asked. Terry knew Victor's *Golden Spud* email password; I was hoping he knew this one.

He shook his head. "Not unless it's the same as the email." Stars appeared in the password box as he typed. When he clicked on Enter, the box turned red. Another sigh of disappointment. "That would have been too easy."

As we pondered our next move, Scott came to the table with two coffees and two pastries. "On the house." He sat down. Terry closed the laptop.

Our guest—or was he our host?—scooted his chair closer to the table. "Sorry about the cryptic message, Fran. I should explain. I was thinking about the conversation with your friend earlier today, and I just wanted to point out that there are always two sides to a story. I'm sure as a journalist you'll learn that no matter what the source is, it's always wise to remain unbiased. To study and evaluate both sides fairly."

He looked at Terry. "Sorry. I'm doing it again. Sticking myself into the middle of a meeting you're having with a friend."

I liked Scott and felt bad that he felt bad, but he wasn't wrong that this was the second time in one day he'd interrupted an important conversation, even if he didn't know how important it was. "That's okay, Scott. No problem."

Terry wore a neutral expression. Was he upset by the intrusion? Or was he thinking about a possible password?

"We're just going over plans for the next edition of the *Golden Spud*. Right, Terry?"

Terry snapped out of his daze. "Right! Always planning the next story!"

Scott stood and waved at the treats he had just brought us. "Great. I tell you what . . . not only is this on the house, but the next time you two are here planning stories for the paper, consider that order on the house too. Perhaps you could also give us a nice review."

I looked at the lineup extending out the door and laughed. "Because you aren't busy enough?"

"I never take my business for granted. You never know what could happen in the future. A global pandemic could force the closure of all restaurants. Then what?" He laughed. "I'll leave you to it."

We watched as Scott returned to the front counter to help with the sudden rush of patrons. Then Terry opened the laptop again. "I can't think of a possible password. We'll need expert help cracking into this file. Victor may have been a pain, but he was smart. Whatever's on here, I have no doubt it's worth reading."

"Do you think there might be evidence against Bobby and Lena? Maybe that was the big story he was talking about, that he was about to bust them for murder."

Terry gave me a sidelong glance. "Are you suggesting that his big story was about *his own* murder? A murder that hadn't happened yet and that he wouldn't have known any-thing about beforehand, and that he'd be unable to write about afterwards?"

"Oh yeah." I would have slapped my forehead, but I had coffee in one hand and my second Danish in the other. "Maybe he had something else on them, and they found out about it and killed him."

"Maybe. At this point, anything's possible. I'll get in touch with Andy and see if he can get into the files on here. You should probably head home and keep a low profile until I call you."

"What about the shoes?"

"What shoes?"

"Victor's shoes."

"What about them?"

I pushed the gym bag closer to him and slowly unzipped it. I pointed at the shoes. "Those shoes. They're Victor's. Lena was holding them when she came into Bobby's room."

Terry's face paled so much that even his freckles disappeared. "You didn't tell me you had those. What are you doing with them?"

"Bobby threw them into this bag, and I grabbed it on my way out of his room. I couldn't let them destroy evidence. They were going to soak them in bleach. Both of their fingerprints will be on them—they both handled the shoes before they were tossed into the bag. I haven't touched them." My skin crawled at the memory of touching the shoes while looking for my phone in the dark. "Well, not by my fingertips, anyway."

Terry's colour, including his endearing freckles, returned to his face. "Fingerprints would be good. Are you comfortable taking the shoes to the police station on your way home? I'd go with you, but it's probably best for me to stay clear of bringing in any more evidence, and I need to meet up with Andy."

"No problem. I can catch a cab."

Terry waited until I was safely in the cab before leaving Jacob's parking lot. He wasn't the only one worried about my safety; by the time I arrived at the police station, my neck was aching from my constant surveillance of the pedestrians and traffic. The poor cabbie looked worried, no doubt thinking he had a crazy person in his vehicle. I made it up to him with a generous tip.

When I entered the station's foyer, the front desk was unmanned, but I could hear David's voice coming from the back. I lifted the countertop as he had done when I was there with Terry, and peeked around the corner and saw a long hallway. Off to the left was a meeting room with a glass wall. Inside, several officers were sitting in a semicircle looking at the back of the room. The door wasn't completely closed, allowing me to hear David's voice, but I couldn't make out what he was saying.

I moved into the hall and put my back up against the wall, then inched toward to the door. Inside was a dry erase board with photos and text. The subject of the photo at the top was Victor Cargo, and underneath it was written the word "victim." Below that, on the left, was the word "suspects," and a single photo—of Terry James.

Chapter 35

BLOOD RUSHED TO my head as adrenalin surged through my body. They still had Terry on the suspect list. And worse than that, he was their only suspect. I wanted to burst into that room and tell them all how far off they were. Why hadn't they considered the backpack he gave them earlier? I was about to push the door open and present them with Victor's shoes when I heard Officer Mather speak.

"Mr. James presented us with a backpack earlier today, claiming it has Mr. Cargo's blood on it. There's no way he could have known it was Mr. Cargo's blood unless he had something to do with the murder. He says someone left it in his car. That's a stretch."

Other officers nodded in agreement. Not only did they not

believe Terry, but they also suspected him even more now that he had shared evidence with them.

"Have we confirmed yet that it's the victim's blood and not just Mr. James's lame attempt to throw us off his trail?" A young male officer with a bushy moustache looked proud of himself for asking this simple question. I wanted to slug him. He was accusing Terry, who was helping them, of falsifying evidence.

"Not yet. Samples have been sent to the lab with a rush order. Once we confirm the blood is indeed from our victim, we'll pick Mr. James up. Until then, we'll continue to monitor the airport and bridge in case he attempts to flee the Island." David was back to referring to Terry as Mr. James, but I guess when you're trying to railroad someone for murder, formality is the way to go.

What happened to David's proclamation that he would approach the investigation with an open mind? He had assured me he would be looking at other suspects. My opinion of the good officer was taking a dramatic nosedive; horses weren't the only ones who wore blinders.

Had he forgotten about the car that had tried to run us over the other night? I'd found the car—why hadn't he? Sure, I just happened to be in the right place at the right time, but still, I found it.

Officer Mather spoke again. "The coroner tells us the nature of the damage to the right side of the victim's face suggests the assailant was left-handed. When Mr. James signed a paper for me the other night, I believe he used his left hand. Of course, that's something we can confirm later, after he's been arrested."

I thought back to the other night at the police station. Officer Mather had produced a document and asked Terry to sign it, but I couldn't remember whether or not he had. Or if he had held a pen at all that night. I couldn't remember Terry writing anything in all the time I'd spent with him over the past few days; we were always using a computer when making notes. What about eating? Or drinking? Which hand did he use?

I pressed on my temple to ease the throbbing sensation that threatened to send me into a dizzying panic. The bag I was holding was getting heavier as I considered the implications of its contents. I'd come here believing I had further evidence that could exonerate Terry, but now I had to wonder if they'd only conclude from it that I was his accomplice—that I was also trying to misdirect their investigation. I turned to leave but wasn't fast enough.

"Franny Fitzpatrick, what are you doing here?"

I stared at David as he closed the door behind him. His eyes, which I'd once thought stunning, now struck me as glaring and dark.

He was no friend, no helper in seeking the truth. He was the enemy, the man trying to put Terry in jail despite claiming otherwise. And I fell for it. I thought he was on Terry's side, that he believed Terry was innocent. I was the one who'd advised Terry to turn the backpack in, and now David and the other officers were using it against him.

"I came by to see if you found any information about that red car. Did you know that Terry and I saw it again today? It's been following us."

"Your friend stopped by earlier, and yes, he did mention it. What are you *actually* doing here?" David stared at the bag in my hand, but that was as close as he was going to get to this evidence.

"I just told you, but I guess the answer is you have nothing more."

"You shouldn't be back here, in this hallway. This isn't a public area." David was annoyed, but I couldn't tell if he was mad—or embarrassed—that a civilian had snuck into the back of the precinct undetected by any of them and seen their murder board. All his talk about TV being make-believe, and here he was using a murder board just like they did on TV. I wanted to chastise him for his arrogance, but that would make things worse.

"I'm leaving. I'll call a cab from the foyer. You can carry on with your meeting, I won't disturb you again."

"No cab necessary. Our meeting is over, and I will happily drive you home."

It would only take ten minutes to get to my home in Sherwood, but that was ten more minutes than I wanted to spend with this man. "No thanks. A cab is fine." Did I have money for a cab? After finding my wallet empty at lunchtime, I'd gone to the campus ATM to withdraw some cash, but I gave all of it to the cabbie who'd brought me here. Stupid!

A ten-minute drive with the enemy would be safer than walking home, and I still hadn't gotten a call back from Uncle Johnny and Aunt Josephine. Should I be worried about them? Did Lena know where I lived?

My heart skipped a beat when I thought about the possibility that Lena and Bobby had gone after my aunt and uncle. Had two murderers tied up my elderly relatives in their home, and were they waiting for me to get there so they could threaten me into silence?

I rushed to the entrance. "What are you waiting for, David? Let's go." This was going to be the longest ten minutes of my life.

Chapter 36

DAVID DROVE THE speed limit to Sherwood, but it felt as if we were crawling. "Can't you go any faster?"

"What's the rush? We're almost there."

I should have told him my fears about Lena and Bobby being at the house and holding my aunt and uncle captive, but he'd just laugh at me. In David's mind, they had already found the guilty party, and it was just a matter of time before they arrested him.

"I need to use the washroom. Scott Jacob was very generous with the coffee earlier." It wasn't a lie—Scott had been very generous.

David shook his head and giggled. "My apologies." He sped up briefly, then eased up on the gas until he was back at the posted speed limit. He was mocking me, but his opinion of me and my bladder control was irrelevant; I needed to get home.

Within minutes we were turning into the driveway of my PEI home. Uncle Johnny's pickup truck was in the driveway, but Aunt Josephine's car wasn't. I hoped they were out together, but my mind turned to other horrible scenarios. What if Lena and Bobby had stolen the car and kidnapped my aunt and uncle, and would later demand ransom for their return? Or the car could be in the garage, meaning there was still a possibility they were being held captive in the house.

I was about to spill the beans, to tell David everything so he would come into the house with me and ensure my family was safe, when Aunt Josephine's car pulled up beside us. She was driving, and Uncle Johnny was in the passenger seat. As they exited the car, they both wore huge smiles.

Uncle Johnny leaned in through the passenger-side window of the squad car. "I don't know what I'm going to tell your parents, Fran, but I believe this is the second time you've been brought home by the police." He smiled at me, amused by his own humour, and headed to the house.

I was happy to see him remove a key from his pocket. It wasn't unlike them to leave without locking the door, but this time, thankfully, they'd locked it.

"Thanks for the ride, Officer." I jumped out of the squad car and gave Aunt Josephine the biggest hug I've ever given anyone, then gave one to Uncle Johnny too. I'd never been so relieved to see two people in my life.

Uncle Johnny unlocked the door and turned the knob, then gave it a gentle push. "You ladies go in first, in case there's a burglar." I laughed at this joke of his that I'd heard a few times since moving to the Island, but inside I cringed at the reality that this time, there actually could have been someone dangerous inside.

I looked back at David and noticed he had turned the car's motor off but was making no motion to get out. Was he making sure we were safely inside before leaving? My anger at him was subsiding.

I bounced in front of Aunt Josephine, wanting to be the first one inside just in case there was an unpleasant surprise—one wearing cat-eye glasses—waiting for us. While my aunt and uncle hung their coats in the closet, I made a quick sweep of the main floor.

I jumped when I came around the corner from the hall-way to the bedrooms and found myself face to face with Aunt Josephine.

"Did you lose something, Franny? Why so jumpy?"

My aunt opened a few cabinets and started to prepare what she, and many older Islanders, referred to as "a lunch." "Your uncle and I were out shopping earlier, then went to a step dancing class. I've always wanted to give that a try." She demonstrated what they had learned, and I had to admit that I was impressed that her thin, aged legs could move so nimbly.

"Very nice, Aunt Josephine. You know, I did lose something. I think I left a booklet down in the basement. I'll be right back." I ran down to the partially finished basement and looked behind every door and around every corner. No one was hiding down there. I returned to the main level and looked out the window of the door that led to the driveway. David was still there. I gave him a thumbs-up and he drove away.

Why did he wait? I hadn't told him about Lena and Bobby, so he couldn't know I was afraid they might be hiding out in my home. Was it because I so readily accepted his offer of a ride, then urged him to speed up? He was a police officer; no doubt he had instincts that told him when someone was worried. I appreciated his response, but now I dreaded that the next time I saw him, he'd ask me what I had been so worried about.

I couldn't have told him what was troubling me—not yet. Terry and I needed to meet tomorrow and come up with a plan. I would send Terry a text to fill him in on what happened at the police station, but first I'd treat myself to tea and a square—or two.

I joined Aunt Josephine and Uncle Johnny at the little table in the kitchen for tea and a selection of chocolate squares, lemon squares, fudge squares, and molasses cookies. I helped myself to a fudge square while Josephine filled our cups with tea.

"Step dancing? That's impressive. How many classes?"

"Once a week for six weeks. If we enjoy it, we'll sign up for the next session. If not, then at least we tried something new." Since retiring, Aunt Josephine had tried a few new things. The house was decorated with her tole painting, a hobby she turned out to be quite skilled at. When I commented on a few pieces in my room and asked if they had bought them at a craft show, she explained that Uncle Johnny, a skilled carpenter, would cut out the wood pieces from a pattern she provided him with, and then she'd paint them.

"Johnny and I may be going to a dance up in Tracadie tomorrow evening. Will you be comfortable staying home alone? We may be late getting home."

My dear, sweet aunt often forgot that not only was I an adult, but that I had grown up in Toronto, where I was often alone, not just at home, but also while travelling to various activities. Of course, she had no idea that I was currently in more danger here on PEI than I'd ever been in the big city, and I had no intention of revealing that fact to her.

"I'm sure I'll be fine. I've had a busy week, so I'll probably just stay close to home and relax. Maybe watch a movie. Or maybe I'll learn to knit so I can fill that hope chest with baby clothes."

I watched them both for a reaction. Johnny suppressed a grin, but Aunt Josephine looked confused. I'd figured out that the hope chest and its supposed purpose for my future domestic life was a joke, but instead of telling them, I decided to play along.

"What baby?" My aunt looked as if she was about to have a coronary event.

"Sorry, I'm just teasing you. No babies. Not for a very long time." I gave her a firm, no-nonsense look. "And no trying to marry me off, especially to men you don't know."

"Well, we know David Hughes well enough." Uncle Johnny snagged a third square. "His father and I worked together on the railroad for forty years, until they closed it down here on the Island."

Uncle Johnny had worked for the Canadian National Railway as a lineman for, as he liked to tell it, forty years and four months. When there was talk of removing rail service on the Island, he took the company up on their offer of early retirement.

"Gave them forty years of my life, and they gave me a watch to say thank you." He shook his head and swallowed his square.

"Is there anyone on this Island you two don't know? By the way, what do you know about Scott Jacob? I know he was a student of yours, Aunt Josephine, but what about later in life? Has he always worked at the family café?"

Josephine got up to add more hot water to her tea. "Oh, he's a smart young man, that Scott is. I believe he completed a Bachelor of Science at UPEI, then went over to the mainland to do a master's degree. His aunt told me that at one time he had a promising career in . . . What is that field called? The one where they look at old bones and old cities."

"Archaeology? Paleontology? Anthropology?" I wasn't sure myself what the difference between the various fields was, but I had picked up a few terms this week from Laurie Lamont and Dr. Watson.

"Yes, one of those." She returned to the table and ate a piece of her cookie. "Hmm. I'm not sure which, but they say he was quite good at it. Very smart. He was smart as a child, so I wasn't surprised when he did so well in college. I don't know what exactly happened, but partway through his master's program... or was it a doctorate? I can't remember now, but for some reason he quit and came home to the Island. His dad was happy he came back 'cause that allowed his parents to retire when Scott took over the café."

That explained a lot; no wonder Scott was so knowledgeable about the things Laurie had been talking about. I thought back to what he had said earlier when I was at the café with Terry. Sadly, I hadn't paid much attention because I was more concerned with talking to Terry about Lena and Bobby, but now I struggled to remember what Scott had said.

It was something about two sides of a story, and not to believe anything without digging deeper. Did he know something about Victor's murder? Victor was in the same field of study that Scott had been in. Why did Scott quit his master's program? *Great, Fran. More questions.*

I put my plate and cup into the sink and said my good-nights, hoping that Lena and Bobby were far away, hatching a plan to escape the Island. I still needed to send a text to Terry letting him know what had happened at the police station, and that I didn't pass the shoes to the authorities.

I froze, then slapped my forehead. The shoes! Panic seized me—I'd left the gym bag with Victor's shoes in David's squad car.

Chapter 37

I DRAGGED MY WEARY body out of bed after another night of interrupted sleep. Almost a full week of long days and restless nights was taking a toll on my mind and body, and not even the arrival of the weekend offered me hope of rest.

For the first time since I was a child, I was awoken several times during the night by nightmares. Zombies were pacing the streets of Charlottetown, all wearing blinders like the ones the horse at the vet college had been sporting. In each disturbing scene that played out in my unconscious mind, a zombie would spot me—then the chase was on. I would run across the university grounds and into a building; the building I entered changed with each dream. The coed dorm, the science building, the administrative building, the Barn. Just as a zombie reached for me, I would wake up, drenched in sweat. Twice overnight I had to change out of wet clothes that were causing me chills.

The last dream was the strangest. I was hiding under a table in Jacob's Café when two giant weathered hands came down through the ceiling and forced a set of blinders onto my head. I screamed, then said, "No! I don't want to be a zombie. I don't want to be a mindless follower of the crowds, to go along with the popular opinion. I want to think for myself. To look at all the facts and present an unbiased report." I struggled with the being from the rafters, but I couldn't get away. The hands were too strong, the blinders too tight. I screamed again, then shot up in my bed.

I remained seated, clutching the sheets against my cheeks for protection against an unknown foe. I was certain I'd identified Victor's killers, but had I? Was my unconscious mind trying to tell me something? So many unimaginable events had filled the past week—was I seeing the whole picture? Did the various experiences fit together? Was I missing something? Maybe I was the one wearing blinders.

Terry and I had agreed to meet at the *Golden Spud* office at 9:00 a.m., and I was anxious to talk to him, but it was only seven thirty. I would have time to shower and change before heading out. While getting ready, I replayed the previous day's events and Terry's last text in my head. The nightmares had me questioning everything I thought I knew about the case. *Forget it, Fran—they were just dreams.*

In his text, Terry had relayed that he wasn't surprised by the news he was still the prime suspect, and he was okay with my having forgotten Victor's shoes in David's car. I wasn't okay with it. Not only hadn't I turned the evidence in, but if David looked into the bag, he'd know I'd been deliberately withholding evidence. Or he'd wonder what kind of maniac I was that I was in possession of bloody shoes.

Since Victor's body had been found sans shoes, it would be obvious to David where the footwear came from. Did the fact that my sleep hadn't been interrupted in the middle of the night by sirens and my arrest mean he had no intention of snooping through my belongings? Or hadn't he noticed the bag lying on the floor of his car?

I quickly dressed, fed myself, and readied my case notes, then realized I was alone in the house. I found my aunt and uncle in the backyard. Johnny was clad in an old pair of overalls from his railway days and a ball cap with a photo of the CN Tower on it. Aunt Josephine, dressed in black polyester pants and a turtleneck sweater with blue-and-black horizontal stripes, was on the deck hanging laundry on the longest clothesline I'd ever seen. It started at the house and ran a hundred yards to the far end of their backyard. At that end was a pole Uncle Johnny had erected twenty years ago when they first bought the property.

I said I'd be on campus all day working on a project, but I didn't tell them that the project was catching a murderer.

My uncle removed his cap and wiped the sweat from his forehead before picking up a basket of freshly harvested carrots and radishes. "Be sure you're home for dinner, Fran. I'm going to cook these on the barbecue tonight."

Uncle Johnny was a master of the art of barbecuing vegetables. It always struck me as funny that he'd have so many vegetables on the grill, there was no room for the meat, forcing my aunt to cook it inside in the oven.

"I'll do my best. I love a good barbecue."

Johnny headed inside, but as he reached for the door, he paused, then turned back to me. "Heard on the news this morning they may have a break in the death of that poor young man on campus."

I wanted to know more, but before I could ask what else the report said, Josephine put a stop to the conversation. "Oh, I don't want to hear about that. Why must the news always be bad?"

She had a point. How beneficial would it be to society if the media reported good news with the same fervour with which they reported bad news? I'd be part of the media some day, and it would be my job, and that of my contemporaries, to make a change for the positive.

My silver-haired landlady, wearing her favourite floppy sunhat, scooped up her empty laundry basket. "Let's get back inside, Johnny. I want to go to the little Superstore to pick up some groceries before it gets too busy."

As I watched my favourite aunt and uncle disappear into their house, I was burdened with a surge of guilt. The feeling I'd had last night, that they may have been in danger because of my actions, overwhelmed me. I should have heeded David's warnings and left the police work to him and his department.

I thought back to the first time I met Uncle Johnny: a few weeks after he and Aunt Josephine were married in a little country church in the town of Millcove, PEI, not far from where my father grew up. They came to Toronto for their honeymoon so the Ontario part of the family could meet Johnny, our new in-law. My siblings, cousins, and I took an instant liking to this burly, curly-haired man who told fun stories and bought us ice cream—extra large scoops, with sprinkles.

Josephine and Johnny had met at a wedding a couple of years before their own. Johnny's younger sister, Claire, was hired on at the school in Charlottetown where my aunt had been teaching for years, and they became good friends. When Claire's wedding day approached, she invited my aunt, who then met Johnny, and "the two J's" had been inseparable best friends even since—even after getting married themselves.

If I had to wait until my mid-forties to meet and marry my soulmate as they had, it would be worth the wait.

I threw my backpack over my shoulder and hopped onto my bicycle. Despite realizing my recent behaviour was foolish and dangerous, I was too deeply involved. I couldn't back down now. We had to clear Terry's name, even if that meant finding Bobby and Lena ourselves.

Chapter 38

A FEW MINUTES OF frantic peddling later, I arrived at the *Golden Spud* office. I secured my bike to the metal bike stand with a ring lock, then paused a few minutes to catch my breath. The pain in my chest was yet another reminder that I needed to get into better shape.

It didn't help that the temperature was steadily rising, and surprisingly, the morning air was heavy with humidity. I was used to this type of weather during Toronto summers, but it was unexpected in early September on PEI. Normally I'd welcome the warmth and sunshine, but I'd ridden harder than I was used to, and had done so without the benefit of water.

I found Terry sitting at his desk. It was obvious from his facial expression that he was in deep concentration, studying something on his computer. To avoid startling him, I tapped lightly on the door before entering.

"Hi, Fran. Right on time." He came over to the entryway, closed the door behind me, and locked it. "Andy's been working all night to crack into the files on Victor's flash drive."

In the room on the other side of the hole in the wall, Andy sat hunched over a keyboard. Two large monitors were situated in a wide V formation on the desk, and his fingers moved like lightning over the keyboard. He paused only long enough to drink from one of the Styrofoam cups on the adjoining desk. The cup trembled as he moved it to his lips, then back to the desk.

"How many coffees has he had?" I counted five cups, but that didn't account for the ones that had been discarded, or for refills.

Terry stuffed his hands into his pockets and turned on his heels, his voice no more than a whisper. "I lost count a while ago."

"You're poisoning your best friend." I marched into the other room, grabbed the empty cups, and tossed them, then filled a clean one with water and set it beside Andy. "Drink this. If your eyes bug out any more, we'll have to use a net to keep you from turning into a gnat and flying out the window. That's if you don't have a heart attack first."

Andy obediently sipped the clear liquid, then grimaced. "Gross. What is this?"

"Water."

He shot me the evil eye; I stepped back. He huffed out his frustration, then pointed at the screen and smiled. "I'm past the second level. Victor has secure folders inside secure folders. The guy either had something big to hide or was a paranoid nutbar." Andy, seeming to instantly forget that other people were present, returned to his task.

I headed back to the main room and Terry said, "Come on. While he's doing that, we can summarize what we have so far."

"You're still the prime suspect, or only suspect. Other than that, we don't know anything more than we did yesterday." I filled a large mug with the thick brown goo from the coffee maker. I'd cut Andy off caffeine for the rest of the day, but I was far from filling my own quota.

"Did you hear anything at the police station before Officer Hughes spotted you?"

I took a sip, added more milk, and sipped again. The sludge in my cup was still light years away from what I would call coffee, but it would have to do. I replayed my visit to David's office in my mind before answering Terry's question.

"There was mention of the coroner's report. One of the officers said the assailant had to be left-handed, based on the damage to the right side of Victor's face." I grimaced at the memory of my discovery but was surprised when the nausea never came. A part of me wanted to cheer, but my newfound ability to remember gruesome details without vomiting was no cause for celebration when one man was dead and another was being falsely accused of the crime.

"Okay, let's start with that." Terry pulled a dry erase board into the centre of the room, drew a table with two columns, and wrote *SUSPECTS* at the top of the first column, and *RT OR LT* at the top of the other.

"Cool, our own murder board."

Terry glared at me, and my other two heads. I was getting used to his annoyance at my poorly timed attempts at humour. "Sorry."

He started to list the names of our current suspects: *LENA, BOBBY.*

"You can stop there. We know Lena and Bobby did it. They had the shoes."

"So did you."

I felt my head tip to one side. What was he getting at? Was I a suspect now? "I don't understand."

"We both know you didn't do it, but if we condemn Lena and Bobby because they were in possession of one piece of evidence, then we must condemn ourselves too. I had the backpack. You had the shoes. We'd be doing the same thing your buddy David and his crew are doing."

"He's not my *buddy*!" Was my voice too whiny? Defensive? "You made your point." I waved at the air. "Continue."

Terry added Dr. Hogg, Dr. Daniels, and Laurie Lamont to the list. "Do you know if any of these people are left-handed?"

I thought back to my encounters with Lena and Bobby. I pictured Lena picking me up from the floor at the library. "Lena! She's definitely left-handed. She grabbed my shirt and lifted me with no effort, using her left hand. One more strike against ole cat eyes."

"Excuse me?"

"Her glasses. Haven't you ever noticed that they look like cat eyes?"

Terry sighed heavily. We were all tired. I drank more brown sludge and thought about my visit with Bobby Burrell.

Bobby had handed me a glass of water. I was disappointed when I remembered that it was with his right hand, but then I pictured him tossing my phone into the gym bag. "Bobby's left-handed. Or ambidextrous. Either way, no way he made such a great toss if he's not left-handed."

Terry wrote *LT* beside Lena's name, and both *RT* and *LT* beside Bobby's. "What about these other three?"

I pictured Christine Hogg lifting her tablet during our interview. "Left! No, wait. She was facing us." I stood up, turned 180 degrees, then put my right hand in the air. "Nope. She used her right hand to lift the tablet."

Terry wrote *RT* beside her name with a question mark.

"Why the question mark?"

"If the drawer was on the right side of the desk, she'd have to use her right hand to retrieve the tablet from it. Using her left hand would be awkward. So, we really can't say she's not left-handed."

"This is making my head hurt."

"It might be the coffee." He was probably right, but we didn't have time to run over to Jacob's Café to get real coffee.

"What about Scott Jacob?" I asked.

"What about him?"

"Twice he inserted himself into a conversation I was having about the case. First when I was chatting with Laurie, then when you and I were meeting. Why would he do that?"

"Did he know what you and Laurie were talking about? Or why you were talking to her? Did he know what you and I were talking about? What would his motive be?"

"You're right. Obviously, I'm still caffeine deficient." I took another sip and gagged. "If only Scott would show up now and interrupt us, just long enough to bring us one of his caramel lattes."

Terry chuckled. "That would be nice. Speaking of your visit with Laurie, did you notice if she's right- or left-handed?"

I scrunched my face, twisted my lips, and stared at the ceiling. Nothing helped. "No. Sorry."

"That's okay. If you run into her, ask her to hold something for you and see which hand she offers up."

"I think it's more likely she'd offer up a few choice words. I think Dr. Daniels is right-handed. I saw him throw his keys into the air with his right hand and try to catch them."

"Try?"

"He missed." I shrugged. "Guess he's not an athlete. Not a baseball player, anyway."

Terry noted RT beside the professor's name, and then we sat and stared in silence at our murder board and list of suspects.

"What about . . . ?" I nodded toward the hole in the wall.

"You're not serious? You still suspect him? The man has been up all night trying to help us."

"Up all night opening folders on a flash drive. How many folders can there be?" I held my breath, sure that my comment was going too far. Terry had complete faith in his best friend, but I still wasn't convinced I could trust Andy. I jumped when I heard his voice behind me. Had he been standing there when I suggested he was a suspect?

"What are you two talking about?" He moved closer to the dry erase board. "Are these the suspects? Cool. Anyway, I have something for you. Follow me."

Chapter 39

I F ANDY HAD overheard me, he either didn't know what I was talking about or chose to ignore me. I was relieved either way. Terry and I followed him through the hole in the wall to his workstation. I suppressed a gasp when I took a closer look at the set-up. On the right side of Andy's desk sat the cup of water I had given him earlier. I wasn't surprised it was still full, but I was surprised by the placement of a pen and notepad—on the left side of the desk.

When I had questioned Terry about Andy's handedness, Terry became defensive and didn't answer the question. Now I knew why.

I would play it cool and keep my suspicions to myself until I knew more. Why would Andy be helping us unlock the flash drive if he was the murderer? The answer was obvious: to throw us off track and buy time to plan his escape. I had no doubt he didn't want his best friend to go to jail for a crime he hadn't committed, but Andy also wouldn't want to land in there himself.

I wondered if Andy had a connection to Lena and Bobby. Another cousin perhaps? I thought about all the cousins I had on the Island who I hadn't yet met—not first cousins, but seconds and thirds. The hostility between Andy and Lena the other night could have been an act to cover up their true relationship. From what I'd experienced so far, I doubted that either of them was smart enough to pull off such an intricate deception. On the other hand, they might be smarter than I'd been giving them credit for, and if they were, could we trust them?

"Fran. Hello, Fran. What are you doing? Are you okay?" Squinting, Terry was standing directly in front of me, waving his hand past my face.

I stepped back, uncomfortable with the sudden feeling of being too close to someone I didn't know well. It wasn't just the physical closeness, but also the emotional closeness to this man I'd only known a short time. It dawned on me as I stood there that my life was now very different than it had been a few weeks ago.

I left Toronto a carefree young adult ready to take on the world, but now I was surrounded by new people and unexpected circumstances. Murder, marmalade, and mayhem. It sounded like the title of a bad murder mystery script.

"I think I need to sit down." I sat beside Andy. I was much too involved in this real-life murder mystery to back out now. I had to trust Terry, and I had to trust his instincts.

Andy pointed at one of the monitors. "It's confirmed—

Victor was some kinda nut. After all the password-protected folders, he's just got two files in here."

My Path to Fame and Fortune
Digging Deeper

Terry grabbed the mouse and double-clicked on *My Path to Fame and Fortune*. "This looks interesting."

Inside the file was a Word document titled *Agenda*. As we read through it, our initial disappointment that we'd simply found Victor's bucket list turned to excitement.

1. Make an appointment to see Scott Jacob at Jacob's Café.

2. Confront Dr. Daniels on the radio.

3. Review Dr. Watson's medical record.

4. Cloud codes.

Terry ran his hand through his hair. "I wonder if you were on to something, Fran."

"What do mean?" I had no idea of which brilliant moment of mine he was referring too.

"Scott Jacob. Why would Victor want to talk to him? Was it about something that led to a confrontation between them?"

I shrugged. "I have no idea. What about the next one? He was going to confront Dr. Daniels about something. In public. What could that have been?"

It was Terry's turn to shrug. "Didn't Laurie tell you that Victor had been snooping around in Dr. Daniels's tent during their expedition?"

I nodded. "Maybe what Victor found in the tent had something to do with Dr. Watson. Why else would Victor be looking at a professor's medical records? How would he even get access to them?"

"Probably found himself a world-class hacker." Andy laughed, which only made me further question his involvement in Victor's murder. Was this an unintended confession? If Andy had helped Victor hack into a doctor's medical records, Victor could have then blackmailed him. We already knew that our murder victim was comfortable taking advantage of people for financial gain.

However, Victor probably knew that Andy didn't have any money and would be unable to pay a ransom, so what could Andy have been afraid of? Had Victor threatened to turn him in to the authorities? If so, what was his motive?

Terry himself had said that, based only on their possession of the bloody sneakers, we couldn't be 100 percent certain that Lena and Bobby were the murderers. My dream last night suggested I was wearing blinders, that I was being narrow-minded. Perhaps my subconscious was trying to tell me something. But what? Lena and Bobby weren't mentioned in Victor's list, but two professors were. Why?

When I'd seen Dr. Watson in his office, he was frail and appeared much older than his age. I asked myself which was worse: killing someone for a pair of shoes, or committing murder to climb another rung on the professional ladder?

I asked, "Do you think Dr. Daniels had something to do with Dr. Watson's illness? It came on so suddenly, and the timing was perfect—right before the Ellesmere Island expedition."

Terry jumped into my line of questioning. "Could that be why Dr. Hogg was telling Victor to back off? To protect Dr. Daniels? But . . . why would she protect him? They didn't even work in the same department." Terry was as confused as I was. We had so many suspects, and a growing number of theories.

"I think they might have known each other before. During their argument yesterday, Dr. Hogg said something about helping him. How did she put it?" I squeezed my brain to remember what I'd overheard. "Something about his promising not to repeat what happened in Hamilton." I lifted my hands in frustration. "That's all I can remember. The scene with Bobby and Lena was so crazy, the rest of the day was a blur."

"I think we can assume Hogg and Daniels have a past. We just need to find out what it is." Terry slapped Andy on the shoulder. "That last point is cloud codes. What do you think that is?"

Andy smiled and puffed out his chest. "Way ahead of you, my friend. While you two were debating the drama of the teachers' lives, I found Victor's cloud account. It'll take me a few minutes to gain access, if these codes I found in the flash drive file are the passwords."

Andy directed his attention from the monitor that displayed the flash drive files to one that had the internet open to a site I'd never seen before. I wondered if it was designed to help hackers break into other people's accounts.

I had to admit to myself that this whole process was stirring up my adrenalin, and I struggled with the conflict raging in my mind: breaking into a person's personal accounts was wrong, but if it helped us to find that person's killer, was it *less* wrong? Was it okay, even admirable?

The excitement of gaining access to Victor's secret notes was overshadowed by the heaviness of my eyelids. "While

Andy's working on that, I'm going to head to the cafeteria to get some real coffee, and food. I'll bring some for all of us."

"None of that decaf stuff." Andy shot me a crooked smile and winked. I wasn't sure how to interpret that. I could assume it was a simple, friendly gesture, but I feared it was something more sinister. Or was he delirious from a lack of sleep? We were all suffering from sleep deprivation.

"Where's Andy?" I was expecting to see him come through the hole in the wall when he smelled the sweet aroma of fresh coffee, but Terry and I were alone.

"I sent him home to get some sleep. He doesn't function well in public without rest." That didn't surprise me. Few of us were at our best on limited sleep, and I could only imagine it would be worse for someone already struggling with anger management issues.

In the short time I'd known Andy, I'd seen a fiercely loyal friend with poor grammar, and a hothead with exemplary computer-hacking skills. Despite his less appealing qualities and my suspicions of him, I wanted to like him—he and Terry had been friends since they were kids.

If my friendship with Terry was to continue, I had to accept that Andy would be a part of my social circle. That is, unless one of them ended up in jail. David still suspected Terry, and I still suspected Andy.

Terry had moved to his own desk and had Victor's cloud account open on a laptop.

I placed the coffees and snacks on the desk beside Terry's. "I have croissants, tiny quiches, and three slices of Black Forest cake."

"Isn't it a bit early for cake?" Terry took one of the coffees and a croissant.

"It's never too early for Black Forest cake, especially from the university cafeteria. They have the best I've ever had. The food is amazingly good for a school cafeteria. True, I've only eaten there a handful of times, but if I had to spend a year living on campus and eating their food, I'd be very content."

Terry gave me a sidelong look. "Good to know. Now look at this list of Victor's folders."

I pulled up a chair and read the text on the monitor. Inside a folder labelled *My Big Break* were four subfolders:

Dr. Watson's Medical Records

Exposing Dr. Daniels–Questions for Radio Show

My Stupid Roommate and How to Ruin Him

A Sporting Good Time

Terry double-clicked on the first folder to reveal a single-page file with an internet link highlighted in blue. He clicked on it, and his preferred search engine opened and took us to a page for a local medical clinic. My excitement grew; we were about to get some answers to one of the many mysteries surrounding Victor's behaviour. But then a pop-up asking for a password appeared on the screen. "Shoot. Without Andy, we aren't going to gain access to this file."

I thought back to my visit with the science professor a few days earlier. "Dr. Watson was supposed to lead the Ellesmere Island expedition but suddenly became too sick to participate. Maybe Victor's interest in his medical records has something to do with that? Perhaps he'd been exposed to something during the trip."

Terry gave me that look again. "He was exposed to something on the expedition he couldn't go on because he was exposed to something that made him sick?"

I sighed. Despite all the caffeine, I was beyond tired, and I wasn't making any sense. "Maybe he was exposed to something here?" I rubbed my face, hoping this would clear my mind.

Terry's face lit up. "You might be on to something. What if Dr. Daniels exposed Dr. Watson to a toxin that made him sick?"

Terry was starting to think like me. I'd have to decide later if that was a good thing or a bad thing. "Would a distinguished professor go to such lengths to further his career?"

"History is full of higher-ups doing horrible things for their own gain, building themselves up, whether for money or fame." Terry closed the folder and opened the next one. Several subfolders appeared.

Kenneth Daniels Undergrad

Kenneth Daniels Postgrad

Kenneth Daniels University of Hamilton

Daniels and Hogg

The petty, immature, gossip-hungry side of me wanted Terry to open the Daniels and Hogg file, but he clicked on the undergrad file. There wasn't much in there, other than a typical CV, or curriculum vitae. It listed Dr. Daniels's academic achievements, including awards, scholarships, and research articles he was involved in, and his extracurricular activities. The latter included shot put, boxing, and wrestling.

Terry typed "Kenneth Daniels athlete" into the search bar, and soon we were looking at an article with a photo of a young science student wearing nothing but shorts and boxing gloves, holding a trophy. His face was swollen and bleeding, but he was beaming as the referee held his arm in the air. The headline read THE CHANGING FACE OF COLLEGIATE BOXING: AN UNBEATABLE LEFT HOOK.

"It changed his face, all right. His face is swollen in that photo, but his nose is still straight and he doesn't have a huge scar across his cheek." I knew nothing about boxing, but the reference to a left hook nibbled at my mind. Before I could ask Terry what it meant, he had opened the next file.

Chapter 40

THE POSTGRAD FILE had a more extensive CV, this time including a list of Dr. Daniels's published papers, teaching roles as a master's and Ph.D. student, and a list of universities he had faculty privileges at prior to coming to UPEI. The last was the University of Hamilton (UH), and it said that he was in line for a tenured position in the paleontology and archaeology department. We already knew that from my discussion with Dr. Watson; unfortunately, it didn't tell us why he left when he did.

"I wonder if there's information in the next file as to why he left UH so abruptly." I grabbed the mouse and clicked on the file named *Kenneth Daniels University of Hamilton*. Two more subfolders appeared. "Andy wasn't kidding that Victor liked to have hidden folders within hidden folders."

I opened the first one and quickly scrolled through a list of teaching assignments and other information that seemed irrelevant to our investigation.

"Whoa. Slow down. We might be missing something important." Terry attempted to retrieve the mouse, but I pulled it away and kept scrolling. I was impatient and jittery; perhaps I had overdone it on the caffeine. I closed the folder and was about to relinquish control of the computer to my colleague when I spotted something interesting.

I read the name of a second subfolder: *Notes for S.J. Meeting*. I paused and glanced at Terry. "Do you think this is about Scott Jacob?"

"There's only one way to find out."

I got the hint and double-clicked. We scanned through the file.

Scott Jacob had been an archaeology and paleontology Ph.D. candidate at the University of Hamilton after completing his master's degree at the same institution. Not only had he been at the same school as Dr. Daniels, but they were in the same department. They would have known each other.

Certain I would regret it later, I shovelled a forkful of cake into my mouth and washed it down with more stimulant. "Why didn't Scott mention this? He overheard at least part of my conversation with Laurie, and he must have known Dr. Daniels. Do you think he's hiding something?"

Terry shrugged. "Hiding what? Being in the same department doesn't necessarily mean they knew each other, or even if they did that they had a cordial relationship, let alone much interaction."

"True." I read on. "This is interesting. It looks like Scott was reprimanded by the university administration." Did we need to rethink putting him on our suspect list? "Do you think Victor found this out and threatened to expose him?" I held my breath at the thought, then sighed. "What if Scott killed Victor to keep him quiet?"

Terry shook his head. "I don't see it happening. Scott's not in academia anymore, so what kind of a threat would it be to have a reprimand exposed? Who would care? Who would Victor tell?"

"I guess it depends on what he got into trouble for."

Victor had a link to a journal article titled "Another Casualty of Academic Bias."

My heart raced in anticipation of what we were about to discover. Did Scott have a motive to kill? Was it a crime of passion? The article in the *Journal of Independent Thinking* popped up on our screen.

I rolled my eyes. "Sounds like a political extremist type of magazine."

"Maybe, or it's as advertised—a journal focused on thinking outside the box. Not following the crowd. Thinking for yourself after gathering all the facts."

Terry's response surprised me, but then I was reminded of the dream I'd had a few hours earlier. When my unknown foe had covered my eyes with blinders, I wasn't afraid of death or having my brain eaten—I was afraid of losing my ability to think for myself. I was afraid of becoming a mindless drone who followed the popular opinions of the time.

The article began by detailing Scott's CV: his educational achievements, including the schools he had attended, the multiple academic awards he had earned, and a list of published papers he had contributed to. The main body of the article, written by Cathy Leaky, listed as one of the journal's editors, was in interview format.

Leaky: I understand that you were dismissed from the University of Hamilton for sharing your religious beliefs with one of your classes. Can you explain to our readers what happened?

Jacob: Of course. I believe that when teaching a controversial topic, it's important to encourage students to look at both sides of the debate. To have them give an ear to each argument so they can develop their own position based on facts. Students should learn how to do proper research, especially nowadays with the advent of social media and the internet. It's easy to read about a subject on the internet and assume you're learning all the facts, not ever realizing that the information you're being exposed to isn't grounded in truth.

Leaky: I have a hard time believing that you lost your position for asking students to think for themselves.

Jacob: I had a hard time believing it when it happened, but sadly, it did. Perhaps if the subject in question hadn't been such a touchy one in the world of academia . . . But I didn't realize at the time just how touchy some of my superiors were.

Leaky: I believe the topic you were questioning is evolution. We learn about evolution everywhere from children's programs on television to high school biology. Why would you take on a subject that people have such strong beliefs about?

Jacob: My goal wasn't to disclaim or even challenge evolution; I merely assigned the students the task of researching it, along with alternative proposals for the origins of life. I stressed that they were to use science, not personal beliefs, when presenting their papers. When we ran into each other off campus, one student later asked me what I believed in, and I told him.

Leaky: And that was?

Jacob: I believe the Genesis account—in other words, I believe in intelligent design. I had never mentioned my beliefs, creation, or intelligent design in the classroom, but that student passed my answer on to a parent, who later called the school administration to complain. That's when my troubles began. I was accused of religious indoctrination of students, and my teaching privileges were immediately suspended. Adding injury to insult, as they say, my research funds were frozen, pending an investigation.

Leaky: They shut you up by shutting you down.

Jacob: Effectively, yes. With no source of income, I couldn't continue in my studies. I tried to play the game and participate in the investigation, but it was more of a kangaroo court.

Leaky: That's a strong claim. How did you defend yourself?

Jacob: I tried to explain that I had simply asked students to think for themselves, because they might be posed with similar questions in their future careers. They would have a better understanding of the basis for evolution by investigating other theories, and the arguments that opponents might use.

Leaky: Referring to evolution as a theory was one of the points the administration used to dismiss you?

Jacob: That's correct. And they continued to imply I was trying to brainwash students with my personal beliefs. I've seen university professors, high school teachers, and even grade school teachers do that with certain beliefs they held—not religious ones, mind you—and I've seen first-hand the damage it can do to young minds. It's another reason I prefer to teach students to think and investigate, not tell them what to think.

Terry stood up to stretch. "Wow. If Scott was going to kill anyone, I think he would have done it in Hamilton."

I had to agree. "If Victor published an article about Scott's beliefs here on the Island, people would be either apathetic or happy about it. I don't know if he would have been given a parade through the streets of Charlottetown, but I'm fairly certain he wouldn't have come off as a villain."

I removed Scott from my suspect list. "Why do you think Victor was investigating Scott? Do you think Victor was a believer in . . . What is it?" I scrolled through the article. "Intelligent design? Whatever that is."

Terry chuckled. "Not likely. And even if he was, he wouldn't have been allowed to publish an article about it in the *Golden Spud*. We have restrictions on the type of material we can publish." He paced the room. "I suppose he could have said something on the radio and dealt with any fallout later, but to what purpose?"

Terry raked his hand through his hair and rubbed the back of his neck. "He was bragging about a big scoop that would make his career in both science and journalism. There's nothing in that article that would have enabled that."

"Yet he wanted to talk to Scott." I stared out the window, pleading for the answers to this newest mystery to appear in the sky. Why did Victor think Scott could help him with his big discovery? We were still no closer to knowing what that discovery was and how it was involved with his death—or if it was even related to his death.

Were we wasting time reading through these files? There was the one about Bobby Burrell and Victor's desire to bring harm to his roommate. Still convinced that Bobby and Lena were the number one suspects, I closed the folder on Dr. Daniels and opened the one called *My Stupid Roommate and How to Ruin Him*. It was obvious from the folder name alone that Bobby and Victor felt a mutual disdain, and I was sure that the motive for the murder was at our fingertips.

No such luck. The folder was empty. Why? I pondered the blank screen. Had Victor not added anything to it yet, or had he deleted its contents? If the latter, why not delete the folder? I thought back to my visit with Bobby Burrell in the dorm room. I assumed he didn't know about Victor's secret compartment and the flash drive, but what if he had? He would have had ample time to delete the information in this folder. However, he would have needed access not only to the flash drive, but also to the cloud account it had taken Andy hours to get into. From what I'd seen of Bobby Burrell, I doubted he could pull that off.

Terry returned to his seat. "That's disappointing. Open the next one."

Without sharing my thoughts about Bobby, I clicked on *A Sporting Good Time*, the last folder in the initial window. It was an Excel file and contained a repeat of Victor's journal, the one hidden in his desk drawer, which detailed his sports gambling scam. More disappointment.

I closed the window and hovered the mouse over the *Exposing Dr. Daniels* folder, but before I could re-open it, I was distracted by the sound of heavy, fast-paced footsteps in the hallway. Terry and I looked at each other; I saw confusion in his eyes, and I was sure he saw the same in mine.

"What do you think that's all about?" I asked.

He shook his head slowly. "No idea, but it can't be good.

The pub and bookstore are still closed. The radio station doesn't start broadcasting until after lunch on Saturdays."

The marching grew louder, then stopped.

Terry waved at the monitor. "Close it down."

I closed all the windows, then pulled the flash drive from the USB port and shoved it into my pocket. Terry hit the power button to the monitors, and the screens went black.

Someone tried the doorknob, but Terry had locked the door after I returned from the cafeteria. The someone then pounded on the door. "Mr. James, we have a warrant for your arrest."

It was David—Officer Hughes. I was livid. How dare he show up with an army to arrest an innocent man! I stood up to confront him, but Terry put his index finger to his lips and motioned for me to sit back down. "There's no point in my resisting. They'll just go harder on me, and we can't risk you getting arrested too."

"How do we know that's not the plan? They don't know I'm in here, but once they do . . ." I couldn't finish the sentence. My heart was racing and nausea was setting in. This had to be how Terry had been feeling all week. Afraid of being arrested for a crime he didn't commit. Of being thrown into jail with hardened criminals. With real murderers. I sat back down and put my head between my legs. It was getting hard to breathe.

"I need you to calm down." Terry rubbed my back.

David pounded on the door again. "Open the door, Mr. James. We have a call in to university security, but if we have to wait for them to open the door, you will be facing a charge of resisting arrest."

"How is resisting arrest a threat when they intend to charge you with murder?" Suddenly, I felt re-energized.

"Listen, go into the other room and stay out of sight. You're right—they probably don't know you're here. I'll open the door and surrender, and hopefully they won't search the office. Once it's all clear, call Andy. Have him call my folks and tell them what's going on."

I headed for the hole in the wall.

"And Fran . . ." I could hear the anxiety and fear in Terry's voice. "Don't let the flash drive fall into the wrong hands. There must be something on there that can help us." He tilted his head and shrugged. "I hope."

As I swung around the corner into the secondary office, I whispered, "I hope too."

Terry unlocked the door. "I'm here. No need to call security. I'll go peacefully."

I wanted to peek around the corner, but I couldn't risk being seen. I pressed my back against the wall and held my breath, fearing that any movement, even a shallow breath, would alert the police officers to my presence.

I finally let the air escape my lungs when the volume of the departing footsteps had declined to the point that I was sure David's army had left the building.

I called Andy, but there was no answer. I sent him a text, then sank to the floor. Now what?

Chapter 41

I SAT QUIETLY FOR a few minutes, waiting for the vibrations assaulting my body to stop before I stood up. Andy wasn't responding to my texts; he was probably sleeping. I'd have to act alone to help Terry, but how? I didn't have his parents' contact information. I'd need to come up with a plan of action while waiting for Andy to wake up and check his messages.

Fearing I might still come face to face with Officer David Hughes, I peeked around the corner into the *Golden Spud's* main office. The man in uniform had a habit of showing up when he was least expected, but to my relief, the room was empty.

I crept to the door to the Barn's main hallway and peered down the long corridor toward the exit. Empty. I made my way partway down the hall until I came to a window, and, continuing to practise stealth mode, peered out. Officer Mather was loading Terry into a cruiser under the watchful eye of her superior, David. When the latter turned to look back at the Barn, I ducked.

I waited a few seconds, then risked another peek. Officer Mather was now seated in the cruiser that held my friend, and David was in the other cruiser. They drove off with their lights on but sirens off. Terry was in the back seat, his head bowed. Thankfully, it was Saturday morning and the campus was empty of any onlookers. I returned to the *Golden Spud* office. I had work to do.

As instructed, I had closed Victor's cloud account when the police arrived, and without Andy, I was certain I'd be unable to reopen it. I could only hope there was some useful information in the flash drive, so I plugged it back into the computer and opened the folder we hadn't looked at yet, *Digging Deeper*.

What were we missing? Were Lena and Bobby killers? Or just insane shoe thieves? I crossed my fingers that the answers would be here, but I was again discouraged. The file was empty.

I had to assume that Victor had moved his important information to the cloud and deleted it from the flash drive. I returned to the file with the codes. Could it be as simple as opening the search engine and looking at the computer's search history?

I gave it a try. I leaped from my seat and punched the air when the page with Victor's cloud account appeared. Terry had closed the window but hadn't logged out, so I didn't need a password. I had full access to the folders we had already viewed, and the one we hadn't—the one I was initially most interested in, *Daniels and Hogg*. I took another swig of my cold coffee, then double-clicked.

Open before me was a bulleted list of the history of Drs. Daniels and Hogg, according to Victor's research. They had worked together at the University of Hamilton in the science department. Dr. Hogg had worked there first, and she hired Dr. Daniels.

Two years later, Dr. Hogg left UH, but Victor was unable to find a reason for her departure. A year after that, she was hired by UPEI's science department in an administrative role that meant she wouldn't be expected to teach or do research. Victor had a list of questions that included: Why did she leave UH? What was she doing during the year between UH and UPEI? With her credentials, why was she hired on as an administrator and not a full professor?

I wondered if the answers to Victor's questions would explain why she was so angry. Maybe something had happened at UH, or during the year between universities, to make her bitter.

Victor noted that Dr. Daniels stayed on at UH for five more years. After leaving UH, he did a semester at UPEI as a visiting professor, then was hired on as an associate professor last year. Victor had the same question I'd had after speaking to Dr. Watson. Why did Dr. Daniels leave UH, going from a position that promised tenure to a junior position?

Dr. Hogg had hired Dr. Daniels at UH, and also at UPEI.

Were they romantically involved? Apparently not, from what I had seen the other day. Unless it was a lover's quarrel. Were they related? Cousins? Kissing cousins? Ick! I needed more coffee. I retrieved the coffee I had brought back for

Terry, thankful it remained untouched. It too was cold, so I headed for the microwave.

Without warning, my caffeine-induced high, mixed with exhaustion, caused my emotions to roller-coaster from one extreme to another. I was sad for Terry and sad for Victor, but I was also mad at them both. Mad at Terry for trusting Andy. But why shouldn't he trust his best friend? Mad at Victor for getting himself killed. But it wasn't his fault someone had murdered him. Why did he have to be so obnoxious, and so ambitious? There was nothing wrong with being ambitious— or was there?

I felt alone. I scanned the empty room, a room that had been full of fellow junior reporters only a few nights ago. Andy was sleeping and unavailable. Terry was in jail. Lena and Bobby were on the run. Greg and Hallie were . . . I didn't know where they were. Should I try to contact them? I shook my head; I didn't know them well, so I didn't know if I could trust them.

For their own protection, I was keeping in the dark the only two people on the Island I knew without a doubt I could trust. Or that's what I'd been telling myself throughout this insanity, but was that really why I hadn't shared the happenings of the past week with Aunt Josephine and Uncle Johnny? Maybe I was afraid they would talk me out of helping Terry in his investigation. The truth was, I didn't want to stop helping him.

My nose was damp from my tears, and time slowed down the way it had that day in the paddock. I was confused and anxious about what was happening. One student dead, and another in jail for a crime he was innocent of. I was scanning my surroundings for a towelette to dry my eyes with when, through the window over the counter, I spotted Terry's little green car with the missing bumper, sitting idle. It looked as lonely as I felt, as though it had been deserted by the world. Left to fend for itself.

My mind wandered from one insane event to the next. The red socks leading me to Victor's body, the car chase, being trapped in a dorm room with probable murderers, my elderly relatives trying to marry me off prematurely, horses walking around with crazy-looking head coverings, police officers with heart-melting blue eyes. Was it real, or was this some extreme reality TV show meant to punk unsuspecting freshmen?

Movement on the other side of the parking lot caught my attention, and in my sights was the dark blue four-door sedan with a gold emblem on the side—a couple of mittens hanging from a string—Dr. Daniels's car! I watched the man in his fedora open the trunk and toss a laptop bag on top of two suitcases. Was he going on a trip?

Dr. Daniels slammed the trunk closed with his right hand, then massaged his wrapped left hand. He had done that when I saw him yesterday, as though his left hand was painful. I stared at the gold mittens on the car door. Were they mittens? I'd assumed that the car belonged to one of the daycare teachers, possibly his wife, but there was no mention in Victor's notes of his being married.

I studied the logo more closely. They weren't mittens—they were boxing gloves, like the ones he was wearing in the photo accompanying that article. What was the headline? I tapped my head; I was missing something important. I tapped my head some more, and then it came to me: The Changing Face of Collegiate Boxing: An Unbeatable Left Hook.

A left hook! Dr. Daniels was known for his powerful left

hook! The police assumed that Victor's killer was left-handed because most of the damage was done to the right side of his head, but what if the killer was a boxer with an unbeatable left hook?

The over six-foot-tall, broad-shouldered professor with a boxing background could have easily killed the much smaller, unathletic Victor. And now Dr. Daniels was making an escape. Laurie Lamont had said that something happened between the two men on Ellesmere Island, and that after they returned, Victor was bragging about a big discovery.

Dr. Daniels had given up a prestigious position at UH, and Dr. Hogg had also given up a more prominent career at the same university. When they were arguing, she mentioned not wanting what happened in Hamilton to be repeated. What had happened? Had Victor discovered the answer to that question and confronted them? What had been so bad that he felt the need to resort to murder?

I had to stop Dr. Daniels from getting off the Island. I started to call Terry but stopped; I couldn't imagine that David would allow his prisoner to answer a call.

David! Heat rose in my chest, followed by the taste of bile, at the thought of him. He was the last person I wanted to talk to, but did I have a choice? Finding Victor's killer was the only way to clear Terry's name. I called David's number. He didn't pick up. Of course not—he was busy putting the wrong man in jail. I left a message asking him to call me back as soon as possible.

Now what? I started to pace, but when the car door slammed, I knew I had no time to think any further. It was time to act. I scanned the room for inspiration.

Terry's keys were on his desk, beckoning to me. I debated

the sanity of following Dr. Daniels. I would have to take Terry's car without his permission. Could I be charged with auto theft? Should I think this through further? No! Thinking was for another time.

I closed the laptop and threw it, the flash drive still inserted, into my backpack. I grabbed the keys and rushed out to the parking lot. I had to stop a murderer from escaping the Island.

Chapter 42

I FLEW DOWN THE hallway as fast as my tired legs would take me. The effects of my fast-paced bicycle ride, followed by a couple of hours of sitting, were now evident in the deep muscle pain I was feeling. With each smack of my foot on the hard tiles, my legs pleaded with me to stop and massage them, but my mind was sharply focused on catching Dr. Daniels.

I was so focused that I almost ran into a smartly dressed middle-aged woman heading in the direction of the pub. I swerved to the right to avoid the collision, stumbled, then regained my footing. I turned back to apologize, only to be met with the shocked look of my Introduction to Journalism professor, Dr. Linda Gayle. The very woman whose class I had walked into late so I could interrogate Bobby Burrell—an interrogation foiled by David's sudden appearance in the coed dorm's lobby. I had chastised myself later that day for making a poor first impression on someone who would no doubt be an important link in my career-driven chain of contacts.

The glass double doors to the outside were within arm's reach—I had to get to the parking lot. Terry's future might depend on it, but *my* future might depend on apologizing for not only almost knocking Dr. Gayle over, but also for being tardy earlier in the week. Self-preservation filled my mind, and I turned around.

"Sorry, Terry," I whispered, then paused to take a breath before approaching my near victim.

"Um, Dr. Gayle?"

She turned around, and to my relief, was smiling. "Yes? I'm sorry—have we met? You seem in a hurry."

I walked briskly toward her. "I was, but that's no excuse to almost run someone over. Please accept my apology."

She extended her hand. "Apology accepted. You look familiar. Are you one of my students?"

I shook her hand, then studied my shoes. "No. I mean yes. I *am* one of your students. Introduction to Journalism, but I'm afraid I was late for the first class. I missed over half of the lecture. I'm so sorry about that. I'd been looking forward to your class, but something unavoidable came up."

"I see." She seemed suspicious of my "unavoidable" claim.

Up until now, I'd been reluctant to let anyone know I had discovered Victor's body unless it was vitally important. Not wanting my professor to think I was a lying, scamming cheat seemed vitally important.

"It's been a weird week, after finding the murder victim's body in the field on Tuesday, then . . ."

As the professor's face went from doubt to sympathy, I was

relieved my ploy had worked. I would deal with the self-inflicted guilt trip later.

"That's terrible. I can't imagine how awful that must have been. I tell you what—why don't you come by my office next week after class and we'll chat about what you missed in the first lecture."

"Really? That would be fabulous. You don't know how much I appreciate it."

"It's my pleasure. I enjoy getting into the thick of investigative reporting in my first lecture to the first-year class. Learning the tricks of the trade, as they say. Gathering information is very important in getting to the truth of a story. We don't want to be narrow-minded, then blindsided by the truth, then later find out we missed important details."

What she was saying reminded me of thoughts I'd been struggling with all week. It was as though I was learning the lesson I had missed in her class in real-life events. David was focusing too much on Terry, and I now feared I'd been focusing too much on Lena and Bobby. Drs. Daniels and Hogg had a lot to hide. What was their truth?

Dr. Daniels! I'd almost forgotten about him.

"Thank you again for your offer, Dr. Gayle. I'll gratefully take you up on it and stop by your office next week."

"No more missed classes?"

I crossed my heart. "I promise." It was a promise I hoped I could keep. I had to find Dr. Daniels, but once I found him, would I be in danger? I shuddered at the thought that I might not make it to class next week, or even home tonight. Why hadn't my phone buzzed, telling me that David or Andy had responded?

I jerked my thumb toward the exit. "I have to run. Sorry."

I spun on my heels and headed for the parking lot, hoping the professor wasn't rolling her eyes or shaking her head behind me. If things ended well today, I'd have an interesting story to tell her at our meeting. I didn't want to think about what might happen if things didn't go well.

The morning's humidity was gone, and I was jolted by a blast of crisp, cool air when I got outside. Supporting my backpack on my shoulder, I headed to the west side of the building where the parking lot was located, but as I turned the corner, I let the bag drop into my hand. I stood and stared at the almost empty lot, where Terry's lonely car sat. Dr. Daniels was gone.

Of course he was gone; I had put my own interests ahead of my friend's and let a suspect get away. *Think, Fran. Where would he be going?*

I opened the driver's-side door and threw my bag onto Terry's passenger seat. I was reminded of the wild ride we'd had a few nights ago and hoped there wasn't any unseen damage to the car. The only visible damage was the missing back bumper. It wasn't surprising that Terry hadn't replaced it yet; he had neither the time, nor the funds, to do so.

I adjusted the seat so I could reach the pedals, then the mirrors so I could navigate safely. I flopped back against the seat and closed my eyes. I said a little prayer, hoping for guidance on what to do next.

There were only three ways off the Island: the Charlottetown airport, the Confederation Bridge between PEI and New Brunswick, and the ferry service from Wood Islands, PEI, to Nova Scotia. If I were a criminal trying to make a quick escape, I'd want to get as far away as possible, as fast as possible.

I checked the flight schedule. The only remaining flight out of Charlottetown was at eight o'clock tonight. The single-terminal airport was too small to effectively hide a man for several hours, so it was unlikely Dr. Daniels had gone to the airport. The fastest remaining route off the Island, with the least exposure, was to drive across the bridge.

I checked my phone's GPS for the fastest route to Borden-Carleton, PEI, then started the engine. With any luck, there'd be a bridge closure this afternoon, preventing the former champion boxer and murderous mad scientist from making an escape.

Highway 1 was the most direct route to the bridge, but there was a red line through the new bypass on the GPS map. I thought back to my conversation with Scott Jacob yesterday, when I met with Laurie; he was taking orders that morning because road construction had delayed two of his employees.

My plan was already falling apart. I couldn't risk getting stuck in a huge traffic jam, and it was the weekend, so there would be a higher-than-normal volume of traffic on the main highway to the mainland.

I studied the map and spotted a small town called Cornwall. When I was a kid vacationing in PEI with my parents, the bypass hadn't been built yet, so our usual route to Sherwood was through Cornwall.

I'll never forget the bakery we stopped at on every trip—they had the best raisin bread I'd ever eaten. It was tradition to buy a couple of loaves for Aunt Josephine and Uncle Johnny on our way to their home. When the bypass went through, that put an end to stopping on the way to Sherwood, but

Aunt Josephine knew that I shared her love for raisin bread, so she made sure that no vacation ended without a trip to Cornwall.

Hoping that late-summer tourists and students heading to the mainland for what was left of the weekend didn't know about this original route to Borden-Carleton and the Confederation Bridge, I set the GPS to guide my way to Cornwall. As I approached the curved hill that would have taken me to the bypass and instead turned toward Cornwall, I spotted the last of the westbound drivers who were stopped, waiting for the signal man to let them proceed.

Was fortune on my side? Maybe Dr. Daniels was stuck in that traffic jam. If he was, I could end up ahead of him. What would I do then? Race to the bridge and wait to see if he showed up? How would that work? I was only guessing that he was heading there. There was nowhere safe near the toll gates to stop and watch for him—not without drawing the attention of the bridge security people.

Then another possibility came to mind. What if he never showed up? That could mean he'd already escaped the Island, or that using the bridge was never his intention. Or maybe he was behind me but had stopped somewhere along the way and changed his plans.

What was I doing? I had no way of knowing if I was on the right trail or wasting a colossal amount of time, but it was too late to turn back. I'd come this far, so I would continue and figure out a plan when I got to Borden-Carleton.

My fears of being on the wrong path were eliminated when I passed the first gas station in Cornwall. Parked at the corner gas pump was a dark blue four-door sedan with two gold boxing gloves on the door. Dr. Daniels had chosen the same detour I had and had stopped for gas.

I looked at Terry's gas gauge–it was close to full. I sighed with relief at not having to take the time to fill the tank, but my heart sank as I pondered my situation. I'd caught up to Dr. Daniels, but that was where my plan ended. What now?

I checked my phone to see if either David or Andy had responded to the messages I'd left them. They hadn't. I sent another text to Andy, reminding him to call Terry's family and updating him with my location.

Then I clicked on David's number, but before the first ring, Dr. Daniels hopped back into his car and started heading west. I ended the call and put the car into drive. I would keep following the professor and try to connect with the police later.

Chapter 43

THE POSTED SPEED limit on this stretch of highway was ninety kilometres per hour, but Dr. Daniels was whipping along at more than a hundred. I stayed far enough behind that, should he bother to check his rear-view mirror, it wouldn't be obvious I was following him.

The sky was darkening as thick black clouds passed overhead, readying themselves to unleash their wet fury on the ground below. I glanced down at the steering column to find the switch for the wiper blades, then returned my attention to the road just in time to see a transport truck in the oncoming lane swerve toward the gravel shoulder. Dr. Daniels had decided to pass an orange SUV on a solid line going around a curve in the road, and had just missed a head-on collision with the semi. Did he know how lucky he was that the trucker had been able to move over in time?

I drew up behind the SUV, but there was no safe place for me to pass it, and I had no idea how fast Terry's car could go. Calling it beat up even before we'd been chased the other night was an understatement, so testing its ability to overtake another vehicle was risky. I anxiously tapped my thumbs on the steering wheel, hoping that either the SUV driver would speed up or there would be a passing lane soon. I was losing sight of the object of my pursuit.

To add to my misery, the clouds let loose with a torrential, blinding downpour. I flicked the wiper control to the fastest setting, but it didn't significantly improve my ability to see the road ahead. The driver of the SUV must have been blinded as well, as he pulled over and stopped on the shoulder. Should I do the same? It would be the wise and safe thing to do, but then I'd never be able to catch up to the professor. Now, with the other car out of my way, I might have a chance of decreasing the space between me and Dr. Daniels. I held my breath and pushed down on the accelerator.

I instantly regretted my decision when the wheels hit a puddle, causing the car to hydroplane. I did what Uncle Johnny had taught me to do: I slowly released the gas, then steered into the swerve. It worked. I had control again. *Thank you, Uncle Johnny.*

I risked a glance at my GPS to see how far away the Confederation Bridge was. The display told me twenty minutes, but that was on a good day when drivers could see where they were going. The display also told me I had driven over the Bonshaw River. I'd heard it was a good place to canoe, and if a person was lucky, they might even have the company of seals. As much fun as that sounded, it would have to wait for another day. A day free of heavy rain, and chasing criminals.

The volume of rain hitting the windshield tapered off, and I spotted a set of lights up ahead. Perhaps Dr. Daniels had slowed down?

No. The lights were white—they were headlights. I was about to attempt to speed up again when the oncoming vehicle passed me. It was Dr. Daniels. He had turned around. Now what? There was nowhere to turn on this stretch of the roadway.

I thought back to the night Bobby Burrell had been chasing Terry and me. What had Terry done to turn the car around? *Think fast, Fran. Don't let your brain take a break. That's it—the emergency brake!*

I grabbed the handle between the front seats and yanked it up as hard as I could, exactly as I had seen Terry do it, but I didn't get the same response from the car.

Instead of spinning 180 degrees, the car came to a sudden stop with so much force that the back wheels left the pavement, and despite the seat belt, I was slammed into the steering wheel.

I struggled to regain the breath that had been knocked out of me and squeezed my eyes shut. I crossed my arms over my chest and let out a groan, then adjusted the seat by pushing it back a few inches. That was a painful lesson to learn; Aunt Josephine had warned me that sitting too close to the steering wheel could be dangerous.

The pain was intense, but honking reminded me I was still on the road. I opened my eyes and saw the same orange SUV swerve around me, horn blaring, and the driver making gestures that expressed his displeasure with me.

Hoping I hadn't done any serious damage to the vehicle, I quickly placed it in park, pushed the emergency brake down, returned the gearshift to drive, and performed a three-point turn on a major roadway. It wasn't my finest hour, and I was grateful there had only been that one witness.

Heading east again, I decided to pull over onto the first exit and reassess my plan. I'd try to reach David and let him know what I'd found on Victor's cloud account about Drs. Daniels and Hogg. I couldn't help but wonder, though—would David care? He had made an arrest, and as far as the police department was concerned, they had the guilty party. I had no proof Terry *wasn't* the murderer, and I wasn't sure if I had concrete evidence that Bobby, Lena, or Dr. Daniels were. How could I convince Officers Hughes and Mather that one of them had killed Victor if I wasn't sure myself who did it?

As I drove the battered vehicle back across the Bonshaw River, I noticed a turnoff to my left. A sign informed visitors that it was the entrance to Bonshaw Hills Provincial Park, and more importantly, that public restrooms were ahead. There was no point in trying to catch up with Dr. Daniels; he had turned around, and I had no idea why or where he was headed. After making use of the facilities, I'd head to the police station and check on Terry.

I crept—or more accurately, bounced—along the pot-hole-laden dirt road, tree branches scratching Terry's car, until I spotted a wooden structure with two doors, indicating facilities for men and women. I froze in disbelief; parked alongside the restrooms was a dark blue sedan with a pair of gold boxing gloves proudly displayed on the driver's door.

Dr. Daniels wasn't in his car. Where was he? I carefully backed Terry's car a few feet to a clearing I'd spotted on the way in, then tucked it behind a grove. I exited the car and approached the edge of the trees. From this vantage point,

I could see not only the blue sedan, but also a small picnic area behind the restrooms. Dr. Daniels was at the edge of the mowed area, swinging a bag.

I stepped forward, hoping to get a better view, but what I thought was solid ground was a pile of twigs covered by decaying vegetation. Several twigs snapped, and a shiver went up my spine. The pain in my ankle was overshadowed by the fear that I'd been heard. To my relief, Dr. Daniels apparently hadn't heard the twigs snapping, but he did turn his head in my direction when I involuntarily let out a gasp. Nuts! I tried to hide behind the largest tree trunk I could find. Had he seen me? Heard me?

Drops of water from the wet leaves were pelting me on the head. I used my fingers to comb my hair back and off my face. The motion reminded me of Terry's habit of combing his fingers through his hair when stressed. I couldn't imagine the enormous amount of stress he must be under right now. I wondered if he'd be bald from excessive combing the next time I saw him.

I had to get out of here and back to town, but before I took a step toward my car, something crashed into the bushes. Had Dr. Daniels tossed his bag there? Why? He might be hiding evidence. I sighed. I couldn't leave now. I needed to find out what was in that bag.

I dared a peek at the picnic area. Dr. Daniels disappeared around the far side of the wooden structure, and then the familiar rattling of a rickety wooden door hitting a wooden frame sang through the woods. He had gone into the restroom. I sprang into action—I'd only have a few minutes to act.

I flew through the grove, stumbling multiple times on wet twigs and plants, to where the professor had been standing.

The corner of a blue-and-green canvas bag was poking out through some shrubbery. Thankfully, the ex-boxer wasn't an ex-baseball player or the bag would have been farther into the bush. As I pushed my way through nature's greenery, my legs got caught up in some vines. I tugged at the vines until they broke away, then reached forward. The bag was just beyond my fingertips.

A fallen tree was to my right, with broken branches around it. I grabbed for one, then dropped it when I spotted a caterpillar crawling toward my hand. *Pull yourself together, Fran. You're chasing murderers. This is no time to be afraid of bugs.* I retrieved the branch, used it to snag the handle of the bag, then whispered, "Yes" in my excitement.

I pulled the bag close to my body, afraid I might drop it. It was wet and smelly, and I imagined it was an old gym bag once used to carry boxing shorts. I gagged at the thought and turned around. Then I screamed.

Chapter 44

D R. DANIELS WAS standing by the picnic bench, his nostrils flared as if he were a bull focused on a red flag. "My, my, what do we have here? A nosy student? You've been following me."

I pointed at my chest and looked at the sky. "Me? Following you?" I pursed my lips, then shook my head twice to seem more convincing. "No. Not me. I'm heading to the mainland to meet some friends. I saw the signs for the restrooms and thought I'd better stop. It's still a bit of a trip to the bridge and Gateway Village. Have you been to Gateway Village? It's a great place to stop for souvenirs before leaving the Island." I was rambling. I loved Gateway Village and its shops, especially COWS Ice Cream, a PEI delicacy.

I shook my head to loosen the cobwebs. *Get a grip, Fran. This is no time to be thinking about ice cream.*

"There are perfectly good restrooms at the village. No need for a young lady to be heading into the bushes."

My story was weak, and I was holding his discarded bag. I wouldn't have believed me either, but I didn't have a better idea. Talking my way out of this was the only hope I had. I raised the bag in the air. "I saw you drop this. I was just getting it for you." I gave a fake laugh and a smile. "You know, it never hurts to suck up to a professor. Can't hurt, right? I mean, bonus marks and all."

The two-legged bull took a step toward me. "Are you even a science student?"

I shrugged. "Well, no, but anyhow . . . How about I just leave this sitting right here"—I lowered the bag to the ground—"and be on my way." I took a few steps toward the clearing where I'd left Terry's car.

Dr. Daniels grew closer and raised his right hand. "Not so fast. Pick up the bag. We're going for a ride."

I picked it up as directed but hesitated. "Um, I don't think so. I've seen this scenario on TV too many times. If I go with you, I'll end up in a deserted area where my body won't be found for weeks, maybe months—if ever."

"Look around you. You're already in a deserted area."

He had a point. I dropped the bag and ran toward the grove that separated me from my ride to freedom, but I was once again reminded I was in poor shape when I stumbled and hit my arm on a rock on the way to the ground. Before I could get to my feet, a strong hand grasped my other arm and yanked me up.

I was now face to face with a man who may have already

killed one student this week. Would he hesitate to do it again? Dr. Daniels's eyes narrowed and his gaze grew cold—so cold that a chill froze my spine as I scrutinized the soulless abyss of his eyes, which reflected a man capable of snuffing out a life.

I struggled to free myself, but it was no use. This ex-boxer was stronger than anyone I'd ever encountered. He removed one of the ties from the gym bag and used it to bind my hands before dragging me to his car, where he effortlessly tossed me and his bag into the back seat.

"You're coming with me. You kids and your cellphones—I can only imagine you've been streaming all this on social media. If any of your pals call the police, I may need a little insurance policy—your freedom for mine." He slammed the door, then got into the driver's seat.

He headed back to the main highway. If only I'd thought to stream this live to social media, but the truth was that even if I had thought of it, I didn't know how. Now I'd never have the opportunity to learn. Trapped in the back of a car driven by a madman, I had to wonder if I'd have any opportunities for anything ever again. I said a prayer; I could think of nothing else to do.

Chapter 45

"LISTEN, DR. DANIELS, I'm not sure what this is all about, but if you could just drop me off on the side of the highway, I'm sure I could find my way back to Charlottetown."

"I thought you were heading to the mainland to visit some friends."

"I changed my mind." Why were we discussing my travel plans?

I'd heard stories of captives befriending their captors—gain their trust and they might let you go unharmed. It was worth a shot.

"Hey, I don't know what happened between you and Victor, but I'm sure you had valid reasons. I mean, from what I hear, the guy was an obnoxious narcissist." My stomach turned at the sound of my own words. Even an obnoxious narcissist didn't deserve to have his brains scattered in a pad-dock, but this wasn't the time to show sensitivity regarding the victim.

The rain had stopped and the clouds were drifting east, allowing the sun to shine through. I loved the smell of the air after a late-summer rain, but all I could smell at the moment was the gym bag sitting on the floor by my head. I was still lying across the backseat.

When Dr. Daniels had tossed me into the car, I landed across the seat, my head just missing the inside metal door handle. My relief at not suffering a head injury was almost dashed when the bag came flying at me. I was lucky again when it hit the floor instead of me.

"I heard you were a boxing champion in university. That's awesome. You must be very strong. I mean, you picked me up no problem. Who else could do that?" I thought back to my encounter with Lena at the library. Apparently, more people than I would have imagined could pick me up with little effort.

Dr. Daniels slammed his hand on the steering wheel. "Stop the rambling. I need to think. If the police stop me, I have you for insurance. If they don't, well, I'll have to figure out what to do with you once we're in New Brunswick. Damn nosy students! Victor was nosy, and look where that got him? He could have kept his mouth shut, but no, he had to be a big shot."

"Um, I'm fine with not being a big shot." I shifted my legs and placed my feet on the floor, then grasped the middle seat belt to pull myself into a sitting position. I was now on the passenger side of the back seat, giving me a view of the mad professor. He had a white-knuckle grip on the steering wheel, his elbows squeezed into his sides as he stared straight ahead. My fear of being killed once he no longer needed me as insurance was momentarily overshadowed by his fixed gaze, and my concern that he'd crash the car before we got anywhere near the provincial border.

"A big scoop!" Dr. Daniels slammed the steering wheel again with his right palm. In the rear-view mirror, I could see his contorted face. "Victor Cargo thought he was so smart." The flaring nostrils of a bull returned when he said Victor's name. "A *big scoop!* He was going to expose me to the scientific community to advance his career in paleontology. What a fool. They would have just laughed him off."

"I'm sure you're right. Fool!"

"Yes, I'm right. Sure, I tweaked the fossils a bit, but I was just showing the advancement of the creature. What's wrong with that? That's how science progresses."

Tweaking fossils? Even my unscientifically trained mind thought that sounded wrong, but I wasn't about to argue with the raging man at the wheel.

"I caught him exiting my tent on Ellesmere Island, and it was obvious he'd been digging through the bones I discovered at our second site. He laughed at me and said he knew I was up to something. He said he'd already been suspicious when Dr. Watson got sick, that it was the journalist in him. Idiot."

Dr. Daniels slammed the steering wheel again. When the car swerved, I grabbed on to the seat belt. With my hands tied behind me, there was no way I could fasten the belt around my lap.

I stared out the window, hoping to see a police cruiser on the shoulder. I could roll down the window with my elbow and shout for help, but all I saw was a road sign informing travellers that the town of Victoria was to the left.

Ahead of us, a small country church, its steeple painted to mimic a lighthouse, reminded me of what I loved about PEI. The countryside, small towns, friendly people, and ready access to the sea in every direction. I had to wonder if this would be my last tour of the Island. If I would ever see it or its people again.

The clock on the front dash told me it was two o'clock. In a couple of hours, Aunt Josephine and Uncle Johnny would start wondering where I was. They were expecting me back for dinner; Uncle Johnny was going to barbecue vegetables soaked in butter, and I was going to miss it. I'd already missed lunch, and now I was going to miss supper. I felt my blood pressure rise at the thought of worrying my aunt and uncle. I didn't want to let this madman continue to hurt people, but all I could do was keep him talking.

"What bones?"

He snapped his head around and stared at me. "*What bones?* Nice try. I knew you were after the fossils the minute I saw you crawling through the bush back there. What bones!" He shook his head in disbelief at what he clearly thought was my attempt at deception. "Do you think I'm some kind of fool? Obviously, Victor shared his discovery with some of his friends."

Stomach acid hit my throat as butterflies danced in my belly. "There are bones in that bag? Real bones? Is that why it smells like that?"

Dr. Daniels's brow furrowed. "What smell? The fossils are a million years old. There's no *smell*."

I nodded and scrunched up my nose. "Trust me, there's a

smell." *It's just not from the bones.* I wasn't sure which was more gross, old bones or old sweat. A debate for another time.

"The bones are from a Tiktaalik. Part of a jawbone and part of a skull, but they were no different from the three specimens found in 2004. What's the use of that? I needed something new, something to advance the field of paleontology."

"Something to advance your career?"

He snapped his head around again, and I was met with a fiery glare.

"Watch out!" I braced my foot against an imaginary brake pedal.

Dr. Daniels looked back at the road and made a sharp turn, shooting us back into the proper lane. He'd drifted into the oncoming traffic and again had almost caused a head-on collision, this time with a tourist bus. *How much luck can one man have while driving so recklessly?* That was one question I didn't want the answer to.

"Victor was too smart for his own good. Unfortunately, that little twerp had examined the fossils closely when I first found them, then later noticed the scratches I made on the jawbone when he snuck into my tent the next day. I caught him and we argued. I told him he was imagining my modifications, and I locked the bones away to keep his prying eyes from them. It wasn't until we got back to Charlottetown that he revealed he'd taken before-and-after photos. He thought he was so witty. 'Before and after your career, Dr. Daniels,' the obnoxious little snot said."

He assaulted the steering wheel a few more times.

"So you did what you had to do. You had no choice—I can see that." I swiped my index finger across my mouth. "My lips are sealed!"

The silence that followed overwhelmed me. My heart rate flew into overdrive, my foot tapped uncontrollably, and I wiped my wet palms on the back of the seat. I had to get out of here, but jumping out of a speeding car with my hands tied behind my back was certain death. My best bet was to keep up the buddy-buddy routine until we got to Gateway Village, then try to get someone's attention.

"So that was Victor's big scoop?"

"I'm sure it was. Fool! He was still a student, and no one would have believed him except . . ." The professor paused. "I don't know how he found out about what happened in Hamilton."

My interest was piqued now, so much so that I drifted from kidnapping victim to journalist. I longed for a notebook and pen or a voice recorder. Was I about to get answers to the questions raised by Victor's flash drive and cloud account?

"Hamilton?" I tried the play-stupid approach.

Dr. Daniels seemed to have descended into his own twisted reality. The glazed look in his eyes made me wonder if he'd forgotten he had an audience. I'd assumed he was talking to me, but maybe he was simply a lunatic ranting to the universe. A crazed killer trying to justify his horrific actions to soothe his conscience. Who hasn't driven around ranting to the wind when upset? I knew I had; the biggest difference was that I've never let my anger boil over into murdering someone.

"Christine was furious when Victor approached her about Hamilton. She'd already been hesitant to give me the job here, but I talked her into it. She's another fool. She backed me up in Hamilton when my creative doctoring of another fossil was about to be exposed to the scientific community. It cost her

her job." He laughed. "They thought it was all her doing, and I stayed quiet. There was no point in both of us getting fired."

Knowing this much about the professor's motive couldn't be good for my long-term survival. I kept quiet, hoping that my guess that he'd entered an alternative reality was accurate, and that my presence had slipped his very warped mind.

"Then someone at the University of Hamilton found proof that I was the one who'd doctored the fossils. Ha! But it didn't matter because they couldn't expose me. That's right!" He shot his hand up in a victory sign. "All the research dollars promised to the institute would have been cut off if I was exposed. And all the research done, not only under my name but also the department's name, would have been called into question. It would have been a financial and political night-mare for the university, so we made a deal and I left quietly."

So that's why he'd left when he was eligible for a tenured position; even Dr. Watson had been puzzled.

Dr. Daniels glared at me in the rear-view mirror. I felt crushed; he was still in this reality after all, still very much aware of my presence. He was willingly telling me information that could seriously damage his career and land him in jail. I swallowed hard at the realization that once we were in New Brunswick, a trip into the dense woods was a certainty; we'd be going in together, but he'd be leaving alone. I wasn't invisible to him, so I'd have to continue the camaraderie approach.

"What about Dr. Watson? Why did Victor want a copy of his medical records?"

As he tightened his grip on the steering wheel, Dr. Daniels's eyelids parted like a Vegas gambler and his hard-earned money. "Watson! He thought he should have led the expedition to Ellesmere Island." The madman paused for a few seconds. "No, I knew that with him in charge, whatever we found would be useless, and I was right. He would have presented the bones as yet another example of a creature already discovered."

My captor slammed on the steering wheel again, with so much force that a cracking sound assaulted my ears. I feared the battering would cause the whole steering assembly to break off and end up in his lap. I prayed that it wouldn't happen.

"The only option was to give him a little something to keep him home. I wasn't trying to permanently damage the man, but he's weaker than I thought. The same amount of the poison barely affected me. I'm not a monster—I made sure it was safe before giving him some."

I couldn't hold back any longer. The let's-be-buddies thing wasn't working, as the man was an unravelling psychopath. I tried a new, more direct approach. "You're not a monster? How do you arrive at that conclusion, oh Mr. Science Guy? You just admitted to poisoning Dr. Watson so you could lead the expedition, you falsified scientific research, not just once but at least twice, and you're kidnapping me."

I was met by a stretch of silence.

"Oh, and let's not forget the worst thing you've done. You killed Victor Cargo!"

The car suddenly decelerated. I flew forward, smacking my face on the back of the front seat. Dr. Daniels wrenched the steering wheel to the right, causing me to fall over onto the floor. I was now once again face to face with the smelly bag of evidence.

"Where are you?" He sounded confused.

I twisted my neck to look up. Dr. Daniels was peering over the seat, a mixture of bewilderment and anger on his face.

"I'm down here. Great driving, by the way."

In a flash, the back door opened and he was lifting me into the air. I was soon standing on the gravel shoulder, my face mere inches from his.

The professor stood in front of me, his arms crossed. "I didn't kill Victor Cargo."

Chapter 46

I LET OUT A sigh. "Could you at least untie my hands?" We were back in the car, once again racing to the Confederation Bridge.

"No."

Dr. Daniels claimed he was innocent in the murder of Victor Cargo, but I didn't believe him. Too much needed an explanation, including the reason for his current state of mind and his need to flee the Island.

"If you didn't kill anyone, why do you need me for insurance? The police aren't going to care that you altered some old bones. Seriously, is *anyone* going to care?"

I thought about Scott Jacob. Yes, many people would care—people who believed in ethical research. People who believed in finding and reporting all the facts, whether those facts agreed with their hypothesis or not. That was truth in science, and truth in reporting.

"I saw Laurie Lamont, another nosy student, snooping around my lab yesterday, and when I went there this morning, the bottle of poison I'd used on Dr. Watson had been moved. Laurie was against my leading the expedition to Ellesmere Island, and she was suspicious of Dr. Watson's sudden illness. When I spotted police cars on campus earlier today, I knew she must have reported me. It would only be a matter of time before they tested the bottle and discovered the truth."

I rubbed my chin and asked myself if I should relieve the man's fears. The police weren't on campus for him but to arrest Terry. If they were going to investigate Dr. Daniels for poisoning Dr. Watson, that would have to wait until they finished unjustly convicting my friend for murder.

"Why all the anger, and why throw the bones into the bush?"

"I can't use them now. What a waste. All that time spent getting Watson out of the way, setting up the expedition, changing sites. What a waste! The fossils are real, and with just a little tweak we'd have had a huge discovery on our hands. It would have been good for the whole team, for the university."

"For *you*."

"And what's wrong with that? I tried to calm Victor down, to show him how damaging it would be to his career if he became a tattletale."

Tattletale? Were we in grade school now?

"No one would have taken him seriously. I told him the same thing I told you—UH couldn't admit to my role in any wrongdoing because it would ruin their reputation. And this new discovery hadn't been reported yet. Even if he did follow through with his threat of announcing his *big find* on the radio, I had a backup plan."

"Oh yeah? What was that?"

"That barista at Jacob's Café. I arranged for him and Victor to meet. Victor's reputation would have been ruined if he was found associating with Scott Jacob."

I bristled at the sound of Scott's name; Dr. Daniels had tried to use Scott's painful past to hurt Victor's future. Scott's name would have been dragged through the dirt of the scientific community all over again. "Why would you want to hurt Scott Jacob like that?"

"Mr. Jacob hurt himself long ago. I suggested to Victor that he talk to Mr. Jacob if he wanted information on the University of Hamilton. I knew that once word got out that Victor was talking to that intelligent design goon, his fate in the scientific world would be sealed. No one would take him seriously."

Did Dr. Daniels really think that revealing what a cold, calculating, soulless creature he was would convince me he wasn't a murderer?

"If killing me isn't a part of your plan, why tell me all of this? Aren't you afraid I'll talk?"

"Talk to who? I just told you that no one would take Victor, an intelligent final year student in the science department, seriously. Why would anyone take you, a freshman who's not even a science student, seriously?" He was sounding a lot like Laurie Lamont.

"The fossils from Ellesmere Island and the bottle of poison are both going to take a nice trip over the side of the Confederation Bridge. Now that I think about it, you did me a favour by fishing the bones out of the bush—it would have only been a matter of time before some camper found the bag. Yup, the bridge is the way to go. No one will ever find them in their watery grave."

Well, wasn't that nice of me? I flung my head back against the top of the seat when I spotted the tariff sign that informed drivers of the fees to cross to New Brunswick. We'd soon be at the exit to the bridge, and I would somehow need to draw attention to myself before we went through the toll gates. If not, we'd be on the barren stretch of road that took us onto Canada's longest bridge and off the Island.

My hands were still bound, so banging on the window wasn't an option unless I used my head. When we'd returned to the car, Dr. Daniels had engaged the child locks on the windows, so using my elbows to roll them down was no longer an option. I'd have to wait until the car slowed, try to open the door, roll out, and deal with the consequences if I survived the impact with the pavement.

The entrance to the toll booths was to the right, but at the fork in the road, Dr. Daniels surprised me when he turned left toward Gateway Village.

"Have you changed your mind? I thought you were running to New Brunswick. You know, running—like guilty people do. People who murder other people."

Steering into the parking lot of a gas station-coffee shop combo, Dr. Daniels ignored me. He pulled into a spot behind the building, opened his door, and turned back to look at me. "You stay here."

I couldn't lift my hands into the air to remind him I was bound, so I shrugged. "Where am I going to go?"

He slammed the door, then walked a few feet from the car before retrieving his phone from a pocket and proceeding, I assumed, to send a text. Once he was done and had put the phone away, he stood with his arms crossed and looking at the far side of the gas station.

I wasn't sure if time was passing more slowly or faster than normal, so I could only guess it was about five minutes before a second car pulled up beside the professor's blue sedan and a woman got out. It wasn't just any woman—it was Dr. Christine Hogg. What was she doing here? Was she an accomplice?

I watched the university administrator stomp toward Dr. Daniels, then shove his shoulder. An argument ensued, but through the closed windows I couldn't hear what was being said. I tried to force my wrists apart, hoping to loosen my bindings. The knot slipped, giving me enough flexibility to scoot my arms under my butt, then my legs. After stretching my arms far enough forward, I was able to put my legs through them. My arms now in front of me instead of behind, I tugged on the door handle and crept out of the car.

I quietly pushed the door closed, then, keeping as low to the ground as I could, attempted to make my way to the front of the vehicle while remaining hidden. My plan was to listen to the conversation, then head for the gas station entrance and call for help. The squatting position was difficult to maintain; I slipped on a patch of oily gravel and let out an involuntary sound for the second time that afternoon. This time it was more than a gasp.

My captor and his friend were soon standing over me. Dr. Hogg scowled at Dr. Daniels. "What's she doing here? What have you done now? I told you to meet me here and I'd give you the plane tickets. All you had to do was wait until the accident on the bridge was cleared, then drive to Halifax, get on a plane, and *poof!*"—she made a *"poof"* gesture with her hands—"you'd be gone." She slapped her forehead and spun around. "Why must you always make things so much more complicated?"

"Because he's a cheat!" I pushed my hands into the ground to raise myself to standing. "And a murderer."

Dr. Hogg's brow furrowed. "A what?"

I stood tall. I was confident I'd caught the killer, and I wasn't going to let him get away with it. "A murderer. You may think he's just a lying, cheating, hoax-creating career killer, but he's a murderer too. Of humans. He killed Victor Cargo, and he tried to kill Dr. Watson."

Dr. Daniels stuck his index finger in my face. "I told you I didn't kill Victor, and I didn't intend to seriously harm Dr. Watson."

"Why should I believe you? You kidnapped me and now you're running away to fly to who knows where. Some exotic island with no extradition agreement with Canada, I suppose."

Dr. Hogg cocked her head. I was uncertain if she was confused, amused, or perhaps a little of both. "You think this guy killed the kid?"

"Yes. He was a boxer—a boxer with a powerful left hook! The police think Victor's killer was left-handed because of the damage to his skull and face on the right side, but it could have easily been a boxer with a good left hook."

I felt smug in my conclusion, but had I said too much? Maybe I shouldn't have been telling a suspect information about a crime scene that only the killer would know. What if I was weakening David's case?

Dr. Daniels shook his head and said, "You have a lot to learn, freshman. I'm not the only one with—"

Chapter 47

DR. DANIELS WAS interrupted by the sound of sirens. I turned around and, to my excitement, three police cars were heading left at the same intersection where the professor had turned. When I turned back, Drs. Daniels and Hogg were racing through a field that led to a large building that looked like an arena.

I jumped up and down, waving my bound arms back and forth. The squad cars—two marked Charlottetown Police and one marked Summerside Police—sped into the parking lot. The doors flew open and several officers, guns drawn, positioned themselves behind the open doors. My relief at seeing this show of force was extinguished when I realized the guns were pointed at me.

I shook my head wildly. "Not me." I nodded toward the field. "Them. They're getting away. He killed Victor Cargo."

Officers Hughes and Mather holstered their guns and chased the professors. David called to his Summerside colleagues to follow him. I fell to the ground, my legs too weak to hold me up any longer. I bent my legs toward me and dropped my head onto my knees. Tremors engulfed my entire body, and the tears flowed with such force, I thought I might drown myself.

"You have no idea how relieved I am that we found you."

I dried my wet face on my shoulder, then looked up to see Terry kneeling in front of me. He took my hands and untied the knot that had held me prisoner. I threw my arms around his shoulders and leaned on him while he stood. Then I hugged him longer than I think I'd ever hugged anyone in my life—for both the physical and emotional support. I feared that if I let go, not only would I fall back to the ground, but I'd also fall apart.

When I opened my eyes, Andy was standing a few feet behind Terry. Conscious that I had just committed a PDA with Terry, and not knowing whether or not he'd be annoyed, I let go of my friend. He had pushed Hallie away when she hugged him earlier in the week. While he seemed okay with the hug I'd given him, I was suddenly confused about my feelings and decided to focus on the matter at hand. "How did you find me? Did they release you? I thought they were charging you with murder. I didn't know if I'd ever see you again."

Terry nodded at Andy. "Andy got your message about Dr. Daniels and your insane plan to follow him."

"Yeah, man, I replied to your text, but you didn't answer. I kinda freaked out and headed to the police station. I told the cops what was going on, and I showed them your text."

I let go of Terry and gave Andy a hug. I had misjudged him; I thought he was capable of murder, but he'd probably saved my life. I could only hope he wasn't aware of my suspicions. Either way, I'd make it up to him somehow.

"They believed my text and let Terry go?"

Terry chuckled. "Not exactly. David said they have DNA evidence that cleared me."

I was confused. "So soon? I thought it took weeks to get DNA results."

"From what David says, it normally does." Terry shrugged, then leaned against the blue sedan. "It turns out the vet college has state-of-the-art equipment that can provide results faster than most crime labs. The vet technicians were happy to help in the investigation."

"Did the DNA tell them who the real murderer is?" I studied Terry's hair. I don't know why my mind was on his hair while David and Officer Mather were chasing the bad guys, but I was relieved to see that it was neatly combed back, with no bald spots. I held back a smile at my observation.

"I don't know. They could only tell me that it cleared me—nothing else."

Terry, Andy, and I watched the action in the distance. Officer Mather tackled Dr. Hogg to the ground, and after a scuffle, she pulled the older woman to her feet and handcuffed her.

David stopped about twenty feet from Dr. Daniels, then yelled at him to stop. When the professor continued to run, David retrieved a taser from his belt and held it in front of him. A popping sound was followed by a scream, and I watched with satisfaction as the man who'd held me captive fell to the ground and writhed in agony. I clapped when David threw handcuffs on Dr. Daniels and dragged him to his feet.

Standing so close to the blue sedan was unnerving; I'd seen enough of that car and wanted to be as far away from it as I could get. I moved to the other side of the parking lot and sat at one of the picnic tables. Terry and Andy joined me.

"How did you know which car to look for?"

"You described Dr. Daniels's car in your text to Andy."

"Yeah. It said 'blue car, gold mittens.' I thought you were loopy until Terry told me that the good . . . well, I guess *bad*"—Andy laughed—"professor was a boxer."

"The police got a report of two cars driving wildly west of Cornwall, near the Bonshaw River. A blue sedan with yellow mittens and a beat-up green car. I assumed you used my car?"

I looked at my shoes and whispered, "Yes. Sorry." I'd tell him about the damage later.

Chapter 48

DESPITE THE CHILLY breeze blowing in from the Northumberland Strait, a crowd was gathering in the parking lot. Three police cars with sirens blaring and lights flashing wasn't a common sight in PEI, so I wasn't surprised that we were the object of everyone's attention, but it made me uncomfortable. How many lives had been ruined because of one man's greed?

This was real-life tragedy, not an event to entertain the masses. Would I remember that fact in the future when reporting on stories? I promised myself I would—that I'd remember that victims of crime have families and friends who might be watching the news.

As David and Officer Mather returned with their prisoners, I swore to myself I would remember that law enforcement officers were humans too. I would remember how events like the ones I'd witnessed this week must affect those in the business of dealing with criminals and tragedies. Can they turn off their on-duty experiences when off duty? And how does dealing daily with the evils of mankind affect their personal lives?

Officer Mather removed Dr. Hogg's handcuffs. "You're not free to go. We have some questions for you before you leave."

Dr. Hogg's eyes darted around the parking lot at the audience, the police, and my friends and me. When she spotted Dr. Daniels, her eyes narrowed and she took in a deep breath. "You fool. I told you to stay out of trouble. I should never have hired you on here. You ruined my academic career in Hamilton, and now you've ruined my administrative career. I had a good thing going here." She leaped at the object of her fury but was stopped by a quick-acting officer from the Summerside squad.

Dr. Daniels instinctively moved away from the angry woman, then turned to David. "Listen, I don't know what you've heard, but I didn't hurt anyone. I certainly didn't kill anyone. You can't prove anything. I want my lawyer."

My blood approached the boiling point. I shot up from my seat and raced to the liar. "*You didn't hurt anyone?* You kidnapped me. And you poisoned Dr. Watson."

David snapped his head around to look at me. "He did what to who?"

"He poisoned one of the other professors. He told me all about it in the car. He wanted a research project all to himself, so he gave Dr. Watson something to make him sick, but it almost killed the poor man."

David continued to stare at me as he adjusted Dr. Daniels's handcuffs.

"Check the bag in his car. There's a vial of poison in there. If you check that against Dr. Watson's medical records, you'll find a connection."

The desperation in my voice must have been convincing. David tightened the cuffs—as evidenced by Dr. Daniels' facial contortions—and retrieved the bag from the back seat of the blue sedan. He shuffled the contents, then pulled out a small clear vial with a black top. He held it up. "This?"

The label had a word I didn't recognize on it—some type of chemical, I assumed. "I don't know what it is, but he told me himself that it's poison. He was going to toss it over the bridge."

Dr. Hogg eyeballed the vial, then leaped at Dr. Daniels again. "You fool!"

David smiled at me. "That's all I need to know for now." He gripped Dr. Daniels's arm tightly and escorted him to the squad car. "Get in." He pushed down the lunatic's head and gave him a shove to "help" him into the car.

I squeezed between David and his car, then dramatically pointed a finger at Dr. Daniels through the open window. "And . . . he killed Victor Cargo."

David pulled my arm away from the suspect and the car, then slammed the door closed. "No. He didn't."

I was livid. How could he argue with me? I'd just caught a killer and he wouldn't believe me. "What about the poison? What about his confession to me?"

"Did he confess to killing Mr. Cargo?" David crossed his arms.

I looked up at the sky. The clouds were gone now, and the sun would soon be setting. The gurgling noises from my abdomen reminded me I'd missed lunch, and that I'd likely miss dinner.

I returned my attention to David. "No. He denied it, but he must have done it." I pointed at the professor again. "If he didn't beat Victor to death, how did he hurt his hand?"

David cocked his head and smiled. Was he amused at my evidence that my kidnapper was also a murderer? "When Andy informed us you were following Dr. Daniels, a uniformed officer was sent to check out his office, and another to check out his home. The hole in Dr. Daniels's office wall explains the condition of his hand."

Our prisoner shrugged and smirked when I threw a questioning stare at him. "I hit the wall, but I didn't hit Victor. I'm wishing now I had. Who was he to mess up my plans?"

What more evidence did David need? "See? He had a motive."

"Having a motive doesn't make someone guilty. Remember, Franny, we need all the facts."

I ignored his use of the name I hated and crossed my arms. I was right. Why wouldn't he believe me?

I didn't have to wait long for the answer to my unspoken question. David said, "I imagine Terry told you we cleared him based on the DNA evidence. We found DNA that didn't belong to Mr. Cargo on his face. When the murderer struck him, she must have injured herself and left her DNA behind. Or more likely, she cut herself when she smashed his head with the rock we found lying beside his body. The blood on the rock was a mixture of his and hers."

Did he say "she" and "her"?

I tried to snap my fingers. "Lena! I knew it."

"Lena Gallant?" David appeared amused.

"Yes. She's related to Victor's roommate, Bobby. They stole Victor's shoes, and they've taken off. I don't know where they went, but you have to find her. She's strong enough to have beaten Victor."

"You can calm down. She and her cousin are in custody, and as soon as we get them off the bridge, we'll check their fingerprints and DNA."

"Their fingerprints will be on the shoes, I'm certain of it." The muscles in my neck relaxed. I hadn't realized how tense I was until David said that Lena and Bobby were in custody.

I scratched my forehead. What did David say? "Wait. Why are they in custody if you don't have evidence that they're the murderers? And what do you mean, when you get them off the bridge?"

"They were driving like maniacs across the bridge when that big storm hit earlier. Their car skidded and they slammed into another vehicle. That put a stop to traffic flow in both directions. Luckily, no one was seriously injured, but it'll take time to clear things up. Once the vehicles are removed, the bridge will need to be inspected for damage."

I was glad to hear that no one had been hurt, but even gladder that Bobby and Lena hadn't been able to make their escape. After the events of the past few hours, I still had a hard time believing that Dr. Daniels wasn't the killer, but the DNA evidence had cleared him. I wondered why I was so skeptical of the evidence.

"Speaking of Victor's shoes . . ." David stood with his arms crossed. "Oddly enough, they somehow made their way into my car last night. Do you know anything about that?"

I gulped. This was it. I'd emerged safe from a kidnapping, but now I was heading to jail for tampering with evidence.

"I took them with me when I escaped from Bobby and Lena, and then I was going to drop them off at the police station but found out you still had your sights on Terry, mainly because he was in possession of the bloody bag, and I was sure I'd be a suspect too if you knew I had the shoes, so I was going to go home and spend the night thinking about how I could give you the evidence without looking guilty." I took a breath.

"You do use a lot of words at times." David smiled. "You're lucky you weren't at the *Golden Spud* when we arrested Terry, because you would have been arrested too. On the other hand, if you had been in jail earlier today, you wouldn't have been kidnapped, so maybe you weren't so lucky."

It was my turn to cross my arms, and I stood tall, my chest out. "If I hadn't been kidnapped, you wouldn't have learned what Dr. Daniels was up to." I huffed, then regretted it. No need to be arrogant.

David laughed. "You have an amusing way of looking at things, Fran."

He turned and headed toward the other officers. As I watched him walk away, my anger toward him subsided. He had been doing his job, and despite my interfering in his case, he was kind enough to call me Fran.

I strolled past Andy and Terry, who were still sitting at the picnic table. I needed to find the restrooms, and a coffee wouldn't hurt. "Do either of you want a coffee?"

They both said yes and gave me some money. I'd forgotten until now that my backpack and wallet were still in Terry's car.

As I rounded the corner of the coffee shop, I noticed a horse trailer with the veterinary college's logo painted on the side. A woman in green scrubs and two younger adults in blue scrubs were putting something on the horse's head. I watched as the young guy scratched the horse's nose to calm him, while the two women slipped a black mask over the animal's head. It was a set of blinders like the ones I'd seen on the horse on campus.

I walked into the store, impressed by the gentle way in which the vets were caring for the horse, but then it struck me: the horse was wearing blinders, and so was I. I had spent my entire day assuming one person was guilty of a crime based on weak evidence. I believe "circumstantial evidence" would be the correct term—I'd have to verify that later.

David had warned me earlier in the week that jumping to conclusions could be dangerous. Scott Jacob had said something similar. I had condemned the wrong man for murder—not that he was innocent of criminal behaviour, but his claims of not being a murderer were valid. He was a liar and cheat in his profession. He was so desperate to get professional recognition, to advance his case to prove the evolutionary process, that he'd been willing to tamper with fossils and publish inaccurate information to his peers.

I sat at one of the booths in the store's café and pulled out my phone. I searched for Piltdown Man and read an article that appeared. It explained that an amateur archaeologist had altered an orangutan's jawbone and teeth, then combined it with a human skeleton before claiming that the bones were from a single ancestor of modern man. Scott Jacob had warned me that things aren't always as they appear, but I wondered how he could have known that the Piltdown Man situation so closely matched Dr. Daniels's. They both involved altering fossils to advance the culprits' standing in the academic world. Maybe it was a coincidence. Or maybe Scott knew what Dr.

Daniels was up to but either couldn't prove it or chose not to get involved.

They knew each other in Hamilton, so perhaps Scott had heard the rumours about Drs. Hogg and Daniels. I couldn't make the connection, because even if Scott was aware of what had happened in Hamilton, he didn't know that Dr. Daniels was my suspect in Victor's murder. I'd have to ask Scott about this the next time I saw him.

I purchased a muffin and coffee for myself and coffee for my friends, then headed back outside. Dr. Daniels was still in the police car, scowling at Dr. Hogg as she spoke with David and Officer Mather.

I sat with Terry and Andy at the picnic table and devoured the muffin, then downed the coffee. We all watched as a white car with blue stripes, lights flashing, approached the gas station from the direction of the bridge. It was an RCMP vehicle with two passengers in the back seat. As it drew closer, I recognized Lena Gallant and Bobby Burrell despite their attempts to shield their faces.

The officer parked and exited the vehicle, then helped Lena get out. My jaw dropped and I froze. Did he know she was a cold-blooded murderer? What if she fled? Why wasn't he taking her to Charlottetown and jail?

David came over to our table. I could only assume he noticed my concern. "I radioed the RCMP and let them know that Lena and Bobby were murder suspects."

As Lena swung her legs around and stood up, I could see she was handcuffed. The RCMP officer cupped his hand around her arm and escorted her toward the building. I guess even criminals need to use the washroom.

It seemed out of place, but I felt a twinge of compassion

for Lena. Was she a murderer? She was goofy and oddly loyal to her cousin—so much so that she was willing to hide evidence from a crime scene. But was she violent? So violent and sociopathic she'd kill for a pair of shoes?

I glanced at the horse trailer when I noticed it backing up, probably heading to the bridge now that the accident had been cleared. Maybe I had some backing up of my own to do. Was I still wearing blinders?

I thought back to the major events of the past few days, including the last words I'd exchanged with Drs. Hogg and Daniels. The latter was in mid-sentence when the Charlottetown and Summerside police arrived. I wondered what it was Dr. Daniels was about to tell me.

"David, would it be okay if I asked Dr. Daniels a question?"

He tilted his head and squinted, then shrugged. "I don't see why not—as long as I'm with you and it's not about any of the evidence."

We walked over to the police car together, and David tapped on the frame of the car door to draw the prisoner's attention. "Fran has a question for you. I suggest you mind your manners if you want to avoid further charges."

Dr. Daniels's nostrils flared and he shrugged. I took that as a willingness to talk.

"Dr. Daniels, I'm sorry I accused you of murdering Victor." It couldn't hurt to try the buddy-buddy approach again—the whole bees-and-honey theory. "Before the police arrived, you were about to tell me something. What was it?"

He slowly turned his head and stared at me. It was creepy, but I held my ground. "I was about to say that I'm not the only one with a powerful left hook. Christine Hogg and I first met on the boxing circuit. She's got quite a powerful left hook herself." He smiled, then stared at the windshield.

David and I looked at each other. Female DNA, a strong left hook, damage to the right side of Victor's head and face, a ruined career, and risk of another professional scandal. As though we had choreographed it, we turned our heads in sync toward Dr. Hogg.

She was standing, her back to us, in front of Officer Mather, and the two women were talking. Officer Mather was making notes on her notepad; I assumed she was taking Dr. Hogg's statement. The police officer tapped her pen on the notepad, flipped it closed, and waved at us. Dr. Hogg turned around. She stared wide-eyed at David and me, then turned again.

She pushed Officer Mather to the side and attempted to run, but Officer Mather had super-quick reflexes. She reached out and grabbed the older woman by the back of her shirt and yanked her to the ground. Officer Mather straddled Dr. Hogg while placing her in handcuffs, then for the second time that evening, pulled her to her feet.

I heard cheering and clapping behind me as Terry and Andy showed their approval.

David walked toward his colleague, but he paused and gave me a stern look. "Stay right here." He then joined Officer Mather in escorting Dr. Christine Hogg to the other Charlottetown cruiser.

As they dragged the angry professor to the car, she started ranting at the world. "Stupid kid! I didn't mean to hurt him. What was he doing wearing Daniels's fedora? I was sure it was Daniels. I thought I was giving him a quick clunk on the head—I knew he could take the punch. But the kid was weak. He went down so fast."

Given this defence of her actions, I wasn't surprised that Dr. Hogg's confession left out the detail about smashing Victor's head with a rock. She claimed mistaken identity because of a fedora, but I couldn't remember seeing a hat when I found Victor's body. I could only imagine what happened to it. Perhaps Bobby had taken it as well as the shoes.

Dr. Daniels's voice came from the car. "There you go—karma, I think they call it. Now I know what happened to my other hat." He laughed. "Victor stole it, and it got him killed. Fool!"

I opened the door to the police car, rolled up the window, then slammed the door. I was done listening to insane comments from the deranged professor. I gave him my best sneer, then stuck my tongue out at him. After his tattletale comment, I couldn't resist.

Hoping no one else had witnessed my childish actions, I joined Terry and Andy at the picnic table. "So how are we getting back to Charlottetown?"

"Andy and I rode in David's car, but we'll take my car back to the university." Terry scanned the parking lot, then gave me the side-eye. "Where's my car?"

I rubbed my chin and sat down. "Well, you see . . . that's a long story."

Terry's hand approached his hair. "Were you in an accident?"

I hesitated. I didn't know how much damage I'd done to the car—or if it would even start. "You may want to get the emergency brake checked, and maybe the alignment." I watched his face for a response, but he was stoic. "When we get the car, please remember that I was trying to help."

Terry smiled. "Of course. You were trying to keep me out of jail. You have no idea how much I appreciate that." He paused. "So let's grab the car so we can get back to town." He and Andy stood up and waited for me to show them the way.

I rubbed my chin. "First we'll have to get a ride to Bonshaw Hills Provincial Park." I said another prayer; I could only hope it was still parked where I'd left it. The keys were still in the ignition.

Chapter 49

THE FOLLOWING SATURDAY, Aunt Josephine scurried around the yard, ensuring that my friends had plenty to eat. When she finished encouraging Terry, Andy, and Greg to help themselves to a third—or was it a fourth?—hamburger each, she came over to the barbecue where I was helping Uncle Johnny remove the latest batch of butter-soaked grilled vegetables.

"There's nothing like fresh carrots and tomatoes from your own garden." Uncle Johnny passed the last tinfoil container to Scott Jacob.

"No sir, there isn't." Scott steadied the veggies in one hand while picking up a tray of pastries he'd brought with him in the other, then headed to the picnic table.

Hallie spotted him stumble on a tree root, released the grip she had on Greg's arm, and ran to steady Scott before dessert met its untimely demise on the grass. She succeeded in saving the day, and everyone cheered.

It had been a week since Terry's arrest and release, and the events at Gateway Village. After the police officer from Summerside had dropped Terry, Andy, and me off at Bonshaw Hills Provincial Park, we were excited to see that Terry's car was where I had left it. To clarify, I was excited to see the car, but from the look on Terry's face, I suspect he had mixed emotions. The tree branches had scraped away huge swaths of paint, and one of the tires looked suspect. We were blessed to have made it back to Charlottetown without a blown tire.

Fortunately, Terry's mechanic was able to fix the damage I had done to the emergency brake. Afterwards, Terry promised to teach me how to properly perform the manoeuvre to spin the car . . . someday. Besides the paint, the wonky emergency brake was the only serious damage incurred by my race to the Confederation Bridge; the tire merely needed some air. To replace the bumper he'd lost when Bobby Burrell chased us through the streets of Charlottetown, Terry would have to wait until he could afford it.

Now, as I watched my new friends laughing together and enjoying my aunt and uncle's hospitality, my emotions were once again riding a roller coaster. It had all worked out for us—the bad guys were in jail and we were all safe. But I couldn't help thinking about Victor's family. We'd met them when we attended the funeral; they were lovely people who'd obviously loved Victor very much, and that made a sad day even sadder.

A gathering with good food and sunshine was just what we needed to lift our spirits—I was grateful when my aunt suggested it. I hadn't wanted to share the events of the past week with Aunt Josephine and Uncle Johnny, but David advised me to fill them in myself before the story hit the media. They took it much better than I expected.

"You see, Franny," Aunt Josephine had said, "I knew a story about your life would be interesting."

"But Aunt Josephine, while you were encouraging me to write about my life, you were discouraging me from writing a murder mystery."

"Oh no, Franny. You can leave the murder part out. No one wants to read about a grisly murder. Simply write about how you helped the police solve a crime. Just not murder." She grimaced, then filled my cup with more tea.

I smiled at my silver-haired landlady. "Okay. I'll think about it."

Uncle Johnny, who'd been quietly listening to the conversation, grinned and shrugged. "I knew you were up to something, but my goodness, I wouldn't have guessed what it was."

I had expected them to panic knowing that I'd put not just myself, but also them, in danger. I was relieved when instead they suggested a barbecue so they could meet my new friends.

"The more the merrier," Uncle Johnny said at the time. "If you're going to be chasing criminals, best we know who you're doing it with."

So I invited the team from the *Golden Spud*, except for Lena, of course. And in appreciation for his kindness to Terry and me at his café during our investigation, I invited Scott Jacob as well.

I shook my head to return my mind to the present and joined my friends at the picnic table. I hadn't yet had a chance to ask Scott about why he'd mentioned Piltdown Man. "So, Scott, how did you know that Victor's murder had something to do with Dr. Daniels tampering with fossils? Divine intervention?"

He smiled and looked to the sky. "Maybe." He laughed. "But honestly, it was purely coincidental. I mentioned the Piltdown Man controversy to you as an example of why it's important to fully investigate all claims. I had no idea what Dr. Daniels was up to here at UPEI or in Hamilton. I did know him in Hamilton—he wasn't very likeable then either."

Scott consumed the last bite of his hamburger, only to find a large scoop of potato salad instantly added to his plate.

"A young man needs a lot of energy. You were always so skinny when you were in my class, and things haven't changed a bit." Aunt Josephine tapped Scott's shoulder playfully. "We'll get you fattened up eventually."

Then my aunt, who could only be described as thin herself, continued her mission to fatten up my other friends by adding a scoop of potato salad to each of their plates, whether they protested or not.

After thanking his hostess, Scott politely ate a spoonful. "On to a brighter topic. Word in the science department at UPEI is that now that the doctors know what caused Dr. Watson's illness, they've treated him, and he's expected to make a full recovery."

My heart sang at this good news. I'd only met Dr. Watson briefly, but he was so kind that day, and everyone I'd spoken to about him since had nothing but good things to say. "That's good news, Scott, but"—I paused, worried my next comment might be insulting or hurtful—"did you know that Dr. Daniels led me to believe that the science community regarded you as a virus to be avoided?"

Scott laughed. "I'm sure he did. As I said, he's not a very

nice person. Very self-focused, and I think he truly believes he's the only one who knows anything about his field of study, and as you've seen, he'll go to any lengths to prove it. The science department is now short a professor, and Dr. Watson came by the café yesterday and offered me a temporary associate position. I had to decline."

"Why? Isn't it an opportunity to get back into the field you invested so much time and energy into? It's not like they don't already know your beliefs, and your teaching style."

"That's just it—I'd still be bound to stick to the status quo. Dr. Watson is more open-minded than most in his field, but even he must be careful not to upset the apple cart, as they say. Suggesting that students should investigate all theories of our origins is simply not acceptable."

"That's too bad."

"Yes and no." Scott poured himself a lemonade, then gulped it down. He wiped his mouth on his shirt, then—as though he was a schoolboy back in the classroom—looked around to see if Aunt Josephine had seen what he'd done. "The academic world is worse now than it was when I was doing my Ph.D. It's not only members of the science department who have to be careful about what they say in the classroom. Educators in every department are becoming fearful that a word misspoken, or misunderstood, could lead to their dismissal. If you're not willing to parrot the politically correct viewpoint, you're done."

I thought about my future—not only the next few years in university, but in journalism. Would I be forced to write what was expected, or would I have the freedom to investigate and report all the facts?

Scott must have sensed my uneasiness. "No need to worry. We have smart young people like you and Mr. James who are willing to seek out the truth and stir things up. With more people like that, things can only get better."

"To the future!" I raised my glass of juice in a toast, and Scott gave it a ceremonial tap with his empty glass.

Terry reached across the table and snagged a pastry from the tray of treats Scott had provided, and one of Aunt Josephine's homemade lemon squares. "What was Christine Hogg like in Hamilton?"

Scott shook his head. "She was actually very nice. It's a sad situation because, until Dr. Daniels came along, she was a team player. She got along with everyone and had a promising future ahead of her." He smiled at Terry, then me. "Nice article, by the way. Until I read your report in the *Golden Spud*, I didn't know what had happened in Hamilton. It sounds like Daniels got his hooks into Christine and led her down a dark path."

"But why did she kill Victor? He didn't do anything to her." Hallie had rejoined Greg and was resting her head on his shoulder.

As a thank you for our help, David had provided Terry and me with the information we'd need to get the scoop before anyone else. In return, we agreed not to print any details that might affect the court case. And much to our relief, neither of us was charged for tampering with evidence after failing to turn over Victor's shoes or his flash drive to the police.

I relayed to Hallie and the others some of the information we hadn't printed in the paper. "Victor threatened to expose Dr. Daniels, which would have caused trouble for Dr. Hogg as well. She feared she'd lose everything she'd gained since moving to PEI."

"She claims she thought Victor was Dr. Daniels because of the hat he was wearing. According to her, Dr. Daniels is the only one on campus with a fedora like that one," Terry said, and poured himself a lemonade.

Hallie nodded. "Mistaken identity."

"Or was it?" My friends all looked at me. What had they said at the police station about Victor's wounds? Before I could voice my thoughts, David's squad car pulled into the driveway. I excused myself and went to greet him. I waved at David.

He exited the vehicle and waved back. "I wanted to come by and give you an update." David peered into the backyard. "Having a party?"

A feeling of guilt overwhelmed me. I hadn't thought to invite David or any of his colleagues. "Um. Yeah. Just the group from the *Golden Spud*, and Scott Jacob. He's a friend of my aunt's. Would you like to join us? We have plenty of food left."

"Thanks, but I'm on duty. Lots of paperwork this week, and I'm a bit behind."

"I guess catching multiple criminals in one day would lead to a ton of paperwork."

"You can't even imagine."

What I could imagine was the ton of school work I had to make up after missing so many classes. "So you have an update?"

"Yes, I thought I'd give you and Terry another scoop. Charges have been decided for all our suspects."

I dug out a pen and notepad from my jacket pocket; one thing I'd learned over the past two weeks was that it never hurt to be prepared to take notes. "Go ahead."

"Dr. Kenneth Daniels will be charged with attempted murder and kidnapping, among other lesser crimes. Lena Gallant and Bobby Burrell will be charged with evidence tampering. We dropped the charges related to use of an unregistered licence plate and dangerous driving because they've been very cooperative. As you know, Bobby is a witness to the murder. He saw the murderer leaving, wearing a fedora."

"That fedora has caused a lot of trouble."

"It certainly has. Dr. Hogg is using it as her defence. She's claiming mistaken identity. She saw the hat, thought it was Dr. Daniels, and struck him. She's being charged with first-degree murder. Her lawyer is trying to get the charge dropped to manslaughter, claiming that Dr. Daniels would have been able to handle the blow, and that it's only because Victor was skinny and weak that he died."

"But . . ."

"But?" David looked annoyed.

"But didn't you say at the police station that the assailant had used their left hand because the injuries to Victor were on the right side of his face and head?"

David shrugged. "Yeah."

"Wouldn't that mean Dr. Hogg was facing Victor when she struck him? Other than their height, Victor and Dr. Daniels don't look anything alike. And I know it was dark, but there were street lights nearby. And furthermore, after she knocked him down, she finished him off with the rock instead of calling 911 and potentially saving his life."

David scratched his head. "Rest assured, we know she's lying, but good for you for figuring it out. You're right, Fran, besides the fact that she was facing Mr. Cargo, she struck him more than once. The damage to his head—"

I raised one hand and put the other one over my stomach. "Please don't remind me. I'm finally able to think about Victor without picturing him lying there in the paddock." Over the past two weeks, I had come a long way from being the girl with the weak stomach, but I wasn't cured yet.

Something was still eating at my mind. "One more question?"

David waved his hand in the air. "Sure, have at it."

"Dr. Hogg knew that Dr. Daniels didn't kill anyone, so why was she helping him flee the Island? What was meeting him with plane tickets all about?"

"Neither of them has explained that—yet. We suspect she intended to shift the blame for Victor's murder to him, thinking that if he *left town*, as they say in the movies"—David smirked—"he must be guilty. A common misconception."

David didn't have to tell me that. I'd fallen victim to that way of thinking myself. "Why did he go along with it? He knew he didn't kill Victor."

"Like I said, he isn't talking. Narcissists don't like to admit when they've bccn had, and no doubt Dr. Hogg somehow convinced him he needed to get away. She may have known he was responsible for Dr. Watson's illness, but unless one of them talks, we have no way of knowing what transpired between them."

"One of the things that made Dr. Daniels a suspect in my mind was his injured hand. Did Dr. Hogg have any injuries?"

"That's another question." David smiled and his eyes fluttered.

Was he flirting with me? He rubbed his eye, then batted at a fly. So not flirting.

"Sorry. I have to ask again. Any injuries to Dr. Hogg?"

"Other than a few scratches and a gash to a finger, nothing serious, but enough to leave a few blood droplets on Victor's shoes, face, and the rock. Dr. Daniels injured himself on the drywall in his office. I don't think that punching Victor wouldn't have caused as much damage to his hand."

The evidence had seemed so clear a week ago. I had focused

on a few facts and accused Bobby and Lena of being murderers, then focused on other evidence and jumped to the conclusion that Dr. Daniels was the murderer. While none of them were innocent of wrongdoing, I'd been blinded by what I thought was clear. Scott was right; I had to learn to look at all sides of an argument, or a story, before assuming that the loudest evidence—or the loudest voice in my head—pointed to the truth.

David opened his car door, then turned back to me. "You've done some interesting investigative work on this case. Have you thought of a career in law enforcement?"

My head swelled a bit at the compliment. "Maybe." I moved closer to the car to shake his hand, but I tripped over a pebble on the driveway. "Or maybe not," I heard myself saying as I flew forward.

When I landed, it wasn't onto the pavement but into David's arms. I quickly pushed myself away from the handsome man in uniform. My heart was racing, and I was sure my face was beet red.

His face was definitely red. *Great! I've embarrassed him too.*

"I was wondering, Fran, if you'd be interested in joining me for a movie this week."

I froze. Was this beyond-handsome man with the gorgeous blue eyes really asking me out? Should I go? For what felt like an eternity, I stood there, unable to speak.

A bird chirped behind me, and I turned my head toward the backyard. Terry was sitting at the picnic bench watching us. Had he seen me fall into David's arms? Why did the idea of Terry seeing that stir up guilt? David was handsome, but Terry was, well . . . he was Terry.

I looked back at David. "Thanks. I appreciate the invitation, but I think I'd better decline." I offered my hand. "Sorry."

He looked over at Terry. "Enjoy your gathering." He got into his car and drove away.

I returned to the picnic bench and sat beside Terry. Uncle Johnny was telling his story about the cat that worked for the railway. I'd heard this one before. Contentment came over me as I sat listening to the birds singing in the trees, and hearing about the antics of railway workers from days gone by.

This story was about a crew who needed a rope strung through a long pipe, so they tied the rope to a cat and coaxed it to go through. Acting in a very uncatlike manner, the tabby did as requested and threaded the pipe. Later that day the foreman asked the railway men if the cat was now on the payroll.

My friends laughed at the story, one of many Uncle Johnny enjoyed telling repeatedly. He told the stories with such animation and enthusiasm that I never grew tired of listening to them. While he entertained the guests with these tales, Aunt Josephine continued to make sure our friends were all fed and comfortable.

I rested my head on my fist. For the first time since finding the red socks in the paddock, I was content sitting among this mix of family and friends on what I considered the world's most beautiful island. I was looking forward to the next four years and the adventures they would bring. As I felt Terry snuggle up closer to me, I wondered if one of those adventures might require a hope chest after all.

Thanks

A special shout out to my friends Mary Asaaf, Laurie Hancock and Anne Mack for painlessly reading through the first draft. Thank you to my editor, Caroline Kaiser, for cleaning up the manuscript, grammatically and structurally, and for all of your sound advice and recommendations. Thank you also to Chrissy Hobbs and Brittany Wilson of Indie Publishing Inc for giving my novel it's professional look.

Author's Note

The campus layout as described in *Body in the Paddock* is loosely based on the real (past and present) UPEI campus mixed with the author's imagination. Some building names are real, others have been altered, and some of the buildings (such as the Barn) were torn down many years ago. Attempting to locate your next class based on the description of the campus provided in this book is not recommended. If you do so, you will miss, as Fran did, a large number of classes and since you are unlikely to have the excuse of helping to solve a murder, it would be an unwise endeavor.

About the Author

Karen Cullen resides and works in southern Ontario, but her heart belongs to Prince Edward Island, the home of her father and her alma mater (UPEI/AVC). When not working, she can be found daydreaming of the day she can return to Canada's Maritime provinces long term.